By CLARE LONDON

NOVELS

72 Hours
Branded
Compulsion
Sparks Fly
True Colors

NOVELLAS

Footprints
Just-You Eyes
Touch

Ambush
Payback
Switch

Published by DREAMSPINNER PRESS
http://www.dreamspinnerpress.com

COMPULSION

CLARE
LONDON

Dreamspinner Press

Published by
Dreamspinner Press
5032 Capital Circle SW
Ste 2, PMB# 279
Tallahassee, FL 32305-7886
USA
http://www.dreamspinnerpress.com/

Compulsion
Copyright © 2012 by Clare London

Cover Art by Anne Cain
annecain.art@gmail.com

ISBN: 978-1-62380-086-4

Printed in the United States of America
First Edition
October 2012

eBook edition available
eBook ISBN: 978-1-62380-087-1

To my family, my friends, and my readers.
Your support makes it all possible.

CHAPTER 1

IT WAS the usual fierce Saturday night debate. Not the one on TV where the studio audience harasses the politician about fraudulent expense claims or there's a juicy sex scandal with a reality show celebrity. No, this was the one in real life, in the flat where I was living, where the bossy gay landlords try to persuade the equally gay but far less social houseguest to go clubbing with them.

"For God's sake! If you could only see the look on your face." Louis stood opposite me in the living room, his hands on his hips, his black trousers clinging low on his slim waist. "You'd think we were asking you to eat your own flesh. It's just one night out, Max, one night among all the others you've wasted since you moved in. We're in Brighton, the south coast's center of gay nightlife, right? You'll have a great time."

"Sure," I said. It was never worth raising your voice to Louis. "Another time."

He rolled his kohl-lined eyes. "No. *This* time. They've got the new lights working on the stage at Compulsion tonight, and I want us all to be there for the show. I want *you* to be there."

"You're pouting, love." Jack stepped beside him, smiling. "Not that it isn't cute, but you're more than a few years off teenager by now." He put his arm around Louis's waist at the same time and squeezed him affectionately.

Louis flushed, but his expression was determined. "So you tell him, Jack. Tell him he needs to enjoy himself, he needs to loosen up a bit and get back into life. He needs—"

"To get out more." I spoke quickly and, despite my smile, a little wearily. "Yeah, you've said that before." I caught Jack's sympathetic gaze over Louis's shoulder. His watchful eyes saw far more of me than I liked. His dark-brown fingers rested comfortably against Louis's pale skin where his lover's satin shirt failed to meet the waistband of his trousers. They were a committed couple and very relaxed together, at least at home. Louis would have been happy to demonstrate their relationship a lot more in public, but Jack remained fairly discreet. Part of that was his own character, and part of it was caution because he worked at a forensic science service company that didn't seem to like its employees having a social life at all, let alone an alternative one. Tonight Jack's hands tightened on Louis and the blond smiled slyly, just for Jack. Yeah, part of it was just that Jack disliked sharing.

I tried my usual excuses. "I'm dog-tired, that's all. I did extra shifts at the site this week and I need some sleep. Plus, those places just remind me I'm not really drinking at the moment. And it's not like I can dance."

Louis lifted his elegantly shaped eyebrows. "Dear God, next he's going to say he has nothing to wear."

My turn to roll my eyes. "Look, guys, you know how grateful I am you put me up, but you don't have to sort out a social life for me as well. I'm good just as I am."

There was a moment's silence as they both looked at me.

"Yes, of course," Louis said in a tone that implied the complete opposite.

"Max, he has a point," Jack said. "You've been a social hermit for months. You never used to be so quiet. You enjoyed clubbing and parties."

"And men—" Louis winced as Jack pinched him. "Well, you did! I haven't seen you date anyone more than once for months."

"It's not a crime." Louis didn't notice my sharp tone, but Jack did, and his eyes narrowed.

"Just come out for an hour or so, okay? We'll catch a cheap pizza at Luigi's on the promenade, then go and see what they've done with the décor at Compulsion. It's not that seedy old place we used to scam our way into after school. No more sticking to the spilled beer on the carpet, no cracked glasses, no broken urinals and that hideous yellow lighting. It's been bought out by a national chain and gone seriously upmarket." Louis was wheedling. On him, it had a certain naïve charm. "You can leave straight afterwards. You don't have to dance. You don't even have to stay for the show."

"But Louis is dancing," Jack added quickly. "Just a couple of places below top billing this time. It's a real opportunity for him. You'll want to see that, won't you?" His eyes shone with pride, making it obvious he couldn't imagine anyone would want to miss it.

I sighed and smiled. "Is that a condition of my tenancy agreement?"

Jack frowned. "You know there's nothing like that, Max. Shit, I wouldn't even charge you rent if you didn't make such a bloody fuss—"

"Joke!" I held up a hand in surrender. Dammit, I couldn't even pitch my humor right nowadays. "Jack, Louis, I'm sorry. I didn't mean it like that. I don't know what I'd have done if you hadn't offered me the room, if you hadn't coped with me turning up on your doorstep at some godforsaken hour of the night with nothing but a bag of clothes and a couple of quid left over from the bus ticket."

"So?" Louis made a show of looking at his watch.

"I'll go and get changed," I said, grinning.

They lived in a small house in Kemptown, built in the 1950s and now converted into two flats. They had the upper floor, which included a small attic. That's where my room was, in the eaves of the building, up a short flight of stairs from the other rooms. There was just enough space for a single bed, a chest of drawers for my clothes, and a small sink against one wall. Since it wasn't really big enough for a guest bedroom, they'd been using it as Jack's home office, I think. The night after I arrived, I caught him shifting a pile of boxes that were full of files and papers, but he insisted it was just a room they used for storage: I was ostensibly doing him a favor by occupying it. In those days, the only furniture was a desk, a chair, and an old couch with ripped covers, but they cleared it all out and brought in a bed shortly after. Louis said it was a friend's castoff, but it looked suspiciously new. I bought myself a small secondhand TV and DVD player, and I'd stayed there ever since. Occasionally I talked about looking for my own place, but they always changed the subject and served up something particularly good for supper that night. To tell you the truth—and nothing to do with the food—I didn't have much appetite to go out on my own.

I was shrugging into my shirt when there was a quiet knock from the landing outside. That was Jack. I zipped up my jeans and opened the door to him.

His eyes flickered up and down. "Purple suits you."

I grimaced. "It's not like I have a lot of smart stuff to choose from." Working on a construction site didn't call for formal clothing, and as for going out on the town—well, I'd just been through that with the guys, hadn't I?

Jack nodded. He was a couple of inches taller than me and far more stockily built. He leaned toward me, his eyes fixed on mine. "If I say you look good, you do."

"Sure." I laughed. "I know you're not coming on to me when you already have your own pretty boy."

Jack didn't laugh back, though we often teased each other that way. Or at least, we used to. But he wasn't angry either. He just looked… concerned. "Give it up, Max."

"What?"

"Making everything a joke, like you're hiding from anything serious. We're your friends, remember? We know you from way back, we know you're a good bloke. You don't have to keep excusing everything you do. And there's nothing to be scared of here."

My mouth was suddenly dry. "I'm not scared. Look, Jack, I'm not keen on getting heavy at the moment. Let's just go out for the meal, right?"

Louis's voice floated up from the bottom of my stairs. "Has anyone seen my black jacket? With the silver buttons?"

Jack smiled, but I knew it was an expression of his fondness for Louis rather than a response to anything I said.

Impulsively, I reached over and took Jack's arm. "I meant it, you know. About being grateful. You're the best."

He nodded, his smile for me now. "It's nothing. Really, it is. We like having you here. We want you to be happy, Max."

Louis came running up the stairs to stand behind Jack. "Ready, gentlemen? Let's get going. I want to be there early enough to get a table by the dance floor for when the club music starts." He leaned up and nuzzled at Jack's ear, slid a hand around Jack's waist, and fondled the front of his trousers.

"We haven't even got out the front door yet," I grumbled. "If you're going to jump each other in my doorway, at least move to the side so I can go on ahead and get my food."

Louis smirked. "We all go together. I don't trust you not to slide away straight after the pizza."

"Just an hour or so, you said. I'll be sociable, I promise you. But then I get a taxi back, okay?"

Louis caught my arm as I wriggled past him. We'd all been laughing, but now he sounded serious too. Seemed they'd launched some kind of pincer attack on me tonight. "Max, we want you to be with us tonight. You don't have enough fun. You always used to."

I bit back the instinctively sharp reply. It'd be unfair when it was nothing to do with them. "I'm fine. Honestly. I thought you were the one wanted to get going?"

He grinned, and we made our way down the stairs and out of the flat together. It was a pleasant walk into Brighton and only a mile or so into the town center. My attic room looked out over the road—a steep incline down to the promenade—and on weekend nights, there was plenty of bustle from visitors to the guesthouses up the street. It had been especially busy over the May bank holiday weekend just passed. During the week was a quieter time, with the distant whine of workday traffic passing along the sea front and the occasional bark from a neighbor's dog. I loved the area—I grew up in foster homes in Hove and Rottingdean. The smell of the sea was in my blood.

Jack and Louis linked arms, and we started the walk down toward the clubs and bars. We'd only get a taxi back if we didn't feel up to walking at the end of the evening, exactly as we'd always done all through our teenage years. Tonight the sea air was salty and slightly damp, the low breeze tickling the ends of my hair on my shoulders. The weather had been largely rain free for the last week or so, with that pale mistiness over the sun that kept the evenings cooler. The horizon was lit by an early evening rose-gold glow, and the sea was settling into low tide. I could hear waves lapping the stones of the beach and the sharp cries of seagulls swooping down to forage. It had been a busy Saturday for tourists, and there were always plenty of pickings. Eventually the birds would become nothing more than familiar silhouettes against the indigo night sky, their cries dying down until morning.

Louis and Jack spoke in low voices, Louis laughing now and then when Jack obviously teased him. They weren't excluding me, but the pavement was too narrow for three to walk abreast, and I fell back a few steps quite naturally. My heart was beating too fast and I was stupidly nervous. What the hell was all that about? It was only a club, after all, and I'd been in plenty of them over the years. *Yeah,* my memories prodded me. *You certainly did that.*

But now things were different. I wanted control over my life, and that was how things had to be. It wasn't an option to go back to those days, was it? To that wild, excessive lifestyle—that limbo time between first growing up and finally getting smart. I paused on the pavement for just one second, wondering whether I'd get away with turning back tonight. I knew I wouldn't.

Maybe, like Jack said, I *was* scared. But there was no way I could tell my best friends why.

CHAPTER 2

GOD, but it was hot in the club! And dark, and loud, and everyone looked pale and virtually prepubescent under the neon lights. I refused to believe I was getting too old for gay clubs at twenty-three—I was just out of practice. Louis had bustled us through the pizza restaurant at top speed, but it meant we arrived at Compulsion in time to snatch one of the small tables close to the bar and in full view of the dance floor. Up until midnight, the music was loud enough to enjoy but low enough to chat. Then the lights started flashing, the music was pumped up to full volume, and Louis was itching to get up and dance. One only half-apologetic glance at Jack and then he left us alone at the table. It wasn't time for his set yet, but he danced for the pleasure of it. He always had. Plenty of eyes followed him into the middle of the wooden dance floor; he was a graceful sway of pale, whipping hair and sexy clothing. We weren't the only ones fascinated by his sensual gyrations, uplifted by the smile of concentrated joy on his flushing face.

Louis Barrington came from a family that had rarely been out of the headlines in one place or another. His mother was a few degrees of separation from European aristocracy but had married into modern money. I remembered how Louis's dad—a big name in London city finance—had single-handedly sponsored a new games hall at our school. Louis was expected to follow in his father's footsteps: he certainly had the brains for it and the drive. But there'd been an awkward couple of years in his midteens when he came out to them, and then when they'd become more or less reconciled to that, he

announced he wanted a career in entertainment instead. And he stood
his ground until they agreed to a drama studies degree in Sussex
rather than the anticipated Oxbridge route. He inherited a small
income from his grandparents when he turned twenty-one, but as far
as I knew, he never called on his parents for anything else. When we
were at Uni together, he supplemented his money with dancing gigs
and joined one of those agencies for theatrical extras. I didn't watch
much TV, but I was sure I saw his face in more than a couple of
crowd scenes.

Louis was no shrinking violet—he'd always stood out from the
crowd, and since he got older and bolder, I could see that he reveled
in it. He was gorgeous and bloody vain, but he was determined too. If
anyone made it to the top in his chosen occupation, Louis would. Jack
told me that every weekend, a small core of fans followed Louis from
club to club, wherever he could find a dance booking. Compulsion
had been closed for a couple of months in the New Year for
refurbishment, but Louis had been on the VIP list ever since the
reopening, and it looked like he'd work his usual magic here as well.

"He looks good, eh?" I tried not to bawl into Jack's ear, though
I'd forgotten how difficult it was to be heard in places like this. Jack
smelled of some exotic cologne Louis had given him for his last
birthday. I bet myself he didn't wear it Monday to Friday at the
science lab, but I didn't tease him about it.

He didn't turn to look at me, but I saw his smile as he gazed at
Louis. "Damn good. If he does well in the guest spot, they're talking
about a regular booking. He'd love that." His smile broadened. Louis
was laughing at something one of his many friends had said to him as
they passed. We couldn't hear him from where we were, but there
was no mistaking the happy way he threw his head back, his eyes
glistening in the lights. "Damn good," Jack repeated, his voice too
quiet for me to catch more than a whisper.

I smiled too. Jack Wallis had been one of the steadier guys in
my group at school, a bit of a geek and always serious. We laughed
tolerantly when he told us he'd be a forensic scientist one day; he was
fascinated by the crime series on TV and wanted to be one of those
who helped the police. Now who was laughing, when he had a good
job and was doing exactly what he planned? And one of the youngest

consultants at the company too. All we knew then was that he was the complete opposite to the extrovert Louis. I don't think we were even sure he was gay, or at least we didn't discuss it with him. Unlike Louis, who was out, proud, and loud, Jack kept that kind of thing to himself. I don't think any of us saw it coming until we found the two of them wrapped around each other at a friend's party, tongues virtually fused in each other's mouths. It was the summer just after we all left school, and they'd been together ever since, all through college. Jack had gone to a Uni in Kent, but he always kept his home base in Brighton, returning every weekend to be with Louis. Eventually they moved into their own flat, and now they were living a grown-up life. Unlike some others I could mention.

I shifted awkwardly in my seat and Jack turned to face me. He stared at me in his direct way. "You know I was only joking earlier, don't you?"

The vibration from the music deck throbbed through the floor, warming my belly. "Yeah, of course." I felt uneasy but managed to grin back. By now we were more than halfway to lipreading over the thudding beat. My chair was knocked by a group of people struggling past the tables to get a drink. I wondered whether to do the same myself: I'd only drunk water with the earlier meal.

"I wasn't lying," Jack said. "You do look great tonight. I can't believe you're not hit on all the time. And you need it. You need *something* apart from work and our company."

Many a true word spoken in jest, I thought. I knew he meant well; both of them did. They just didn't know what I'd been through—and what I wanted to leave behind. They thought everyone wanted to be like them. "A soul mate like yours?"

Jack may have flushed; I couldn't really tell in the reflected lights from the bar. "If you don't feel comfortable here, don't let us keep you—"

"No." I reached over and gripped his arm. "I didn't mean that. I'm jealous, I expect, that's all. Things have come together for you two, whereas I…." I wasn't sure where that sentence was going, so I let it slip away.

"It will for you too." Even over the noise, I could tell Jack was choosing words carefully. Did I really need handling with kid gloves? Not for the first time, I wondered how the hell I appeared to other people. "You've had a hard time, but you're on the right track again, right?"

"Right." I nodded, more to satisfy him than myself.

But he was relentless tonight. In a very different way from Louis—in a far more assertive way, I must say—and I was caught off guard. "Look, Max, you haven't been out with anyone since you came back to Brighton. That's—"

"A couple of months," I muttered.

"Almost six," he replied smartly. "But there's no shortage of guys looking your way, so why not? You're bright, you've got a steady job now and some money. And you look okay."

"Thanks," I said drily.

He laughed. "I'm not trying to drag you into the Louis-Jack connubial bliss club. But you always loved attention."

"You mean sex?"

"You say that like it's a bad thing. You never thought that way before." He shook his head, still smiling. "But not just that. You were more lively, more tactile. I mean, you're still generous with yourself as a friend, but don't you need something else for yourself?"

"More trouble than it's worth," I replied. I wished the music would stop, that Louis would come back to the table. I needed to distract my well-meaning friend, and soon.

"You know you can talk to me if you ever want to, about while you were away...."

I sucked in a breath. He must have caught the expression on my face because he shook his head again, acknowledging my resistance. It wasn't going to happen. I couldn't bear them knowing about it all, realizing what a mess I'd made of everything. How I'd disappointed everyone, including myself. No, I never wanted to tell them the whole sordid story.

I dropped out of Uni just before my final exams, much to everyone's shock and disapproval, and left my digs shortly after. I must have known what a short-sighted decision it was, but my boyfriend at the time had been based back in London and offered to get me a job there. My blind lust colored it a much better opportunity than it ever was. I'd already discovered I was a crappy student, even though I was interested in my Media Studies course. In reality I partied too much, couldn't settle to writing up assignments, and spent all my money on fast food. The struggle outweighed the benefits, in my opinion. I expected to be chucked out at any time, so I just jumped first. Or that's what I told myself.

Jack and Louis were the only two of our group who stuck with me. They never gave me a hard time about dumping everything without a word. Jack had just passed his driving test and bought a small car, and on the morning I left Brighton like a humiliated gunslinger on his way out of Dodge, he offered to take me to the station so I didn't have to drag my case up the hill. It was some hideously early hour of the morning too. It shamed me now to remember how I wouldn't let him get out of the car to see me off, in case he tried at the last minute to stop me.

After a while, I sent them a mobile contact number. Nothing else, and I made them swear not to give it to anyone. They went on to finish their degrees that year and get jobs and a happy home life, like I could have done. Maybe. They had no idea what I went on to. I told them I'd moved to the bright lights for fame and fortune. They didn't know my shit of a boyfriend never got me a job at all and very soon afterward was my ex. They didn't know the stream of casual jobs I chased after, the one-night stands I lost count of, the crappy dives I begged a room to sleep in, the weird friends I started to hang around with purely by virtue of the fact that we were all either homeless or jobless—or both—at the same time. I called Jack and Louis and we talked now and then. But I'd never been very good on the phone, and I never wrote or e-mailed. I didn't like to tell them exactly where I was or what I was doing. Partly in case they asked whether it had been worth it; partly because, after a while, I was ashamed to talk about it. Our lives became less and less comparable.

Those bright lights tarnished really bloody swiftly.

To give them their due, Jack and Louis never complained about my fitful friendship, and hardly anyone else asked after me. I kept in touch with some of my foster families with Christmas and birthday cards and the rare e-mail, but my placements got shorter in duration as I got older and mouthier and determined to look after myself, so I never expected anyone to follow up on how I was doing. Instead, Jack and Louis chatted to me when I did call, and when that started to be less and less frequent, they told me I could always come to either of them, if and when I needed to.

And then one day I did.

"Take it easy," Jack said. He'd leaned close to me over the table while my thoughts were miles away. "I didn't mean to hit a nerve."

"You didn't." I'm sure he was really thinking, *What the hell happened to you, made you so touchy?* In the background, the music changed beat as one of the club dancers stepped onto the small stage beside the music desk. There was a ripple of listless applause.

"Was it someone special, Max?"

"What are you talking about?" My thoughts were turning toward escape. It was cowardly, but I started calculating how long it'd take me to reach the taxi rank.

"Whoever you were close to, in London. If it all went wrong, you know Louis and I want to help. No point bottling it up."

"Leave it, Jack." I could hear the growl in my voice. My heart rate was increasing. "You don't know anything about it."

"Then tell us. Tell *me*." There was a determined cast to his dark eyes that made me nervous. He was moving onto dangerous ground— dangerous for me. "It's eating you up, Max. Maybe you don't see it, but you're a shadow of yourself sometimes. At least, of the mate we used to know."

"I'm fine."

He bloody well ignored me. "Time to come out of the shell, right? If it was something bad, you're back with friends. And if it was something good, well then, don't dump the memories along with everything else. You shouldn't be afraid to take people to heart. Don't you think you deserve that?"

Don't you think…? Did Jack have any idea at all of what I deserved?

"What did he—?"

"There's no one!" I slammed my hand down on the tabletop, making the beer bottles rattle alarmingly. The heat rose up through my body, raging in me, bringing me almost to my feet. "He's dead! He's *dead*, okay?"

CHAPTER 3

THANK God the music had started up again at its loudest, or security would've been on their way over. I'd thrust my head forward, glowering at Jack, and a couple of people at the table next to us swiveled around on their seats, startled by my voice.

There was a shocked, still moment between the pair of us, even amid the throb of dance music and the rise and fall of party voices. I stared at Jack and he stared back, eyes wide. It was obvious we were both startled at how things had slipped out of control.

"Come out to the lobby," he said. "It's quieter there. Please, Max."

I followed him, mainly for the sake of making amends. There were still patrons lined up there, paying for their entrance, but the noise level was much lower. There were also several padded chairs set against the wall, and Jack pulled me over with him to sit in a couple of these.

He leaned forward, his hand on my knee. "Shit, Max, I'm so sorry."

"Jack, it isn't what you think, you know?" I could hear the break in my voice even as I fought to control it. "I'm the one who's sorry. Yelling at you like that, I just…."

"It's okay."

I took a deep breath. "It's not. You're right. I'm just not ready to talk about it yet. There was someone, but not in the way you mean. Not a lover. He was a friend. Someone I thought a hell of a lot of."

Jack nodded, his strong hand back on my arm. "I didn't mean to stir things up. Shit, Louis will…." He shook his head.

"He'll go ballistic?"

Jack grimaced. "Yeah. He says I'm to leave it alone—to leave *you* alone. Says we have to let you open up in your own time. Give you time to…." He shrugged. "Whatever."

Whatever. I didn't want to talk about this, even though Jack was obviously worried. And me? I sat in a virtually public place as if I were totally alone, trying to shake off a creeping depression. I felt withdrawn from everything around me, inside a bubble of lonely misery, isolated in the middle of the fluorescent-lit lobby of a busy club on a Saturday night.

In my mind, I was scared again. I was on a cold, cracked London pavement around the back of Soho, crouched over a crumpled and bleeding body. The night air was rank with the smell of smoke, weed, and spilled alcohol. Tacky neon lighting gave a sickly cast to the scene, accompanied by the distant bass beat of dance music from a nearby building. I was crying outside a club just like this one. It looked like some cheap, corny set in a movie about the capital's seedy underground.

But it wasn't a scene from a film—it was a memory of real life. It was vivid because I'd been there—I'd seen the man's blood as a dark shadow in the artificial light, the puddle underneath his torso creeping slowly and irresistibly across the concrete, his life leeching away with it. My cheeks were wet with tears of shock and grief, and my hands shook as I grasped the lapels of his coat, trying to keep him with me, trying… to make it not so.

"Max?" Jack's hand pressed more tightly.

That was the day I realized everything had gone wrong. My move to London should have been a great adventure, a way to express my rebellion, releasing my much wilder side, embracing the independent *me*. Yet there I was, on my knees in a charity-shop shirt and worn jeans, sobbing pathetically over my only real friend, who lay dying in the street while everyone else backed off, scared. And I was fucking scared too.

"Max!"

This time I turned to face Jack, the club coming back into focus around me. "Sorry, man."

"Tell me," he said. He couldn't hide the urgency in his tone.

"Stewart Matthews," I said. "That was his name. About twenty years older than me, well educated, from a good family. A really great guy. Always reasonable, always fair, even when I was the most trouble I've ever been."

"This was when you were first in London?"

I nodded. "It wasn't… what I thought it'd be." Jack was obviously a damned good friend, because he didn't interrupt, just waited for me to go on. "I was lost, Jack. A real fucking mess. I never thought I was vulnerable, but I saw so many that were… and then I realized I was headed the same way. Thinking I was so bloody clever, picking up with a crowd because I wanted to belong, not because I felt good with them. And out of control. Too fucking fond of grabbing what was on offer, too greedy, too easy. That's all I ever was."

"No," Jack said, sounding fierce. "That's not bloody true."

"Stewart was a youth worker at a local center. He knew a lot of the kids on the street wouldn't come to the center unprompted, even if they needed help, so he used to go out to meet them. Just for a chat and an occasional coffee, you know?"

"You liked him."

"Yeah. He was great to talk to. We had a similar sense of humor. I could talk about my Uni days without being mocked about getting above myself." I smiled through the sadness. "He reminded me of you guys in some ways." I suspected it was more like Stewart reminded me of the days when I had a decent place in life.

The friendship stalled my destructive tendencies for a while. Stewart pulled me out of the crowd, encouraged me to help him with his work at the center. We mended the pool table, set up a bike repair stall, ran a couple of football tournaments—laughable shambles but careless fun. He talked to me about things beyond the next packet of smokes and how to avoid the landlord at the latest squat. He wanted to help me, but he never pushed too hard. Knew he shouldn't have to, that I had to find that way myself. It was obvious he'd already found his own place in life—a job he enjoyed, satisfaction, respect. I wanted that too. I always knew it, even while I was chasing the kind of excitement you get from booze and one-night gropes in dark, dirty back streets.

"Max?" Jack was looking worried again. "Do you want to tell me… how did he die?"

All of that satisfaction and respect crap didn't save Stewart in the end. He picked me up one night outside the local club on Dean Street, where I was doing some unofficial cleaning work, and we were going back to his flat for coffee. We had plans to discuss the center's forthcoming Christmas celebrations. It was a humid, misty autumn night, and although the main streets around Soho were familiar, many of the cut-through alleys weren't safe. London was a teeming mass of excitement and opportunity, but danger as well—like any major city. Too much sordid social history, too many shadows.

We took a route around the gardens at Soho Square, despite the area's dodgy reputation at night. It wasn't as if I hadn't been through there plenty of times with no trouble, and we wanted to catch the tube at Tottenham Court Road out to Stewart's place in Camden. But before we even made the turn at the end of the road, one of the shadows darkened ahead of us and materialized into a man in a hoodie. Stewart and I both hesitated, and I caught a glimpse of something that glittered. I barely had time to form the word *knife* in my mind before the guy put his head down and barreled into Stewart.

It all happened too quickly. People say that, don't they? But it was true that night. Stewart went down on his knees on the pavement with a guttural *oomph*. Acting purely on instinct, I launched myself at the guy. Yeah, me, Max Newman—tall and skinny, who never darkened the door of any gym, who had no relevant qualifications except for an occasional scrappy street fight at pub closing time over possession of a spliff. I punched him clumsily in the stomach before he kneed me in the balls and ran off, back toward the club we'd just left.

When I rolled over, wheezing, I found Stewart lying beside me, still and pale on his back on the cold ground. A few people who'd been leaving the club at the same time gathered at a cautious distance. No one spoke. A slow trickle of dark liquid eased out from under Stewart's coat, following the path between the paving stones. No body movement, no expression on his face, no flicker under his closed eyelids. There was no sign of the knife, but it was obvious Stewart had been stabbed. I just couldn't—wouldn't—understand why.

"Mugging," I said slowly, dully. "They said it was a random mugging." The club where I'd been working was small but fashionable and often featured in the city entertainment press. But it hadn't always been that way. Before it was taken over the previous year, it had been a seedy, dull little place, long overdue for renovation and making do with facilities that would never have passed a Health and Safety check. It was a haven for lost youths who hadn't anywhere else to go apart from a grubby shared room—yeah, just like me. It also attracted more than its fair share of local gangs and dealers. I guess some of them hadn't moved on yet.

Stewart's youth center was rough and ready, based in a local church hall, but he called it a refuge, and he set it up for those very lost youths who still caused trouble on the streets. He was proud of it and had all kinds of plans for decorating it and bringing in modern facilities and games equipment, but he never had enough authority, and definitely never enough cash. To some of the guys who hung around the club, he was a joke. A couple of times he got beaten up, so I was told. But he kept on trying, chatting to anyone who welcomed him, offering company at the center without strings, and maybe some other future in life.

Until they took his life away from him. What kind of fair was that?

But what was worse, and despite what I told Jack, I'd always suspected it wasn't a random mugging. Stewart only ever carried a couple of tenners in his wallet, and in his pockets were his keys, a Travelcard, and a disposable lighter. He liked the red ones with the Arsenal crest stamped on them. He didn't smoke, but it was his favorite football team, and offering the lighter for their cigarettes was one of the ways he got chatting with kids.

He still had all of it on him after he was stabbed; it didn't make sense. That night, as I knelt beside him, crying, I knew I had to pull myself together enough to yell for someone to call 999. But I knew he was already dying. So that's when it happened—something more cowardly, more disgusting than I'd ever done before. Something I wasn't going to forgive myself for, not for a very long time.

I ran away.

What could I say in my defense? I'd personally tried to find an excuse for months and failed to find anything comforting. At the time, I was confused and scared and looking for a chance to break away from that lifestyle, but that didn't excuse the fact I left Stewart dying on a pavement, victim of a horrible crime, alone and abandoned by anyone else who knew him.

That was the point when I decided things had to change for me. That *I* had to change them. I'd stop the drinking and casual sex and the abuse of whatever other substances were on offer. I ran away from those bright but destructive lights and found myself back in the place I grew up. Back to the sea, to the couple of friends I had left, and a different life. It was a sorry flight, an escape, or maybe a new start—a refuge of my own.

I wasn't too sure at the moment which.

THE throb of the club beat seeped into me, jolting me back to the present. I focused back on Jack's look of concern. He was mercifully silent, perhaps realizing I didn't want to go into any details. To be honest, I didn't think the words would come out. And it was all behind me now.

Wasn't it?

The music never stopped, but it changed to a cheeky fanfare, announcing that Louis was ready for his spot on the small stage beside the music desk. This time there were encouraging catcalls and clapping from the dance floor. Jack and I both stood up, looking back toward the entrance to the bar. Jack's eyes flashed with excitement, and his attention was obviously torn between supporting me and following Louis's set.

"Go and watch from the front," I said.

"You—"

"Go!" I pushed him none too gently, but I smiled to let him know it was fine with me. "I'll follow in a minute."

With an apologetic shrug, Jack left the lobby and hurried back to the dance floor. I followed more slowly, watching Jack wriggle his way through to the front of the crowd to watch the show. I stayed at the back. Not that Louis wasn't exciting—his dancing always was. Tonight's set was based on a pastiche of *On the Town*, complete with full US naval uniform, at least when he started. His style was a mixture of the athletic grace of Gene Kelly and the blatant sexuality of the best kind of pole dancer. He lost most of his clothes by the end of it, of course, but he had the kind of attraction that made guys remember his face as well. Something about the smile: half-mischievous, half-provocative. There was plenty of applause and whistling, so it was obviously a popular session, and I was confident they'd want to hire him regularly. He hadn't found any acting roles recently, so it'd be a bonus for him and Jack to have extra income coming in.

I glanced at my watch: it was nearly 1:00 a.m. The music shifted tempo again and the lights dimmed on the stage. The set was over and general dancing started up again. The crowd in front of me split into smaller groups, some of them moving onto the floor, some of them retreating back to the bar. I made my way to our previous table, and Jack came to join me.

Louis came over to us, his bare limbs shining with sweat as he batted off a crowd of clamoring, ever-hopeful hands at his arse. His eyes were bright and fierce, his smile elated. He'd slipped on a clean sleeveless shirt over a pair of his own brief shorts, but Jack told me the two of them wouldn't stay at the club much longer. Louis was always keen to get home and washed up properly after a dance spot. For the time being, he slid into the seat beside Jack and their existence shrank back to each other. With a happy shake of his head, Louis refused my offer of another bottled water, and I don't think either of them noticed when I left the table and went over to the bar.

I ordered a beer for myself. Tonight it tasted as sharp as if I'd been waiting for weeks, not days, for a drink. I savored the cold, blissful shock of it in my throat, the dribble of condensation on my hand from the bottle. Glancing back over to the table, I saw Jack and Louis had been joined by another couple of friends. They were all laughing, distracted. I finished the first beer quickly and ordered another. I meant to take my time drinking this one, but the cool liquid was both stimulating and seductive. I was still shaken from my talk with Jack, so I found a spot at the bar where I could lean on the counter, resting my back against a pillar. It meant I wasn't jostled too often by other customers and I could look back over the seating area. The hope was that I'd calm down and recover my equilibrium, but the cruel, sorry memories of London wouldn't leave me alone. I lifted the bottle to my mouth and back down a few more times and felt my mind retreat into itself, away from the hubbub and flashing lights. When I nodded to the barman for a third beer, I felt a residual sway in my body. Shit, I *was* out of practice.

This time I was handed a paper napkin with the bottle. I glanced at it, intending to discard it back on the bar. It was a promotional sheet with "Compulsion" written across one corner in bold but elegant script. Below that was printed "a Medina Group venue" and the website details of the new owners.

My stomach clenched. The words blurred slightly as my head spun with both anger and shock. It was a coincidence, wasn't it? I peered at it again as if I'd discover I'd misread it. *Wishful bloody thinking.* I crumpled the napkin with more force than was necessary and dropped it back on the counter.

My memory flared again: that hideous night when Stewart was knifed, and my struggle to get any help or acknowledgement. I sucked in a breath, my skin prickling, as cold as if I were outside again in the friendless night. I recalled the way people moved away quickly rather than get too close to secondhand horror; my despairing glance back at the club, and the bouncers standing like immutable rock outside the doors, careless of what was happening; the people shapes blurring in my tears, shifty shadows in the neon light from the club's sign…

A light that flickered through the name in some fancy designer script but still clearly announcing: "a Medina Group venue."

CHAPTER 4

I GRIPPED the edge of the counter, suddenly dizzy as I rested my half-full bottle back on the top. It was then, while I was trying to come to terms with way too many disturbing memories, that I saw him. A man who stood at the other end of the bar, nursing a clear drink, leaning casually on the shiny beer-stained surface. Just another guy, I told myself.

I didn't listen.

He was as tall as I was, dressed in similar black jeans, though they were better fitted than my low-slung style, and snug around his compact arse. His shirt was long-sleeved, tucked into his jeans and buttoned to halfway up his chest. It was pale, perhaps a cream or a gold color—I couldn't decide which under the dim lighting. I could see the shadows of a well-developed chest under the fabric, wide shoulders, and skin that was darker than mine. Mediterranean, maybe. It was a look I always liked.

Of course, I didn't ogle men, not nowadays. I kept my head down and my needs tight inside. Had done since… well, since I came back to Brighton, according to my would-be matchmaking friends. I'd be lying if I laughed off what Jack said earlier: I knew I got plenty of come-on looks when I was out. And I had dated—well, now and then. I just didn't let it go any further than casual. It was the safest strategy I could think of. That rush of lust and excitement and carelessness had led me into trouble all my adult life. I was determined to control it now.

But tonight I gazed at *him*. I don't think I could have said exactly what caught my attention, but I was suddenly, startlingly hooked. His face was in profile, but I could see slightly more than half, and he was very striking. *Way* beyond striking. His eyes were shadowed by heavy lids, and he had a strong jaw and a slightly hooked nose. He wasn't one of the cute twink dancers or muscled beach boys that clustered in here over the summer months; his features were more mature than that. I wondered how much older than me he was—probably only a couple of years. He had night-black hair cut very close to a well-shaped head, a neat mustache, and a trimmed beard framing his jaw line.

As I watched, he sipped at his drink. Slowly and deliberately, like he wasn't particularly thirsty but wanted to be doing something with it. His mouth was wide, though the lips were pursed together. Even at this distance and under the fitful light, I could see them glistening with the liquid. I found myself wondering what they'd taste like: how rich they'd be, how responsive. I recognized the feeling, of course, deep in the pit of my stomach, perhaps a little lower. *Long time no see*. But I was just as sure that it wasn't going to get a hold of me, not like it used to.

And then he turned his head and looked straight at me.

His eyes glittered; he blinked slowly. I told myself he couldn't have known for definite I'd been watching him. It was too dark and busy at the counter, and we were too far apart for that. Bartenders darted back and forth, sweating and grinning and shouting out orders; beer bottles chinked together and shot glasses lined up, sparkling with weird layered concoctions. But the man's eyes stayed on me—wide and deep colored, reflecting the glint from the optics on the wall and absorbing it at the same time. The effect was hypnotic. Things stood like that for all of ten, maybe twenty seconds. Then he lifted his glass very gently, saluting me, and his mouth twisted into a slow, encouraging smile.

No, I thought.

His head inclined a little, as if he were calling me over. He didn't say anything, though there was no way we could have heard any words over that din.

No, I thought again. I knew that game too well to want to play it, right? But my feet moved instinctively. A group of men in matching leather shorts, braces, and firemen helmets had just arrived at the bar beside me. They were shouting and laughing as they handed out bottled beers among their group. I pushed right past them, and walked over to the mystery man.

I stopped close enough so no one else would force their way between us but far enough apart that we wouldn't touch accidentally. His eyes were still on me, but he'd put the glass back down on the bar. I don't know whether it was the fact I'd been drinking or the astonishing glow in those fabulous eyes, but an aura sparked off him like electricity. I didn't even have to touch him to feel it. The current ran through my whole body.

I knew this was a really bad idea. I didn't have the time or appetite for strange fascinations or lustful hookups, not even with a man whose grip around a plain glass made my nerves shudder with the anticipation of feeling that grip on *me*. No, I wasn't into the party and club life anymore; I didn't want to catch anyone's attention. I wanted to keep myself to myself and try to get things straight in my life. Definitely.

So what the hell was the matter with me tonight? I was staring quite openly at him. Bloody rude of me. Maybe he reminded me of Stewart. The same shade of black hair, the same lean face, maybe a similar determined look in his eye. By the time I got closer to him, I saw they actually looked nothing alike. But perhaps that was why I was drawn to him, who knows? It wasn't enough to explain the thrill inside me.

I was struggling to speak—my throat was as tight as a fist. My nerves were strung as tightly as a guitar string and hummed excitement about as tunefully. Inside my jeans, I felt my balls shift and lift with physical need.

A *really* bad idea.

"…drink?"

It was still difficult to make out speech, but I got the word from the movement of his lips. He was watching my mouth, maybe for my reply, maybe just for the hell of it. All I knew was, it was very arousing. His eyelids slid down over dark-bright eyes and back up again. It was as if he wanted to take full measure of me in those brief moments.

I shook my head.

He frowned. "You look like you could use—"

"I've had enough tonight—"

We spoke together, then both laughed. I'd tuned into his voice, or maybe we were both speaking louder to be heard over the music.

"I look like I need a drink?" I asked.

"Like you need something," he said, his voice deep. He leaned into me and I smelled him—slight sweat from the damp skin around his throat, the tantalizing trail of an unknown but probably expensive cologne. It wrapped itself around me as strongly as a real and irresistible binding.

"You were watching me," he said.

I blinked hard, trying to think of something cool to say. "Just watching. That's all."

"It's okay. It's good." His eyes were still on me, a smile teasing the edges of his mouth. "I was watching too."

"Me? I didn't notice."

He nodded and shrugged. "You weren't meant to."

"Why?"

He frowned again. "Why? Because it doesn't matter. Because I wasn't...." He never finished the sentence.

"You didn't want me to notice?"

His shrug was almost imperceptible. "I said it doesn't matter."

"Maybe it does." I didn't know what had got into me, challenging him like this. It felt weird and confusing, and I wasn't in any mood for stupid pickup games. But something warm and irresistible crept along my veins, and I knew the seductive feeling had nothing to do with the mass of bodies around us. "Tell me."

He frowned as if puzzled. "I'm not here for anything in particular. For any*one*."

"Me neither." We both stared each other down for a few more seconds, our concentration giving that whole exchange the lie.

"Okay." His smile was slow, and I felt stupidly pleased to take it as the first climbdown. "I know somewhere we can go. Want to come with me?"

Did I? Hell, yeah.

I FOLLOWED him, never more than a foot behind, as he cut his way through the gyrating bodies on the dance floor toward the back of the room. We still hadn't touched in any way. I probably looked calm, but I felt like a lamb to the slaughter, and I knew in my heart that was exactly what I was. I told myself we were going to find a quieter room and talk, we were going to share a joint, or maybe I'd take him up on that offer of a drink. After all, we couldn't do much of that over the noise and scramble in this place. And then I'd get that taxi, go home, make strong coffee, and write the whole damned evening off to a moment's madness.

He stopped at the far wall in front of a door. It was flush against the dark paintwork and wouldn't have been noticed by most of the clients there tonight. There were no signs on it, nor a strip handle like the usual fire exit. A member of security stood nearby, and as we approached, she turned as if to stop us. But she stepped back when the man from the bar made a slight gesture with his hand. Then he pushed the door as if he knew it'd be open, it slid outward easily, and I followed him through.

It closed behind us with a heavy clunk, and the sudden drop in noise was a shock. I could only hear the beat of the music now, a regular throbbing bass that seemed to make the whole wall shudder. We'd stepped right outside of the building, and the chilly night air sent goose bumps along my skin after the heat of the dance floor. I took a quick glance around, wondering if this had been the most deceptive throwing-out I'd ever encountered, but I wasn't back out on the street. It was an enclosed space like a backyard, with brick walls of head height and rubbish bins full of plastic bags and packaging over in one corner. A couple of security bulbs were placed high on the back wall of the club, giving a pale, misty arc of light across the area in front of the doorway. Something moved behind the bins—maybe an urban fox. I heard the sudden rustle of dislodged cardboard and saw tiny eyes glinting warily in case we threatened its territory.

And then a hand landed heavily on my shoulder, I was spun around so my back hit the cold bricks of the nearest wall, and the mystery guy's mouth was on mine. Not a word, not a request, just hard, wet lips crushing mine and a fierce tongue pushing for admittance. My palms were flat against the wall, but he didn't try to hold me there. It was enough that his mouth claimed me. I surrendered immediately and willingly and damn, *damn* eagerly!

I'd always had a healthy libido. At least, that's what I called it, if and when I felt I should be kind to myself. I liked to touch, I liked to kiss—I liked sex. At least… I used to. But it hadn't always gone well. Jack joked about it with me earlier, but that had been one of the reasons I left Uni so easily. I'd been both excited and confused at the freedom I had there, almost scared to realize how quickly I could get carried away with it all. But I rarely held back. Within a few months of moving into the student flats, I gathered a complex and varied sexual history. I don't think I was indiscriminate—just hungry. And I'd always been attracted to the person, not just the body. Or so I justified it, until I reckoned I needed a wider and more exotic playground, and I moved out at the first tempting offer.

Like I said before: a case of jumping before I was pushed.

But I could genuinely say I'd rarely felt this rush of consuming, desperate *lust*—not since I was a teenager, first discovering I liked men and all their strong, sweaty, solid sexuality. Tonight I felt swamped by a terrible need, just like this guy had said. A purely physical reaction that made my head spin and my heart tighten in my chest. A deep desire to touch—to grab—to *possess*. I didn't know if the urgency was coming from him or from inside myself. His hands roamed over me as greedily and fiercely as if he were afraid I'd escape, so it seemed he felt the same way. Harsh breaths escaped him like gasps, as if he was startled or angry about it. I was too consumed by my own desire to ask which it was. How long had it been since I'd had a fuck? I genuinely couldn't remember. Something strange had happened tonight, from the minute I saw him. Something had loosened all my bonds.

We never spoke a word, though I'd have found it difficult with his probing tongue inside my mouth. I opened up even faster than he asked of me and I sucked him in, rolling my own tongue against him, tasting the hot skin and the cool taint of iced vodka in his mouth. He was panting, and I knew damn well that *I* was.

We broke apart from the kiss and his hands landed back on my shoulders like a blow, pressing me down the wall. I struggled for a minute, not sure what game we were playing. I clapped my hands onto *his* shoulders, acting instinctively, seeking to restrain him in return. I tried the same pressure myself, seeing if he would buckle instead. To see who'd surrender first.

Something flared in his eyes, but they were too close to me and he was too much of a stranger for me to understand it. But there was excitement there, and a challenge that I'd never had before.

"Get down," he growled. Out here in the fresh air, his voice reverberated in my ear. It was richer than I'd heard in the club, a match to his dark good looks. I slid, less than elegantly, down onto my arse.

When I glanced back up, I saw tall, shadowed buildings looming above my head from over the wall. Nothing but the featureless rear view of converted flats, where no one would venture out again until the brighter morning. This yard was obviously private. It was quiet except for the beat from the club behind us and the occasional wailing siren from the direction of the marina. It was a pregnant quiet, as we waited for each other's next move. I was fleetingly thankful the night was dry; I knew we weren't going back inside for a while yet.

His gaze had followed my path—my surrender—and now he reached for my hair, tangling it between his fingers. "I like this," he said.

I'd been white-blond as a child, or so the care system told me. There were no photos I ever saw, and over the years it turned a darker shade. Sometimes, covered in brick dust, it looked gray. But boyfriends had told me about the glint under certain lights, gold like an old sovereign. I wore it to my shoulders and never even tried to tame the curls.

"You got a name?" I struggled back up onto my knees. He'd turned around so his back was against the brick wall now. He was fumbling with the button of his jeans with one hand, his other grasping the back of my neck. And I was letting him. "*Any* name?"

He glared at me like he might tell me to mind my own business, but something in my face must have caught his attention. He hesitated and then smiled. "Severino. *Seve*." He pronounced it with a lilt on "Seve" that caught in his throat. A gentle accent, probably Spanish, only obvious on particular vowel sounds. Pretty damn sexy.

"I'm Max," I replied, but he didn't look as if he was listening. He tightened his grip on me, and his eyes glinted in the dim light, his gaze fixed on my mouth. Night shadows skimmed across the left side of his body, but under the open collar of his shirt, I could clearly see the olive tint of his skin, the muscles tensing in his sinewy neck. He opened his mouth, then closed it again. I watched the throb in his throat as he swallowed.

"This isn't…."

What? Was he having second thoughts? I wasn't in the mood for indecision. Every animalistic feeling I'd bred over the years surged to the surface, and I knew this had to be. "You want this?" I said roughly.

His eyes narrowed. "Of course."

We'd asked and accepted the terms. I grasped his thighs, leaned forward, and shamelessly mouthed the bulge in his jeans.

CHAPTER 5

SEVE groaned aloud and his hand slid up the back of my head, pushing me against his groin. I could feel the heat on my cheeks even before I reached my hand up and tugged down the zip. He hissed and his hips jerked. My nose rubbed against warm cotton briefs, the smell of skin and arousal like nectar.

No hesitation: the need in both of us was implicit. No "please." No "thank you." I grasped the thick cock as if it were the Holy Grail, peeled it out of its swaddling fabric, and took it fully into my mouth.

"Fuck." His whisper was so soft, I wasn't even sure I'd heard a coherent word. He pressed himself back hard against the wall. I leaned my weight against his legs, grasping the creased denim of his jeans, and began to move my mouth up and down, dragging my tongue along with it. The smell of his balls was musky and erotic, the dark, rougher pubic hairs tickling at my nose. His cock was thick and hot in my mouth and tasted like nothing on Earth. I couldn't possibly have forgotten how good a cock could taste—the sharp tang of living flesh on my tongue; the wrinkles of skin smoothing under my lips, stretching over a swelling shaft. I could feel the pulse of the vein along the side of it, could taste the droplets of precome as they oozed out of the slit for me to suck up. His hips strained against my hands as he thrust into my mouth in a parody of fucking, and his fingers gripped my hair close to the scalp. But he had no need to force me up and down. I was sucking for my own delight as well.

I hadn't done this for *so long*! I reckon I'd always been pretty good at it. The pleasure returned in a rush of sensation, and I tried very hard to pace myself, to control the excitement that was racing around me, making my hands clutch too tightly at his muscular thighs, my mouth suck too greedily at his dick. But he didn't complain. Maybe he liked it that way. Our combined breath was short and rasping, and when I glanced up, I could see a mist from his mouth as he panted his body heat into the rapidly cooling night air. My head bobbed back and forth, my mouth making soft suckling noises, and his grunts accompanied me. I wished to God I could get a hand down into my own briefs and relieve the ache I was suffering there.

I don't know how long it took. I was lost in the rhythm of sucking, and it seemed like I'd been pressed close to his groin forever. My mouth had always been filled with this flesh; my lips had always been bruised against his taut skin as I satisfied our hunger, deeper and harder. I felt a shudder deep in his balls and the catch of his breath as it announced the imminent end. But even as my heart raced at the thought of swallowing him and my lips tightened, he yanked my head back and slid me off.

Panting, I licked my swollen, frustrated lips and lifted my head to stare up at him. He still gripped me tight, but his eyes were half-closed. His chest heaved with breaths too shallow for comfort, and his thigh muscles twitched under my touch. His cock jutted out into my face, red, glossy with my saliva, and acting bloody angry at being denied. He looked superb: a vibrant, aching statue of a man, and I wanted so much more of him that I felt a physical hurt.

"You want to fuck me?" My voice was hoarse as if I hadn't used it for weeks. I knew what I was asking. It was all part of the strange surrender that had consumed me this night—I was contemplating letting some near stranger bury his cock in my arse, and I seemed to accept it as okay. Welcomed it, in fact.

"Yes." His tongue slipped out and moistened his lips. He bent his head forward, gazing back down at me with half-focused eyes. "*Yes!*"

I stood, my knees shaky. He watched me as I slipped open the button of my jeans and unzipped myself. I was standing there in an open yard and I was going to strip myself for this man to fuck me. Let's face it, it wasn't going to be comfortable. We were standing on a barely swept concrete floor with a brick wall for a view, surrounded by bags of rubbish and spied on by passing foxes. What's more, anyone might come out of the club and find us.

Which was the dominant feeling—terror or excitement?

I slid the jeans down my legs and flipped my briefs down after them. They caught on my erection, sending a shivering ache up to my groin. My dick was damp at the tip, swollen and desperate to be free of the cloth. I kicked the clothes off over my boots, my movements clumsy but determined, and pushed them away to the side. I hoped they didn't land in anything too sordid. I stood there in my crumpled shirt and footwear, nothing else. The night air rustled gently against my shirttails, blowing soft trails in the hair on my legs and tickling under my balls. I wondered when I'd last fucked in the open air. My memory wasn't up to scratch at all tonight.

Seve was breathing very heavily. He stared at my body, desire glittering in his eyes like fireflies. "Turn around."

He had a London accent, but the sensuous roll to his pronunciation made my skin crawl with excitement. I felt him move up behind me and his cock nudged at my arse cheeks, catching on the edge of my shirt. He was a shaft of pure heat under the silk. His hands landed on my shoulders again, and he pressed me forward so I had to throw out my hands to protect myself. I was forced up against the wall, my back bent in a concave shape. His hand slipped down to my buttocks, touching me there, firm, possessive. He shifted a knee between my legs and spread them further apart.

My cock bobbed rather perilously near the brickwork. This was going to hurt one way or another.

"You got a condom?" I was horny but still bemused at the way things had gone so fast, so fiercely. And unused to this whole thing: it had been a bloody long time since anyone took me.

"I… no." To give him his due, this whole thing seemed to have taken Seve as much by surprise as it had me. He cursed softly. His hand paused in smoothing my buttocks, creeping around inside the crack, brushing at my hole. I just about stopped myself pushing back against his fingers, begging for more.

"It's okay, I have." I couldn't believe I was saying this. "In my wallet." He bent down and I heard him scrabble around in my discarded clothing. I wondered if the fucking thing would be out of date by now—one of the guys on the construction site had slipped it to me a couple of months ago, just for a laugh. I'd never intended to use it. I heard Seve give a small, tight laugh. He'd obviously found the sachet of lube my mate had added as well. Well, now he'd know what sort of slut he was dealing with, wouldn't he? I flushed with embarrassment, but I knew we didn't have any kind of conversation going where I could explain that I wasn't like that, really. And anyway, it looked like I *was*, didn't it?

"Now," I said. "Do it now, Seve. Don't make me wait."

My cock hung down between my legs, and I clasped it tightly. It was hot and heavy and the new pressure was a welcome if temporary relief. Seve pressed up close, leaning on my back, his breath steamy at the nape of my neck. I felt the open zip of his jeans snagging at my thighs and his cock teasing between my cheeks. My hole clenched then flexed in desperate, needy confusion, trying to prepare for him coming in. I was dead scared that he'd never *get* in—I had to be tight as a gnat's arse from lack of recent attention. But from the soft, slippery touch of his cock on my chilled skin, I knew he was protected and lubed up. And then—*oh fuck*—there was a similarly slick finger pressing gently into me, probing and stretching the entrance.

Another thing I'd forgotten—the blessed, unmistakable delight of being fingered! My back arched shamelessly now, my body reaching for his touch, and I whimpered. His other hand twisted itself tightly into my hair and held my head back. The fingers slid in and out of me a few more times, then exited abruptly. His cock brushed there instead, a slightly clumsy prod against my hole. I opened my legs wider and my arse presented itself into his hands. I wanted him so badly I thought I was going to spontaneously combust.

He let out a deep, guttural sound in my ear and pushed into me. I yelped and jerked with the shock, but his arm gripped my waist and held me tight. He pulled back a little, then thrust more deeply, and my body moved with him. The momentum pressed me further against the wall so my forehead banged on it. I turned my head, preferring a grazed cheek to a concussion. He straightened again, pulling me slightly back, and started to fuck me with a steady, strong rhythm. I wondered, with fascination and desire in equal parts, how long he could last. He'd been ready to come only moments ago. But there was no sound from him or shiver in his body that made me think he wasn't in total control.

"I need…." I gasped, not really knowing what the hell I was saying and far from coherent in the middle of a fuck at the best of times. But he obviously understood me because his right hand left my waist and came down to my groin. He batted my flailing hand aside— I was doing a pathetic job of pleasing myself because my concentration was far, *far* away—and he fisted around me with perfect precision. There was lube on his palm and my dick was leaking with eager precome, so his grip was slick and effective. I moaned loudly and began to thrust into his hand. We moved in tandem, in the same rhythm. His fingers slipped firmly up and down my cock, teasing the excitement further up from the coil of lust deep in my groin. Seve may have had control of his bodily responses, but I was hurtling over the edge too bloody soon. We rocked together, nothing to be heard but the wet slap of sweaty flesh against even more sweaty flesh; the harsh grunt of a body slamming against another; the panting of two people concentrating on what must be surely one of the most pure, physically satisfying feelings ever discovered.

To my shame, I climaxed only a few seconds later. Fuck, I don't think I'd ever felt so good in my life, plus I'd had no practice in controlling the suspense in oh so many months. My body wanted to hit those heights and wanted it *now*! I gulped and sobbed and pumped out hot, creamy seed all over his hand. I looked down through ecstasy-blurred eyes as strings of it splattered onto the rough ground at my feet.

He let out another guttural moan. I was probably like a vise around his dick, but I didn't have any kind of control over those muscles at that moment. But as I started to relax and slump under his body, he clutched me back around the waist and started to speed up his fucking. I could hear his heart hammering against my spine, and the shudder I'd been waiting for in him started to run down his torso. I could feel it at my hips, feel his legs crushing against mine, his groin trying to sink even deeper into me.

And I was the one doing this to him.

"*Shit*," he hissed into my hair so that I barely heard him. His fingers pinched at my skin and he bucked a couple of times. Then I felt the erratic thrust and the catch of his breath that declared—in my experience—he was coming.

He groaned aloud and his body shuddered. In the distance, a car horn sounded from a motorist angry at having to wait behind someone at the lights. I thought I could hear the insistent throb of house music played at top volume through its window as it passed up the street on the other side of the wall. And then the silence fell around us again.

SEVE groaned with some kind of relief and straightened up. He pulled cautiously out of me, then peeled off the soggy condom and threw it into a pile of overflow rubbish by the nearest bin. I heard the soft plop as it fell onto a pile of dusty cardboard.

I realized how little our skin had touched, though my arse and legs were bare and his jeans were still wide open at his groin. I struggled to regain my breath. When I craned back to look over my shoulder, I saw his cock hanging out, fallen limp now against the denim, shining in the semidarkness with a sheen that was made up of the remnants of his come and overenthusiastic lube. Besides the sex, there'd been virtually no other contact between us. He tidied himself back into his underwear and jeans. His zip rasped in the quiet air.

That's that, then. Talk about a soulless fuck.

He cleared his throat and said, "That was really… good."

Good? I searched my mind for some withering response and fell short. I stretched my way upright, still leaning on the wall for much-needed support. My shirt fell softly over my bare groin, and I winced at its touch. What the hell did I have to complain about? I felt too good for snark and too well fucked for protest. It had been the hottest, fiercest, most exciting fuck I'd ever had.

"Yeah." I hesitated a moment but then just added, "It was. Thanks." I bent and grabbed at my jeans, then tucked in one of my legs to start dressing myself. I hissed in frustration as I got tangled at the knees. Shit, if I'd known I was going to need to pull my clothes on and off quickly, I'd have chosen to wear sweats instead. Seve caught my arm as I staggered, and I bit back more thanks. Not that he hadn't earned it, in more ways than one.

He was all zipped up, all done and dusted and calm as anything. Maybe there was something still lingering… a breath heavier than before, a flush on his smooth skin? I was sure he'd been blown away by it as much as I had. He wasn't rushing off, after all. Nor had he tried to slip me a twenty in payment for services rendered. Dammit, I knew I was being a hypocrite. I was creating melodrama around something that had been perfectly clear to both of us—nothing but spontaneous lust, nothing but a fast and furious race toward mutual satisfaction. And I'd welcomed it wholeheartedly.

"I've got to go." I stumbled out the words. So much for any witty repartee.

Seve frowned, a brief crease on his brow. "Okay, Max." That deep, steady voice, like he hadn't just fucked me to a sob, like he hadn't just come like an enthusiastic porn star himself. But I was absurdly pleased he'd remembered my name. "If that's what you want."

I blinked hard. "Yeah. Um… my friends? They're still in the club."

He shrugged and his smile had an arrogant, harsh twist to it now. "Push the door hard. Security will let you back inside. They know you're out here."

"You coming too?"

His dark eyes blinked as if I'd startled him. "No. I have things to do."

He fell silent again. I just stared. Even allowing for this whole weird scenario, he didn't seem much of a conversationalist. There was a single bead of sweat shimmering at his left temple. Once I'd seen it, I couldn't seem to tear my gaze away.

"I'll see you around," he said.

Before I had a chance to return the farewell, he turned away. I watched him walk diagonally across the yard and let himself out of a small access gate. The shadows were deeper there, and all I could see of his head and shoulders was silhouette. He shut the gate firmly behind him, and I heard his footsteps fading away, heading toward the main street.

I leaned back against the wall for another ten minutes or so, watching my breath huff out on the increasingly nippy air and waiting for the soreness in my arse to ease off. I wished like fuck I was still smoking.

CHAPTER 6

"MAX, you're not sleeping well, are you?"

I peered up over the top of my book. I immediately forgot what had been on the page, despite having skimmed over it four times already. One-man-against-the-world thrillers were proving way too implausible for me. "Sorry, Jack. Have I been disturbing you or something? I only get up for a drink or a read."

Jack was standing in the doorway of the living room, wiping his hands on an apron with "Kiss Me Quick" on the front. "Or to cook something. Or to have a shower."

I flushed. So perhaps I'd been a pain in the arse this last week. But I had things on my mind. Things that kept me awake, that nagged at me, that refused to be laid back to rest.

Jack wriggled out of the apron and threw himself down in the armchair opposite me. "It's not a problem for me. I sleep little anyway. And Louis expends all his energy dancing and socializing, so he'd probably sleep through the Second Coming. It's you I'm worried about."

"No need," I said hastily. "But sorry if you're losing sleep over me. I'll stop roaming about at night. You need your rest to keep up with the new job."

Jack had recently been promoted. His employer was working closely with the local police on a new initiative against drug crime, and Jack had been co-opted onto the liaison team. Louis all but itched with pride whenever he tried to explain it to me, with me smiling and trying to look like I understood every word.

Part of the reason we'd built such a strong friendship at school was the complementary mix of our three personalities. Jack was the steady achiever, Louis the smart extrovert. I was… well, what was I, apart from the bridge between the two? I'd been one of those guys they all said had great promise. I was the one with plenty of energy and drive—I'd *do* something with my life. Unfortunately it didn't take me long to start misusing that energy, kicking back at authority as soon as I was old and big enough to stand up for myself. Not that the school wasn't good, that the teachers weren't sympathetic to teenage boys. Shit, I wouldn't have had their job for all the tea in China and places beyond, especially with kids like me in the class. But I was full of aggression and bravado and the confusion that comes at that time. Bloody hormones in a rage too. What was I really doing with my life? I was setting the scene for a few messy years, is what.

I was high maintenance. And I always fought to go my own way, even when no one was challenging me. I always took the difficult route, always expected struggle and opposition. I got into fights, was disruptive in class if I didn't understand the subject, and came in late, hungover, and sometimes stoned. Louis and Jack tried to rein me in. Tried to convince me I wasn't a moron and shouldn't act like one. That I could understand mathematical principles, carry out a successful science experiment, and write something more lyrical than my name on the toilet wall. But I was just too far up my own arse to listen to my peers.

It was a small miracle I lasted long enough to get to Brighton University. In fact, I think the school head put in a few words for me, just to get me that one last chance. The three of us were still together, the Uni life was good—it should have been a brave new world for me. It just didn't go that way.

The partying had started in the late school years. I knew I was gay from an early age, knew I was highly sexual as soon as I learned enough about it. And I liked the thrill of finding out how my body worked—I liked to see the games we were all starting to play with each other, the drama and the physical excitement. And I found I was particularly adept at all of those. I kept fit and I had the gift of the gab to pick up casual partners. I was enthusiastic too.

I lost my virginity in Compulsion, the first term of Uni. It was called something like Beach Bubbles then and was into the cocktail crowd. Clubs changed their names a lot according to fashion and to new owners. I was only just legal—not that that had stopped me drinking illegally for the past few years—and I'd scammed my way into an over-twenty-fives night with a fake ID. I picked up a pretty fit bloke and we were all over each other. Can't even remember his name or if we swapped any details except the "yeah, right now" look. We stumbled into a cubicle in the gents', full of beer and a smoke and laughing at something that probably wouldn't have been funny to anyone sober. And so it happened. Made me wince a bit, and it was over in the time it took to pull a vending machine condom on and then peel it clumsily off, but I was excited at the way it made me feel. Loved the power of how it obviously made *him* feel too. By the time I'd got through that first term, I was well on the way to quantity over quality. Didn't have much idea of inhibition; restraint was an alien concept. Yeah… if you'll pardon the pun, I was way up my own arse.

"Max?" Jack was frowning at me. "You look miles away."

Not just miles but years. Or maybe not even that long ago. Jack wasn't entirely right—I *was* sleeping at night. But it was so restless that each morning I felt as if I'd had no rest at all. Louis usually teased me because I was difficult to wake in the morning—I was notorious for sleeping like the dead, just like him. *If there's a fire*, he'd say…

I'd burn, would be my flip reply.

And that's what seemed to be happening to me now. I was burning up, but with needs and wants, not flames. Last Saturday's escapade had nagged at me every bloody night this week. I was disturbed out of all proportion. I mean, life went on, regardless. I worked extra shifts at the construction site, I cooked a couple of suppers for us at the flat. I thought about changing my job or signing up for night-school Spanish or getting my hair shaved—all the usual nonsense that went through a bloke's head during the day. But I just couldn't settle. I scooped up a bunch of secondhand thrillers from the charity shop to read in the evenings, and I even tried watching the TV soaps with Louis. He'd recently filmed a minor part in one of them and now he was hooked on the whole damned lot, but I eventually drove him mad asking who was related to whom all the time. Nothing eased my mood. I found myself pottering around the town in my lunch hour, wondering whether to buy another good shirt or two and trying out samples of men's cologne. I'd never bothered about those things before. I nearly got discovered by one of the site managers— also on lunch—as I was thumbing through packs of new underwear. Decent but way too expensive stuff. Totally weird.

I was burning for all sorts of other reasons. Something had lit up under me, and I couldn't put out the heat. "What's the time?" I asked.

Jack blinked hard, distracted just as I'd hoped he would be. "Eight p.m. Why?"

"I'm going out for a drink with one of the guys from work. I'll… I said I'd meet him at eight thirty."

Jack didn't grace that with a reply, just peering at me. What, he didn't believe me?

I got up, showing off my firm intention to go out. "Is Louis dancing at the club tonight?"

"No, he has the weekend off. He's round at his mother's for the monthly visit, but he'll be back soon. He's bringing in some good wine. We're celebrating our anniversary tonight."

I smiled to myself at the sudden flush on his face. Did he really think I hadn't noticed the extra candles on the table, the smoked salmon chilling in the fridge, the smell of something special in the oven to follow? They were over each other like treacle on special occasions. What's more, they'd appreciate me going out, even though they'd never ask.

And I wanted to get out of the flat. I wanted some space to think about it all. To try to calm my restlessness. To shake off the smell of Seve that I imagined still lingered in my nostrils, and the abrasion on my fingertips from clutching at the rough bricks of that backyard wall. To relive the memory of him behind me, the press of his body, panting, gasping, thrusting hard against my back. Deep up inside me, stretching me, filling me. His unfamiliar but firm hand around my dick, tugging me along with him, ripping a reaction from me that had been as deep as it had been dirty.

Shit. I was shocked at myself. Why couldn't I get this into perspective? It had just been a quick, fierce fuck at a club, a whole week ago. It's not like I hadn't done it before. Yeah, I was trying not to make casual sex with strangers a habit nowadays, but I wasn't giving it up for life, was I? *Yes, you were,* prompted my nagging conscience. It was part of my old life, not the new. I seemed to be having trouble with the separation.

Seve didn't feel like a stranger. All I could think about was him.

That night, I never met anyone for a drink. In fact I never had any intention of it. I went straight to Compulsion.

HE DIDN'T appear until after midnight. The dance floor got darker and hotter and noisier, and I'd cursed my fixation at regular intervals ever since I arrived. I was drinking beer again and had been leaning against the bar for hours like some lazy whore. The number of approaches I'd turned down was five so far: four guys, one girl. I started out civil, then got progressively sharper. When the next person approached with the same hopeful leer and what he thought would be a seductive line, I glared so hard that I saw him pale. He veered quickly off in another direction.

And then Seve was there beside me. I never saw where he materialized from. His smell was spicy and teasing, and suddenly I was awash with all the other sensual memories of last Saturday. I swallowed hard, determined not to behave like some horny teenager, and turned slowly to face him. His long-fingered hand was curled around a drink as before, and his smile was almost sly. He had the same jeans on, I think, but a darker shirt with some kind of green shine to it. There was a slim silver chain around his neck and a tiny silver stud in his ear. The beard was newly trimmed, the skin of his cheeks and throat smooth.

He nodded at the retreating clubber. "Not your type, Max?"

He remembers my name. Something twisted painfully inside me. I'd been thinking he spent the last week fucking so many strange blokes in the backyard that he'd never remember just one.

"Don't know." I was having trouble making my tongue work— just the sight of him did things to me that I'd hoped were long buried. I dropped my gaze away from his. "Been a while since I even thought about what my type is."

"A while?" That bloody voice—soft, rich, cool. "Since last Saturday?"

I know I flushed. I prayed that the lights were low enough that it wouldn't look too obvious. "Yeah, well, last Saturday was—let's say—unusual for me. Can't say it's on my regular weekend list of Things to Do."

"Me neither."

I felt him staring at me and I met his gaze. His eyes flashed like fireworks, like warning flares. He was still smiling, but his expression was guarded, with pursed lips as if he wasn't sure what else to say.

"You come here often?" I blurted out. *Shit*. And after I'd been so rude to those others tonight, coming up to me with far more original chat-up lines.

"I do now," Seve said.

I started to laugh, then bit it back. "I'm not asking for me," I said with a grin. "It's just I haven't seen you around before." I tried to remember what the club had been like when I last came to see Louis dance, before it was sold into its latest guise. That was over a year ago, of course. I was sure I'd have remembered a bloke like Seve, however crowded the place had been.

He paused before replying. "I haven't been in Brighton for long." He shrugged very slightly, his muscles moving like the last gentle ripple of an evening wave on the beach. "I'm with the new management."

It figured. The way he seemed to exist apart from the crowd of dancers and drinkers; his confidence with the club; the way he got past security.

"Do you have a problem with that, Max?"

"No way. I mean… no. Unless I'm causing you trouble as a customer, of course." I laughed again, realizing how stupid that sounded the minute the words left my mouth.

But maybe the embarrassment was all on my part. Seve certainly didn't seem disturbed by my prattling—far from it, in fact. If there was one thing I could recognize in a man's eyes, it was lust, and I suspected Seve's was reflected in my own. His smile creased the corners of his mouth—his lush, greedy mouth. The mouth that I wanted to be touching very, *very* soon. My gut ached, and I felt warmth creeping down my spine like heated goose bumps. And I knew the feeling wasn't because I'd been drinking.

I knew I had to keep cool. Then I looked into his confident gaze and thought, *Who am I kidding?* "Look, Seve. About last Saturday—"

He interrupted me. "You want some more?" He put his drink down beside mine on the bar.

"Yeah." I knew he didn't mean the beer. And I knew he knew I knew. *Whatever.*

"But?"

I stared at him. "But what?"

He shrugged again. The fabric of his shirt shifted on his shoulders. Even over the deep, throbbing beat of the latest dance number, I imagined that I heard him sigh. The chain glinted in the hollow of his shadowed throat, and he casually ran a single finger down the side of his glass. My jeans went unbearably tight around the crotch. Fuck it, what was going on with me?

"It looks to me like you do have a problem."

"Me? A problem?" I stared at him and he stared right back. He was reading something in my expression that I didn't know was there. Something that was holding me back from him, from the pleasure he was offering me. Was he annoyed? He might just turn around and leave. Fuck, I didn't want that to happen. But I also didn't know what I was getting into if he stayed.

His white teeth teased briefly at his lower lip. "You're not sure. I don't know whether it's about me or yourself."

I blinked hard. What the fuck? "It's not a bad thing, to want to know what's going on."

"No. It's not. Have you always been like that?"

I flushed. "No." *But that's how I want to be now.*

Seve nodded. "You're right, it's not a bad thing. What can I tell you?" He stood in that relaxed but assertive way, his shoulders back, his neck tight. *Fucking gorgeous.*

"Okay. Who are you, why are you here?"

He shook his head a little impatiently. I wondered if he had other *things to do*, like he'd said last Saturday, but when it came, his answer was calm and his tone pleasant. "This club is part of a newly formed franchise. The owners have other clubs opened or scheduled to open soon. I'm interested in a career in the entertainment business, so I was recruited for this job at Compulsion during its reopening." He extended a hand with a wry twist of his mouth. "My name is Severino Nuñez."

I took his hand. It was warm and the handshake very firm. "Max Newman."

He held my hand for a few seconds longer than was usual, but I wasn't pulling away either. "Are you sure now, Max?"

Irritation spiked through me. "What the hell kind of a question is that? I was making conversation, that's all. Like normal people do."

He dropped my hand and his eyes widened.

I sighed and took a step backward. "Fuck, I'm sorry. I'm just...." Mixed up? Horny? Both?

Seve took a step forward to close the gap again, and he smiled. "You startled me, that's all. You like to talk, don't you? To argue as well. You're very...."

"Very what?"

He didn't finish. His gaze slid down to look at my mouth, and the desire in his eyes sucked any resistance out of me. I let out a breath that had been building tight in my chest. He looked intrigued now, and I remembered his reaction last week, when we struggled, very briefly, out in the yard. So perhaps he liked a little resistance.

"Come with me, Max," he said. Very low, very quiet, but full of promise. I might not have heard the words because of the noise surrounding us, but I read those lips. In the middle of the heat of the bar, I felt a chill. He moved away and walked right past me.

I turned and followed him, just like before. There'd never been any doubt I would.

CHAPTER 7

WE DIDN'T go out through the back door this time. Seve led me out of the dance area, across the lobby, and toward the exit. Did he have a place nearby? "Where are we going?" I asked.

He didn't answer, just moved confidently through the crowds of people moving to and fro, pausing for nothing. The dance floor lights were flashing behind us, the noise level loud and distracting. There was a roar of approval from the dancers as the DJ segued into a medley of eighties hits. Seve led us to a short flight of uncarpeted stairs behind the entrance desk. It was roped off as private, and a couple of security men nodded to him as he lifted the rope and slipped through. I ducked under as well. One of the security men continued to follow our path with angry, half-hooded eyes. But the lighting was dim on the staircase, so perhaps I was imagining it.

I concentrated solely on following Seve. Every step was firm, his movement elegant. I'd rarely seen a guy so physically sensual and yet so obviously masculine with it. I felt clumsy compared against him. The stairs led to a small landing with a couple of closed doors. Both of them had a spy hole looking out and a small gilt plaque saying "Private." No one was around, though I could hear the bustle at the entrance down below. There was a security keypad on the wall, and Seve pressed a few buttons, quickly and confidently. There was a soft *snick* as the lock disengaged; he pushed the door open and gestured for me to go ahead of him.

I went in, of course. It was dark, and for a moment I couldn't get my bearings. Seve had followed on my heels—I could feel his breath on my neck—and as I groped around for the light, he kicked the door shut behind us. The room felt small and the air stuffy. The thud of the door was reminiscent of our exit out of the club the previous week, but this time I was being captured indoors rather than thrown out into the fresh air. I still couldn't find any switch, but Seve eased past me and clicked on a lamp.

It was some kind of office-cum-storeroom. The lamp was on a table pushed to the back of the room, with a plastic chair tucked up against each end. There was a computer on the table, but I didn't see how anyone could comfortably work, because it was surrounded by box files, reams of copy paper, and a pile of neatly folded towels that looked like they'd just come back from the laundry. On one of the chairs was a tall box with torn flaps at the top and polystyrene chips scattered around the bottom. The packaging had obviously spilled out when the box was opened, and now it looked bizarrely like snowdrifts at the base of a cardboard tower. Three filing cabinets lined the left-hand wall, and a dozen or more boxes covered the wall to our right. From the print on the sides, the boxes seemed to contain cleaning and catering supplies. They were piled high and deep, leaving very little floor space for two men to move about. I considered another of my lame witticisms along the lines of "nice place you have here" but managed to keep it to myself. I wondered what the hell he was up to. "I'm with the new management," he'd said. Obviously he wasn't any kind of cleaner, but he could have been anyone from bar supervisor to finance manager and still know the security codes to the storeroom as part of his job. Maybe we were going through here to a larger office, but I couldn't see any door except the one we'd originally come through.

Seve reached his arm across my body and flipped off the lamp again. Immediately we were plunged into darkness, with no windows to the outside world and barely a sliver of light around the close-fitting door. I took a step toward the table, or so I thought, and almost tripped over one of the boxes of supplies. A crinkled strip of something fluttered up and brushed across my cheek. I shivered in shock until I realized it was probably a stray edge of shrinkwrapping.

I was fighting to focus my sight in the blackness when a hand gripped my arm.

"Can't wait," Seve said, his voice a hoarse purr.

He kissed me then, just as shockingly as he had the first time. His mouth was hot and damp on me, plundering my own, his tongue probing behind my teeth. His beard felt rough against my skin, the short hair scraping across my jaw. He nipped at my lower lip and started undoing the buttons of my shirt with deft fingers. At the same time, he slid his wet tongue out of my mouth and ran it around my cheek and out to my temple. Along its path, his lips pressed against my skin, kissing me with possessive care. His hot breath tickled the hair I'd tucked back behind my ears, and his hands caressed my chest.

I shuddered with pleasure. It seemed like forever since I'd had this kind of attention. A few words, a kiss that was more like an attack—that was all I'd had from Seve so far. That, and a bloody good fucking. What kind of relationship potential was that? Yet tonight, this was pure indulgence—even though it was already heading way beyond a kiss.

He wriggled his hand down between us to undo the button and zip of my jeans. He wrenched them down, dragging my boxers with them. I wriggled until I got my feet free of the cloth, but it was difficult to move with hardly any space in the room. And now I was naked from the waist down. *Again,* I thought, more than a little disorientated. Seve was all over me, hands at my groin, pushing my flapping shirttails out of the way, fingers sliding in between my tensed thighs. His features were half-hidden in the dark, but he remained a very tangible man, his body pressed against mine. He cupped my balls, his palm even warmer than my furred, tightening flesh, and his eyes glinted in the shadows. I saw the occasional flash of his teeth as he grinned or grimaced—I wasn't sure which. He never said a word, but I happily surrendered to those sweaty, demanding hands in the stuffy air of the storeroom, allowing him to hold me. To grip my waist, to curl a fist around my aching cock. To do whatever he wanted with me.

There were soft moans of satisfaction, and they weren't only mine.

He pushed me back until I felt the edge of the table on my arse. Then he slid his hands under my bare buttocks and hoisted me up onto the top of it. There was only a small square of available space—half the box files immediately slipped off the table, and the towels flattened out underneath me, their softness a welcome cushion under my bum. Seve pushed the other files off impatiently and let them crash on the floor. It felt a little like that scene in *A Streetcar Named Desire* when Brando angrily sweeps away the crockery to show how *he's* gonna clear the table. My shoulders were pressed hard against the cold surface of the back wall, and Seve leaned in against me, holding me in place. He twisted awkwardly, shaking off his shirt, fumbling with the waistband of his jeans. Then his hands gripped my thighs and pulled them apart.

My cock was damp at the tip and straining shamelessly to the heavens. He tugged me farther toward him so that my arse perched on the very edge of the table. I wanted to grab on to something as an anchor, but I didn't think the computer monitor was stable enough, so I just spread my hands on the tabletop and hoped for the best. My fingers caught the edge of a pack of paper, and it tumbled off after the files. By now my back was bent awkwardly and my feet were waving in the air. My knees were wide apart—I was completely, brazenly open for him. I knew that at this angle, if there'd been enough light, he'd have been able to see all of me—my dick, my balls, my hole. I felt horribly exposed and even more shockingly excited. A blob of precome dripped onto my belly, and I could smell my eagerness.

Seve suddenly took one hand away and turned his head so he was totally shadowed. He seemed to be groping around in the pocket of his jeans. All I could hear was the sound of his harsh breathing. When his hand touched me again, it was covered with something cool and slippery. *Lube.* I shifted, trying to get more comfortable, and one of my joints cracked. My heart was hammering. Then his fingers slid into me and I moaned more loudly.

He loomed over me again, his eyes wide and knowing, his mouth searching for mine. I sucked hard on his tongue, desperate because I knew what was coming. He wriggled forward, rubbing his groin against mine. His cock was free of his jeans, the satiny sheath stroking my length, tugging my own skin up then back down again.

The suspense was almost unbearably exciting. When he moved against me, our chest hair brushed with a thin sheen of sweat. I grasped him with one hand and held on. The hair on his forearms was damp already.

He'd come prepared this time. Or maybe last Saturday's condomless status had been the exception. When his stretching fingers had finished their work in my arse and his cock nudged up against my entrance, it felt slick with latex and lube. I was really glad I didn't have to bring up the subject again. I also didn't need him to spread my legs even farther, but I let him, because it was a touch from him—an intimate one. He slid his hands under me again and lifted my thighs a couple of inches off the bench, propping me on my tailbone. And he entered me like last time. *Hard.*

A groan escaped me, probably too loud considering I had no idea who might be passing outside the room. We both grunted and started moving together. He was face-to-face with me this time, though his features were gray in the half-light. But it was good to feel him flush up against me, and I hung on to him as best I could. He had more hair on his chest than I did and he was more muscled, even though I was fit from work on the site. He smelled great, whereas I was sure I smelled of too much sweat and beer. Each time he thrust into me, I was knocked back against the wall, but I clenched my thighs around his hips and let him dictate the pace. It was a bloody exciting angle for me. He hit my prostate more often than not, and several times I had to hold myself back from arching right up and falling off the table. My cock was squashed between us, rubbed to maximum sensitivity by the skin of his belly and begging for release. His knee knocked against the table leg, and the last of the box files teetered on the edge, then fell. We rocked on top of the table, not caring. The towels slid away from under my arse, and when I flung out an arm, looking for better purchase, I thumped the tall box on the chair. The cardboard gave a *whumph* sound, and I heard the squeaky puff of more polystyrene chips flying through the air.

"*Max.*" I barely caught Seve's whisper. His breath blew out over my neck. "Touch yourself, Max. I can't...."

I peeled my hand away from his shoulder. He adjusted his stance so that he could still balance me on the table and continued to thrust into me, his thighs under mine, the open zip of his jeans starting to scratch at my exposed skin. I didn't care. I fisted my fingers around my cock and started to pump.

Seve's breath hitched and his head dropped. Even in the dark, he was watching me jerk off, my hand squeezed up between our bodies, twisting up and down my swollen shaft. His teeth tightened briefly on the skin of my shoulder.

"*Close*," he hissed and started to thrust into me more quickly. I reckoned I could feel him thickening inside me. I squeezed both the muscles of my hole and my hand around my dick, eager for completion for both of us. Seve was going to come soon, and I was either going to be flattened against the wall or plonked down unceremoniously. There was already a nagging pain in my lower back from trying to keep upright as he fucked me to a blubbering wreck. But I didn't need much help at all to get there—my climax came rushing like a geyser and my hand became a blur as my eyes filled with tears of excitement.

"Seve… *shit!*" I moaned aloud, and the last things I saw before the ecstasy robbed me of sense were his eyes opening wider in the half light and a shocked smile on his face. Even as my hot come hit our stomachs and began to dribble down between us, he gave a shout and pushed hard against me, forcing me back up against the wall and pressing finger-shaped bruises into my buttocks.

Gotcha! I thought wearily and triumphantly.

IT WAS eerily quiet in that tiny room, despite our ragged breathing. I untangled my legs from around his hips and he pulled his cock slowly out of me. With a wince, I sat back properly on the table and let my feet land on the floor. I was in dire need of proper support. My whole body ached and throbbed with the climax, the excitement, the physical strain.

"You okay?" I whispered into the darkness.

He nodded. I felt it because his head was bowed against my shoulder. He reached out a hand to grip my waist as if he were supporting himself as well. "Your head," he muttered.

Huh? I put a hand up, wondering why he was suddenly worrying about it. I found several chips in my hair and pulled them out with an irritated grunt. They were squashy between my fingers and shone white in the dim light. *Great*. Not only did I presumably look well fucked, I was also a lookalike for Frosty the Snowman.

"Hell of a squeeze in here." It was a feeble joke of mine, I knew, but to my surprise, Seve chuckled softly.

"Hell of a *good* squeeze, though."

I wasn't arguing with that. Just wondered what I was going to say now. How do you follow a fucking like that? Judging by my earlier pathetic "come here often" gambit, I knew I was out of practice in sweet-talking my partners. I didn't think Seve was looking for that, anyway. If I even knew what he *was* looking for.

I reached down to the floor, fumbling for my jeans. He let go of me and took a step backward. My boxers were pushed into my hand, and I felt Seve's sweaty palm against mine. "Thanks," I mumbled.

Silence as I dressed myself. I was sticky all over my stomach, and I had to peel another polystyrene chip off there as well. The spunk was already drying, and I knew it'd be a really itchy treat when I walked home. A couple of the towels had tangled around my ankle like overeager children, and when I stood up, I stubbed a toe on one of the fallen files. I thought about moving to the doorway, but there was something scratching against the back of my thigh that was either a horny dog or an oversized toilet brush, and I wasn't sure of the best escape route. Did we need some sort of security code to get *out* of here, or would I end up trapped with my postcoital aches and pains until someone came to restock the ladies' toilets?

But a crack of light suddenly speared across the floor, and I saw that Seve had opened the door back out to the club. The noise level increased from downstairs—I heard someone shriek with laughter and the swell of sing-along to a Kylie hit. I could see Seve's silhouette against the hallway light; then he turned back to look at me. He'd run a hand through his hair and it stood up spikily, despite its short length. But his shirt was rebuttoned carefully, and the jeans looked like they'd been molded to his body at birth.

I suspected I looked like I'd been dragged through the proverbial hedge and then back again, just for the hell of it. He was staring at me, so I guessed that must be it. *Game over*. I knew my cue when I heard it. Licking my lips, I said, "So. Um. I'll be...."

"Going?" I thought I heard a sharp edge to his voice.

"Guess so." What was I meant to do? Thank him for the hospitality? For the fuck? Some weird X-rated spin on "Thank you for having me"? I straightened up, determined to regain some kind of dignity. It was bloody difficult, is all I can say. My legs felt like jelly and my heart was only just settling back to a steady rhythm. I stared back at Seve, his body still half in darkness, preventing me from seeing everything his expression might tell. I stared at his strong profile, his perfectly controlled limbs. At the glimmer of saliva on his lips, the shape of the lush, plump lips that matched the mark of teeth on my shoulder....

Yeah. Bloody difficult.

It was a long—and itchy—walk home.

CHAPTER 8

THE following Saturday, the flat was turned into a kind of actors' commune as a whole group of Louis's drama friends came around to help him learn his lines. He'd landed a return scene in his TV soap— "unprecedented feedback for your interesting interpretation of a minor character," his agent, Grace, had told him, though none of us had any clue as to how far her tongue was in her cheek at the time—and the excitement was racked up high.

I knew most of Jack and Louis's friends by now, but I couldn't help feeling awkward when they came around en masse. Especially when I got elbowed out of the living room for the third time, squeezed between Harry—a very tall, booming-voiced Goth who quoted Shakespeare mixed in with swearing that would embarrass a navvy— and the Vs, a trio of petite girlfriends who were of completely different ethnicities but all wore the exact same pink tutu outfit over their matching skinny jeans. I never found out whether they actually all had names beginning with *V* or whether it just made it easier for everyone to remember them. When I tried to reach the kitchen but found Bob and Bryan—an inseparable pair, with Bob the most outrageous snoop and Bryan with the hugest appetite I'd ever known—arguing in the hallway about which bey-otch should have won *what* at the BAFTAs, I surrendered the battlefield to them all with a rueful smile and decided to hide out in my room.

I paused at the foot of the stairs. Louis's laughter rang out from the living room. Someone had taped the episode of the soap he'd been in, and I heard the series theme music start up on the TV. Looked like they were settling in for a fan review session.

"Max." Jack touched my shoulder, and I turned. He was flushed, clutching a chilled six-pack of beer and three family-sized bags of snacks to his chest, obviously on his way from the kitchen back into the fray. "Come on in with us."

In the background, the girls shrieked in a trio of octaves when Louis obviously came on screen. Someone laughed and belched and someone slapped them—at least, that's what it sounded like. Out in the kitchen, the arguing couple decided they needed Lady Gaga at top radio volume to accompany their raised voices.

I winced and Jack laughed. "I know. You'd rather get the hell out of here."

I'd been considering burying myself upstairs with a beer, my headphones, and rock music, but Jack's words shook my already wobbly nerve a different way. "Yeah," I said. "I'm just going to change my shirt, then I'm going into town."

Jack didn't exactly raise an eyebrow, but his expression went carefully blank. "Anywhere good? I might join you."

I shook my head. "You have Rehearsal City to manage."

"No he doesn't," came Louis's voice. He'd come up the hallway behind Jack and now rested his head on his boyfriend's shoulder, staring at me. "In fact, I think I might join you as well."

"You're preparing for your big break."

Louis snorted. "Cute, Max. It's twenty lines and a cup of cold brown liquid on the café set. It's hardly Les Mis. I'll probably not be asked back again."

"Bollocks," came Harry's voice from someplace above my head. He loomed a good six inches over all of us. "The lady doth protest too much, methinks. He'll be a fuckin' star."

Louis grinned but kept his eyes on me. "Harry, you're a silly tart, but a loyal one. Anyway, I need a break, and I'm going out with my friends."

"So what are *we*?" wailed one of the girls from the other room, obviously eavesdropping. "Don't leave us behind."

"Where's my bag?" called another.

"Behind you, you stupid cow."

"Don't call me that!"

"Wait for us!" Bob called from the kitchen. He and Bryan had stopped arguing long enough for Bryan to make a plate of sandwiches, and he was finishing off the last crust.

Jack rolled his eyes. "Looks like we're all coming, Max." He put the beer and snacks on the bottom of the stairs up to my room. The girls spilled out from the living room, and Bob and Bryan joined us in the hallway. It was starting to look and feel like some kind of rush-hour bus queue. Bryan bent down quickly to pick up a bag of tortilla chips.

"Greedy bastard." Bob jabbed him in the ribs and Bryan shrugged, unapologetic.

"I was only going for a bite to eat and a drink," I said in mild protest.

"Works for us." Jack slung his arm around Louis's shoulders. "I want more time with this one before he goes off to film in London."

"A few days away, that's all," Louis scoffed, but his eyes danced at Jack's attention. "And Grace says I'll be stuck in some small, shabby B&B, nothing glamorous. Minimum expenses, mostly my own makeup, no guaranteed callback." To my amusement, Grace seemed to spend a lot of her time managing her clients' expectations downward. "But maybe I'll get some free time to look around. I haven't been up to the smoke for a long time. You'll point me to the best places to go dancing, Max, won't you?"

I froze. Everyone else must have picked up on the sudden tension, because they all stopped talking and turned to look at me.

"You from London, man?" Harry asked me. "Would I were in an alehouse in London! Right?"

"Just…." I swallowed quickly. "Stayed there for a while."

"Fuck," Louis whispered, not quietly enough.

"London's a big place," Jack said, his voice steady. "Max isn't some kind of walking A to Z, Louis."

Louis laughed carelessly, placing his pale, elegant hand over Jack's dark one. He was a much better actor than people gave him credit for; I expect only I noticed how tightly his fingers closed on

Jack's. "Of course, yes, it's a huge city, and Max was only passing through, right?" He grimaced at me, apology in his eyes. "Stupid of me. I didn't mean to… anyway, people, this is my chance for the big time, isn't it?" He wriggled out of Jack's grasp, shaking his blond curls and seeking the attention back from the others clustered around us. "No time for dancing! I'm sure Grace will have me reading Stanislavski rather than Maeve Binchy every evening. I'll have to sneak ten minutes away just to call home and weep about my boredom. Now, has anyone seen my denim jacket?"

"Whereabouts were you in London, man?" Harry was peering at me from under a straggly jet-black fringe. "Gotta fuckin' love the vibe up there."

"London?" One of the Vs peered at me, her head on a level with Harry's elbow. "You're so lucky. I'd love to go there. Were you working? Did they replace you? If you know someone and could put in a word for me…."

"No," I said. She blinked hard so maybe I'd pitched my tone too sharp. "I don't know anyone there anymore."

"Let's get going, everyone," Jack said, his hand on the front door.

"Bob, Bryan, was my jacket in the kitchen?" Louis called overloudly. "Help me find it, will you?"

They were doing a brave job, running interference for me.

"I'll go and get changed," I said. "I'll be ten minutes." No one replied, but Jack stepped to the side so I could dash up the stairs. As I pushed through the door of my room, all I could hear in the hallway was a long sigh from Louis and Bryan's open-mouthed crunching of the tortilla chips.

THE casual drink out with friends didn't go so well, or maybe it was just me. We ambled down to the prom again and, deciding we were hungry for a proper meal, sat down at one of the seafront fish and chip restaurants. It was warm enough to stay outside under the flapping red awning. The smell of chips covered in salt and vinegar was familiar and comforting, and we all tucked in apart from Louis, who picked at a chicken salad, continuing to chat and entertain us with stories of the TV actors off set. The gulls cried overhead and a couple of kids shrieked at each other on the beach, playing catch with a bunch of damp seaweed fronds. Music from a jukebox wafted out the open door of a nearby amusement arcade. But the group had lost some of its liveliness. Harry had dropped both the swearing and the quotations, and Bob and Bryan couldn't find anything more interesting to bicker about than how much ketchup Bryan should or shouldn't put on his double saveloy and chips. The Vs met up with a couple of other friends and drifted back out on the pavement, making plans for the rest of the evening. Obviously whatever one did, they all did. They were very sweet.

And all through his meal, Louis sent me pleading looks. I smiled at him, hoping he'd see it as forgiveness. It wasn't a problem that he'd let slip I'd been in London for a while. After all, it was true, wasn't it? Just not something I wanted to dwell on. I think the others had picked up on that. I caught a few curious looks coming my way, though I didn't flatter myself I was that interesting.

The evening got chilly, so we moved on into the town and one of our favorite bars just inside the Lanes. Jack wanted a drink, though Louis was itching to go dancing. He'd eased off on his dance gigs when he got the call for the TV work, but we all knew he missed the excitement—and the limelight. After a couple of pints, Harry left to visit his Goth friends in a pub up Ditchling Road. The Vs had already gone to catch a recommended drag show back in Kemptown.

"You all coming to the show?" Bob asked us. He was shrugging on his jacket, ready to follow the Vs. "She does a fabulous Judy."

"And there's food at the bar," Bryan added.

"You're always bloody hungry, man." Bob rolled his eyes.

Jack smiled. "No, thanks. I've got work to do tomorrow, preparing for a case meeting on Monday. A couple of beers and a chat is all I'm up for tonight."

Louis sighed but he was smiling too. "Me neither, guys. I'm with the homebody here."

"Max?"

"No, thanks."

Jack was peering at me. "But you're not coming back with us?"

I didn't remember saying that, at least not specifically. "No. I'll probably stay in town, have another drink somewhere else. Then go on to a club."

Jack nodded, never taking his eyes off me.

"Which club, man?" Bob asked.

Both Louis and Jack were staring at me now. Had I suggested I was looking for a snack of babies' heads or threatening to run amok through the Lanes with a machine gun? No, just another drink, just a trip to a club….

"Compulsion," Louis said into the pause. "That's where you're going, isn't it, Max?"

I nodded.

"Where Louis dances?" Bob said. He and Bryan were blissfully unaware of the fresh tension between the rest of us. "Yeah, we've been a few times since it got taken over. It's a good location, near the marina but not too far out of the town center."

Bryan snorted. "The drinks are too bloody expensive."

"Who are the new owners?" I thought I sounded almost careless.

"It's part of a chain. Some franchise, I suppose, though there's family money behind it." Bob's nosiness asserted itself. He was always the first to read the entertainment and society pages in the newspapers, and urban myth had it that he loitered around the local fish and chip shop most nights, just to borrow the old copies of *Celebrity Hassle* or whatever those weekly glossy magazines were called. "The top man's name is Medina. Alberto… Alvin, something…."

"Alvaro," Bryan offered.

Bob nodded—they were used to helping out each other's conversations. "He made his money in some kind of exporting. Don't ask me exact details, because I don't do the business pages, but now he's launching out into entertainment. There are other clubs in Manchester and Newcastle. A small venue opened in London last year."

I may have made a noise in the back of my throat; I didn't mean to.

Bob continued with oblivious enthusiasm. "He's going to refurbish the whole of Compulsion over the next twelve months, which will be fucking great. The carpet near the bar was starting to feel like glue, and those dance stages aren't too sound, are they?"

This question was aimed at Louis, who nodded in mute agreement. He glanced at me, obviously not sure whether to be worried or puzzled. I hadn't given my flatmates much to go on, but I imagined they could see how tightly coiled I was.

"Not my scene. Too hot, too loud," Bryan said, wrinkling his nose. Bob grinned, leaned forward, and smacked a kiss on Bryan's creased brow. Bryan pushed him off but with a grudging smile. "And the duty manager turned us out last time because we didn't have our ID on us."

Bob grinned. "Our fault we look like twinks, eh?"

"Speak for yourself," Bryan replied. Everyone laughed together.

Except for me.

"You can't blame them, trying to keep the club clean," Bob said.

"Like hell they are." Bryan snorted.

"What do you mean?" I said.

"The Medinas are crooks," Bob said, taking up the narrative. "It's common knowledge. They were raided by the Drug Squad when Manchester opened, and there was some problem in London too—they had to call in extra security for a while."

"The bloody club owners are usually the ones behind the trouble in the first place, right?" Bryan added.

"Cynic." Bob squeezed Bryan's arm and planted another kiss on his cheek. Bryan flushed but seemed to like it.

"How on Earth do you find all this out?" Louis asked Bob.

Bob shrugged. "I listen. I read."

"You snoop," Bryan grumbled.

Bob ignored the jibe. "And there's that new man at Compulsion, the one from Medina Head Office, who's meant to be overseeing the new look. He's Spanish or something like that. Very sexy, from what I've heard."

"What you've *read*," Bryan grumbled. "Judging by those fucking gossip rags you wank over."

Bob yelped in protest and they tussled together for a moment. When Louis yelled at them to stop they broke apart, flushed and half laughing, half snarling at each other.

"You'd think he'd take more care what he does in Brighton," Bryan said. "Or *who* he does. What with him being part of the family."

My gut clenched. "What?"

Bob glanced at me, alert at last to something in my tone. "He's a cousin or nephew of the Medinas. I can't quite remember, but I can look it up for you. Apparently he's done the business degree and stuff, and now he's claiming his place in the family firm. He's only ever been some kind of playboy, or so the mags say. He's gay but not exactly monogamous. Last seen wearing a whole bloody boy band on his arm, sort of thing."

"What's his name?" Jack asked.

"I've got to go," I said. The chat stopped and everyone turned to look at me. "Catch you later, okay?"

"Max, I'll come with—"

"I've got my key. Don't worry about locking up the flat." I was already backing off, shuffling farther up the street, watching their surprised faces retreating to the background. Then I turned and all but ran in the opposite direction.

SEVE stood as before, at the bar. People pushed past him, grabbed drinks, and stumbled away, laughing and shouting. He still stood there. A couple of large guys were close by, and I thought I recognized them as having been security on previous nights, but they didn't specifically turn his way. No one else approached him, though I saw plenty looking. *A better protection strategy than mine*, I thought sourly. But I was equally pleased that he wasn't being pursued tonight. I didn't know what I'd have done if I'd seen him pick up someone else.

"Max, here you are." Jack appeared at my shoulder, bringing us drinks. I'd forgotten how good he was at sports in school, and he'd easily caught up with me on my way here. I couldn't, in all honesty, tell him to get lost. And I didn't want to, of course, I just wanted— well, I wasn't really sure what.

I hadn't assumed that Seve would be here again. If he were really this big shot from Head Office, I supposed he had to spend time at the club, checking things were going okay. But he must have staff to do that, as well. Was he here for business or… what else? I didn't know what free time they gave big shots. I couldn't imagine it was much. Was he one of those career men who lived in—and above—the shop?

Essentially I didn't know anything about him except his name, some basic info about his job, the fact he thought I talked too much— and the feel of his cock inside me. Kind of a strange reference, eh? My mouth was dry again, despite the drink Jack had just handed me and I'd taken a swig of. My legs felt weak and I felt dizzy. I was beginning to realize that being fucked by Seve was maybe more than just his hands on my skin and his dick up my arse.

He turned so his back was against the bar, and then he looked over. I was ridiculously excited when his gaze fixed on me, like he'd been waiting only for that. We stared at each other for a moment, neither of us changing position or making any other move. He was in the ubiquitous black jeans, but matched tonight by a short-sleeved T-shirt in some kind of dark-blue satin. A black leather jacket was slung over his shoulder. Had he just arrived? Or was he ready to leave already?

The evening was becoming surreal. And to be honest, it hurt to stand there, with Seve only feet away. I wanted to go to him. I wanted to touch him again. If he lifted that glass as he'd done the first time, with its subtle invitation, I'd be there in a second.

"You okay?" Jack was a blur at the periphery of my sight.

"Yeah, of course I am."

"You've been distracted all night. All week, actually, like something's nagging away at you. And the way you dashed off…."

"I'm fine. Honestly."

"Was it Louis mentioning London? I'm really sorry about that."

"No." I shook my head to reassure him. "There's no problem, Jack."

Jack didn't answer. He followed my line of sight to Seve at the other end of the counter, then looked back at me. "You and him?"

I knew not to insult Jack's intelligence by denying it. "We just met. Nothing special going on."

Jack obviously chose not to insult my intelligence in return by telling me I was talking bollocks. "Is that the Medina bloke Bob was talking about?"

"I don't know. Haven't had time to find out for certain."

Jack's voice was low. "And you're not bothered about taking it. The time, that is."

I bit my lip. I still didn't turn to face him, but I could feel his gaze on me. "It's not like that, Jack. *I'm* not like that, not anymore. I'm taking things a step at a time."

Jack sounded angry but not necessarily with me. "I know I've been pushing you to get out more…."

"Jack? I've got it all under control."

"You know we don't judge—"

"Of course I know—"

"We just want you to be okay," Jack finished over my protest.

"I said I'm fine." He meant well, I knew. But he would've had to be blind and stupid to miss how I gazed at Seve, how my whole body leaned toward him. However, I was surprised to see that Seve seemed to be the same. He continued to gaze at me, that slow smirk teasing at the corner of his mouth. I saw his gaze flicker to Jack, then back to me. A lifting of his lids; a lazy droop back to cover the flashing eyes. It was all the encouragement I needed, and I pushed away from the bar.

"Max." Jack sighed as if he didn't know what else to say.

To my shame, my mind wasn't on my friend anymore. It wasn't really there at all. It was reaching out for Seve—reaching for his sharp, rare words, for his fingers inside me. For his goddamn arrogance. For the careless pleasure he'd given me.

"Is this really what you want?" Jack's voice was soft, barely heard over the music ringing in our ears.

I glanced back at him. "What? It's just a bit of fun."

Jack shook his head. "I know you, Max. The way you act around him… it's like you've dived straight in the deep end, and to hell with the lifeguards."

"What are you talking about?" But I realized how well Jack *did* know me. He knew what I was thinking and where I was going. Probably what I was going to do. But I wasn't ready to share my feelings with anyone yet, not even my closest friends. Hell, I wasn't quite sure what highlights I could censor for him, anyway. "Get off home, Jack. Louis will be waiting for you. Thanks for following me, I appreciate it. But we both know I'm a grown-up now."

Jack smiled, though it looked strained. "What I know is that you deserve the best, Max, whatever you think of yourself. Be careful."

I grinned. "What are you, my mother? One more time—I'm fine."

I watched as Seve slipped the jacket over his shoulders and also pulled away from the bar. He started to walk toward the main exit with a long, slow stride. He wasn't deliberately trying to leave me behind, I was sure. But an irrational panic rose up in me, in case he did. I grabbed my coat off the back of the chair. My eyes followed the broad shoulders and the muscled arse.

And then so did my legs.

CHAPTER 9

I MADE my way out of the club, weaving through bunches of people making their way in, ebbing around me like a human sea. The lights from the entrance desk in the lobby were too bright for me, and bursts of music followed in my wake every time the door opened to let someone in. By the time I emerged into the cool night, Seve stood at the curb, leaning back against a BMW. It looked very expensive and very smart, with midnight-blue paintwork like his shirt tonight. Seat covers as black as his hair. Woodwork on the dashboard as rich as the color of his skin. *Shit*. I had this thing bad.

I looked around but no one was asking him to move his vehicle on. It was nowhere near chucking-out time at the pubs and clubs yet, but I was pretty sure it was a restricted zone even for taxis. The bouncers stood at attention by the club entrance, silent and apparently unbothered, with aviator shades that hid their eyes. Bloody stupid at night, I thought. And it meant I couldn't see if they were looking at him or not. I drew a deep breath and went to meet him at the car. "Yours, Seve?"

"Yes."

Was he going to ask me to ride with him? Was I going to see something or somewhere that told me more about him? Or would we just drive to some lay-by along the coastal road, park beside a deserted café where the tea cakes and ice creams were locked away for the night, and then fuck away frenziedly in the backseat? *Stupid teenage melodrama.* But I knew the strength and irrationality of my need.

"Something more to say, Max?" He sounded sharp. "I see it in your eyes. In the way you stand there."

I thought about what Jack had said about being careful. He'd obviously picked up on something about Seve even in that brief time. He was worried, though I didn't know the exact reasons. Was *I* worried? "I need to know more."

"What about?"

"You." All he did was raise an eyebrow and I filled with warmth from my toes upward. "Something more than that, Seve."

He smiled and nodded. "Will you get in the car first?" He glanced up at the indigo sky, lit in patches by the neon lights from the club and nearby marina buildings. "The forecast is for rain tonight."

I ignored that. "Tell me. Are you the guy they sent in to oversee the refurbishment at Compulsion? One of the Medina family?"

For the first time, I saw a flicker of unease in his eyes. "Yes. But you know that already, I'm sure. Anyone here would tell you."

"But *you* didn't. You said your name was…." I struggled, briefly, to remember. "Nuñez."

He shrugged. "My mother is a Medina. My late father was called Nuñez. I am the nephew of the owner of the group. Does it matter?"

"You didn't say," I persisted.

"Maybe I didn't want you to know then. Maybe I didn't want to waste time talking." His voice tightened. "I applied for the job with everyone else, Max. You should know that I am qualified—that my position is earned."

That wasn't the point, but I wasn't discussing that now. "You're a company employee, though, right? You follow the company rules, agree with corporate strategy. And you're family too, so you know what really goes on in all the clubs."

He frowned. "What are you talking about?"

I shook my head, impatient with the anger that washed over me and with my inability to express the pain inside.

"Get in the car, Max."

Behind me, a group of young women on a hen night shrieked with laughter. Two guys on the other side of the road were having an argument, maybe a lovers' tiff. "No," I said, even as I took an instinctive step toward him. "This isn't going to happen."

"Why not?" He reached out his arm and brushed a finger down my arm. Even through my shirtsleeve, I felt the heat from him. "We're free, we can do what we like. Don't tell me you don't want more. It's magnificent, yes?"

Fuck, yes. "No. Leave me. I'm on my way home."

"Is it because of him?" Seve looked back toward the door of the club. "The man you're with?"

"Jack? We're…."

"Just friends?"

"No!" I was angry for different reasons now. "Not *just* friends! He's a bloody good one, the best. He cares about me and that's fine by me."

Seve stared at me as I fidgeted there on the pavement. I could feel his gaze as if it burned through my clothes. My body was shivering at the thought of his hands on me, and my cock was swelling at the mere smell of his cologne. He shifted a little and I wondered with a sudden glorious wildness whether he was feeling the same discomfort. But why should he? He'd called all the shots so far. I was just the easy target.

"Not always, though, is it?"

"What?"

He sighed. "The interference. It's not always fine. People may mean well, but they can't know what you're really like, what you really want. It used to be like that for me too."

"Used to?"

He shrugged. The muscles under his T-shirt flexed, promising so much that I felt the aching heat in my groin. "Now my life is my own affair. What I do, who I do it with. It's nothing to do with anyone else."

I looked over at his flash car, his expensive clothes. Imagined his well-paid job, the salary he commanded, the staff he'd be in charge of. *A whole fucking boy band on his arm*.... "I don't think we're remotely the same."

He didn't reply, just looked at me. In that moment I saw the hunger in his eyes and—yes—a brief flare of uncertainty. I took a step back, away from him. I was trying to leave. I really was.

"He's with the blond one, isn't he? Your friend?" He seemed to smile at the thought.

I knew he meant Louis. Everyone knew Louis at the clubs—he was a local dancer. He was the ripple of lightness and grace that turned heads as he passed. He was the one who drew the crowds, who would be a star one day, who got hit on every time he went out. Not *me*. "Yeah, he and Louis are a couple. They've been together for years."

His smile broadened. "I thought so. I was tempted by him a couple of months ago when he started his gig at Compulsion, but I never got any positive reaction from him. I assumed he must be taken." There was a twinkle in his eye—a kind of mischief. "A man like that wouldn't be free for long."

I was horrified at the wave of nausea that engulfed me. "You made a play for Louis?"

"No, I did not pursue it. It was obviously a mixed message from him." Seve twisted his body to ease the car keys out of his jeans pocket. It was an elegant, sensual movement. It looked like he was trying to be careless, but from the way he turned his face, sneaking a look at my expression from under his hooded lids, he knew he'd shocked me. In fact, he was bloody enjoying it. "He looks like he needs it, doesn't he? Needs a fuck. The way he moves, the looks he gives a man... like he's asking for it. All the time."

"Louis is definitely not like that. You...." I caught my breath. "You're an arrogant prick, you know that?"

Seve just smiled as if, yes, he did know. "I said it was a mixed message. I thought it was a come-on for me, but it's just the way he is." He turned to face me again, his eyes sparkling. As cars passed the club, the illumination from their headlights swept the side of his face and neck. "And you're very defensive, aren't you? Why would you care?"

Yeah, why would I, apart from his careless disrespect of Louis? Shit, was I *jealous*? Startled that Seve had been attracted to one of my friends before he even met me? I'd never been in this situation before—in direct competition with a mate. It'd be amusing if it wasn't so... so....

"I'm glad I waited, though," Seve was saying. He rolled the keys around in his palm, back and forth. His gaze ran down my body, trailing hot slices of need in their wake. "The messages are a damn sight clearer from you."

"You reckon?"

He smiled slowly in reply.

It's just sex, I told myself. My head whirled. *I'm just a willing arse. Look how he talks about it... about* me.

"Will you get in the car now?"

I paused. I wanted something else, I guess. Some other word. Whereas my cock—I sighed to myself wearily—just wanted *him*. Seve dropped his head back, stretching his arms out behind his shoulders. Cracked the joints of his fingers as if he'd been still for too long and needed action. He moved with the restrained energy of a wild cat, like something feral. Something predatory.

He replied as if he'd heard my thoughts and was angry or tired of them. "You just want to talk more, then? Or do you want to fuck?"

"That's my only choice?" I snapped back.

Suddenly there was that flash of uncertainty again. This time he was the one to hesitate, his free hand lifting from his side, reaching for me. His breath was warm on my cheek, and I thought he'd try to grab me. But instead, he ran his fingertips along my jaw and then to my ear. He touched me as if he were blind, trying to gauge the shape of my face. His breathing was faster than before.

"Max?" He said just my name, his voice low and softly questioning.

Hell. Before I could even think about replying, he leaned even closer and put his mouth on mine. I found myself sucking on his tongue, hot and needy. He had his answer. I was sure people were staring at us as they passed on the pavement, but I didn't care. I gripped his arms and pressed as close to him as the contours of my body allowed.

Out of the corner of my eye, I saw the bouncers move uneasily. Behind them, something—or someone—else stirred. A shadow passed across the side of the building, like someone had dodged back out of sight. You know that feeling, when you don't see something clearly enough to know what it is, but your sixth sense alerts you to trouble? The hairs on the back of my neck sprang up like I was a guard dog and I'd heard a key in an unseen but forbidden lock. Was it another security man? Just one of the partygoers?

A group of young men pushed past us with a wolf whistle or two, on their way to the club entrance. Distracted, I pulled away from Seve.

And I got in the car.

WE DIDN'T go anywhere special—no exclusive party, no discreet bar, no guided tour of where Seve lived or played. But at least he never took me to that bleak, windy lay-by I'd imagined. Instead, we drove for fifteen minutes or so in silence toward Hove, where we pulled into the tree-lined car park of a small guest house. Seve switched off the lights and turned to me.

"You mean you were listening when those guys outside the club said get a room?" I quipped.

Seve didn't answer. He reached to the dashboard and pressed an unidentified button. With barely a jolt, the back of my seat started to recline. After the initial surprise, I released my seat belt and lay back, savoring the luxurious leather upholstery underneath me as it moved. The doors were a snug fit, and no noise intruded from outside the car. On the roof, I could hear the first patter of raindrops, as forecast. I hated the rain, though I wasn't sure that justified driving to some unfamiliar place with Seve just as a way to stay dry. There was no movement anywhere else in the car park. The trees shaded us from the guest house itself, and I guessed every sane person had left their car long before now and gone into the warm, comfy rooms.

"You forgot to make a booking?" Another of my feeble jokes, but I felt aggrieved. "Or you need a couple of quid toward the cost?"

"It's not that."

I felt vulnerable, flat on my back on a car seat that was larger and comfier than some beds I'd slept in. And Seve looming over me from his side of the car. "I don't understand you at all."

To my surprise, he didn't come straight back with a snappy protest. Instead, he gazed at me, the reflection from a nearby security lamp in the car park flickering in his pupils. "Then we're well matched. I don't understand you either."

I laughed. It was a loud sound in the claustrophobia of the car, in conflict with our stilted breathing. "I thought you'd had plenty of experience with guys."

"I'm not talking about *guys*," he said. "I don't understand *you*."

"Maybe you should have stuck with the boy band."

"Boy band?" He frowned. "What the hell are you talking about?" Then his eyes widened with anger. "Those fucking journalists. I tell them to keep away, but they keep calling. I have no time for their stupid gossip magazines."

"You're obviously news." I shrugged. A new business venture in Brighton's clubland, a franchise with links to other UK cities, a family manager who was young, gay, sharp, and fucking gorgeous. Yeah, what wasn't news about all that? Especially the manager's sex life.

"Max?" Seve was staring at me again. "You don't believe everything you read in that trash, do you?"

"Hey!" I held up my hands in mock surrender. "I don't believe everything I read *anywhere*. It's none of their business who you fuck."

"Who they *say* I fuck." He seemed disproportionately angry about it.

"It's none of my business either," I said. The words felt like individual lumps in my throat. It was bizarre, arguing about his sexual diary when I was stretched out under him and aching for him to bend down. Aching for him to fuck *me*. If things continued like this, I'd start to dwell on the thought of him lying on a bed, panting and naked apart from his sweat, with three or four ridiculously cute pop stars, their lips on his skin and the trail of hair on his belly, their hands curled around....

Yeah. Looked like I *was* jealous, though it was neither sensible nor my right. I started to struggle back up to a sitting position, but his hand landed firmly on my chest.

"Get back down." The growl was back.

"You want to do it right here?" I peered out the car window. The rain was running freely down it now, the lingering drops glistening like little silver Christmas tree lights against the darkness outside.

"Right here, yes," he hissed. "I do it when I want it, *where* I want it. That makes me hot. It's more exciting, more risky. Don't you agree?"

"I—"

He laughed softly. "But I know you do—because you came with me again."

I didn't have any other defense. It was true. When Seve leaned over the central console and put his warm, moist lips on my neck, I welcomed it, wriggling on the seat to get a more comfortable position. He slid his hands up under my shirt, pulled it out from my jeans, and jerked the buttons apart with such impatience that one of them sprang off into the depths of the car. His palms were damp with sweat and his fingers were rough. When he ran them up my chest to my left nipple and twisted it sharply, I yelped.

"Hurts, Max?"

I lay back against the cool leather and panted. "Like hell it does."

His smile made a damp shape on my belly where he kissed it. He licked up from my navel to the other nipple. He flicked it back and forth with his tongue, occasionally sucking it between his pursed lips. I felt the vibration all the way down to my toes, and my knees pushed out against the sides of the seat cushion.

Seve laughed softly, running his free hand down between my thighs. He teased at the seams of my jeans, the material now sticking to my skin with my own sweaty desire. "Soon, Max. Soon I'll fuck you." He cupped my groin, rubbing firmly up and down my thickening dick. It made the ache much, much worse. I heard a zip go, but to my selfish disappointment, it wasn't mine. He slid a hand up to grasp me by the neck again, and for a few long seconds, he thrust his tongue into me, moaning his lust into my mouth. I grabbed him in return, trying to get a grip on his cropped hair, holding his head close.

Then he pulled away. He was panting too, and he fumbled under his own seat with clumsy movements. The back of it jerked down, though it didn't settle as flat as mine—just enough for him to lie back. His hand was still on my neck, and he tugged my head over his prone body. When he pulled open the flies of his jeans with rather gratifying impatience, I saw he had no underwear on. The cloth parted and his cock was there, nestled against crisp dark curls, already filling and straining to get out into the night air. The skin was flushed and dark; the tip was weeping for attention. My mouth watered.

"Suck me again." His whisper was hoarse. "It was so good."

I bent awkwardly from the waist, avoiding a minefield of buttons and switches, and leaned over him. I trapped his nearer arm under my body and went down on him with as much enthusiasm as the first time. He jerked at my first touch and my head banged against the edge of the steering wheel. But then he settled, letting me suck down toward the base of his cock, and I began slowly to torment him. I licked and sucked from his balls right up to the hot tip of his shaft, shining in the dark. I could taste the drops leaking out, feel the ripple of excitement inside its sheath. I wondered how long this rock-hard dick had been aching for this, and how the hell Seve had managed to concentrate on his driving with this in his jeans, clamoring to get out.

His free hand clutched at my hair, pushing my head up and down. Damn, but he liked it. Pleasure was bubbling deep in his groin, I could feel it in his pulse. The hairs around his cock tickled my nose, and the soft furring at the tops of his thighs brushed my chin. I could feel his balls tightening and his cock throbbing on my tongue. He'd come soon. I opened my throat to take it all in.

"No!"

Like the first night, just as his climax was beating a path to escape, he tugged at my head, trying to pull me away. Tonight, though, I wasn't going to take it like that. Perhaps I was getting bored with the whole submissive thing. I growled in my throat, tightening my lips on his cock. I resisted him.

"Max!" He faltered, maybe nervous that if he pulled too hard, my teeth would scrape a deep and angry passage all the way up that very, *very* sensitive flesh. I continued my sucking because I wanted to taste him. I *really* wanted to.

"Fuck it, wait...."

I could feel him struggling with the need to climax, the rising ecstasy. He tried to slap my head away, but I caught his hand and gripped him by the wrist. I pressed his arm back against the window so he was trapped on both sides. And still I savored him. "You want me to fight you?" I murmured into the soft skin around his dick, dragging it up over his slit then peeling it back down with my lips. "Is that what you want?"

"You have to stop...." But his hips bucked up into me regardless.

"I don't have to do anything just because you say so. I want to swallow it, Seve." I rolled my tongue around the rim of the head, my voice muffled by my mouthful but the words as clear as I could make them. "I want to swallow *you*."

When I glanced up, he looked shocked. "That's not what hap— oh *fuck*!"

I spat more saliva out to ease the way and I tightened my mouth. His cock jerked. It was reaching for my throat, I could feel it. I remembered someone telling me once I gave really good head. "No one ever did this for you, Seve? No one ever tasted you? Swallowed you?"

His silence was enough answer. *Damned if I won't enjoy being your first.* And then he gasped and the flood came. His hips crushed me up against the steering column, his fingers dug into my scalp, and he keened his essence out into my mouth, pumping again and again, hot and sharp tasting and richly thick.

Shit, but I also remembered how good come tasted!

CHAPTER 10

FOR the next few moments, things were awkward. Seve lay back on his seat, gasping for breath, the aftershocks still shuddering through him. I licked at his softening cock for a while, and then I levered myself back over onto my seat. I wiped my mouth carefully and teased out a thin hair stuck on my lower lip. I relaxed back as well, aware of the pressure of my own hard-on. Neither of us spoke. The only sound was our panting and the thrum of rain on the car. The air felt tense, as if it were shrinking in on itself.

Something had changed in the balance of things. Perhaps because I'd snatched control from him at the last minute? Perhaps because I'd done something for him no one else ever had? No, I was kidding myself. More likely it was because I'd pissed him off. I was meant to be the bottom in all this—to do what I was allowed, what I was told. Wasn't that how it'd been so far? But now we were stuck out here together, and if either of us was unhappy with it, well, what would we do? I, for one, didn't know *where* the hell I was.

And perhaps I just thought too much.

I flipped the button and zip of my jeans and slipped a hand inside. I wanted to touch my swollen cock. Yeah, I wanted Seve, but above all, I wanted the friction. I gasped with relief and started to rub myself up and down as teasingly and as slowly as I could stand. My eyes were half-closed with the relief, but I knew Seve was watching me. In the shadows of the car interior, he rolled over and braced himself on one arm, looking down on me.

"*Seve,*" I murmured. His name sounded good on my lips.

"Take them off," he whispered. "Keep touching yourself, but take the jeans off."

It was a challenge, but I somehow managed to wriggle the jeans and boxers down my legs and to pull one foot out. I could move more freely now. I stretched out on the seat, then bent the leg nearest the window at the knee, and arranged myself in a better grip. The windows were steaming up nicely, and I was panting heavily again as I worked myself toward completion. The car rocked underneath me.

"Going to come soon." I sighed. "You just going to watch?"

"No," came the whispered reply. He seemed to have recovered his composure. Possibly his libido as well—I had no idea what sort of stamina he had. "Turn over, face toward the window. On your side."

More wriggling until I lay on my side, watching the window, opaque with our lusty breath and spattered with channels of heavy rain. I kept pumping—I was leaking all over my hand, and the movement was slick and fast now. Then I felt Seve's hand close over mine and I paused for a second.

"Keep going." His mouth was at my ear. He nipped at my lobe, and the sudden pain jarred with the increasing pleasure. He moved my hand aside, then ran his own up and down my length a couple of times, cupping his hand over my tip so that I gasped aloud with the sensation. Then I realized what he was doing—he was collecting the precome on his fingers. My heart nearly stopped with excited anticipation.

"Keep going, I said."

I did. I wasn't far off climax now. And then I felt it—Seve's fingers up between my cheeks, ghosting at my hole and teasing the soft skin behind my balls. I strained to reach him, strained to receive him. His fingertip slid into me.

"*Fuck.* That'll do it." I groaned in extra emphasis. Even as he probed for my prostate, his palm flat against my skin and another finger seeking entrance, I felt the uncontrollable throb in my cock. The seed burst out over my belly and his hand, dripping onto the seat. I shuddered and moaned, and the car's suspension bounced under me.

Seve's soft chuckle tickled my ear.

Still moaning, I slid down from my climax. Calm returned to my spinning senses. But Seve was still fingering me. He'd dragged himself half off his seat and half into the space between us, which must have been damned uncomfortable. I dreaded to think where the gear stick was resting. His chest pressed against my back, and I could feel his thighs nudging hard against the backs of mine. Should I suggest moving into the backseat for anything more? I could feel the heat of him behind me now, the thick, solid column of his cock rubbing up against my arse. He must have pulled his own jeans down, because I couldn't feel that nagging nuisance that was his zip. Just hot, firm flesh. He prised his knee in between my thighs, lifting my upper leg until it hung over his hip.

"Here?" I gasped.

"*Now.*" His voice was hoarse.

Even as I wondered what the hell lube he was going to use and how in God's name I was going to get my leg far enough over on this narrow seat, or if my cock had any appetite left after basking in the afterglow of its climax—he slid the second finger into me. It was wet and warm with my come, and I moaned with need. Stretching my upper leg up and forward so that my knee banged on the inside of the door, I grabbed the handle as an anchor. My nose was squished up against the upholstery. I heard Seve flip open the glove compartment and then fumble with a condom. When his cock came back up against me, it was cool and still almost dry. *Not like that, you don't.* "Use my come," I hissed. "The rest of it." No one was going to rip me apart, however much I wanted him.

Seve crawled his fingers around to my groin, where a sticky puddle had dribbled from my navel to my pubic hair. He scooped up what was there: a generous handful. I lay still, bracing my limbs, listening to the upholstery squeak as Seve shifted and rubbed my seed over his cock. The flesh would be red-angry; he'd be impatient. I could imagine every detail going on behind my back. My own skin was tingling back to life at the thought. Then he rolled hard against me again, gripping my waist, forcing his hip under my upper thigh. And he pushed his cock into me.

I've always liked being bottom, though with Seve I hadn't had the option of anything else yet. But I wasn't bothered right now, because it was so damn *good*. It was briefly painful, there wasn't much room to maneuver, and my leg started shaking from the tension of holding it up and out of the way. But Seve must have recovered quickly from my sucking, because it took him only a few minutes of thrusting into me before he came again. Just a few minutes, plenty of stifled groans, and more abuse to the car's suspension.

I was half-erect, but to be honest, the way I was cramped against the side of the car wasn't conducive to another climax. When he shuddered inside me and finished, I let him ease himself out and fall back onto his seat. Something creaked, and I didn't know if it was the gear stick or the steering column. Or me. My hard-on was dreaming of past glories, but very shortly they'd sink away to mere memories.

"You're amazing." The words were spoken almost dreamily. It didn't sound like Seve's bold, aggressive tone at all. And that was more or less the only way I'd ever heard him.

I was shaken. I wasn't sure he'd meant me to hear it.

For what seemed like a long time, I was silent, staring at the black rectangle of the car's window. Seve was too. It was as if neither of us knew what to say. I listened to his breathing beside me, and when I glanced over, I could see his chest rising and falling. His face was turned up to the roof of the car and his eyes were closed. I should have felt at peace like that too. Lively sex, a fantastic climax, no irritating postcoital chattering.

But my mind was in turmoil. I wanted to sleep; I never wanted to sleep again. I wanted to touch him; I wanted to push him away. I wanted just to hold him… to hear his voice… to listen to his laugh. Then to fight the fascination he awoke in me. I was an emotional mess, and it wasn't just a result of the sex.

I also realized I wanted to leave.

"Take me back to town," I said. My voice was stark in the cold, clear air. The car was chilled by the rain, and our bodies were starting to shiver.

"What?"

"Take me back."

It sounded like Seve held his breath for a moment. Then he shifted clumsily, pulling the condom off into a tissue, and drew his jeans back up his hips. I did the same, cursing the narrow space, ignoring the awkward imprint of the seat belt clasp on my thigh. I hitched up my seat and Seve started the car.

The side windows were still fogged, but I thought I saw a pair of car headlights spring alight just as we pulled out of the car park. There was no other traffic around. The other car followed our route for quite some way until it finally turned off by the pier and we drove farther along the promenade toward the marina.

Seve dropped me off near the club and drove away swiftly. Since I'd asked him to go back, everything had been in complete silence.

A COUPLE of weeks later, Louis caught me in the kitchen while I was washing up after our late dinner. Well, not that I was making a break for it, but he stopped in the doorway, effectively blocking my exit. I wiped the last couple of plates slowly, wondering what was coming and suspecting I already knew. He had a particular look on his face, one of *those looks* I hadn't seen since I was a kid and was caught stealing sweets by the old ex-soldier who ran the corner shop. A mixture of anger, admonition, and understanding. Very difficult to balance, all of that. Louis's acting experience inevitably stood him in good stead.

"Max?"

I sighed to myself.

"I'm worried about you."

"In what way?"

He peered at me, suspicious of my calm. "This man you're seeing—"

Is that what I'd call it? *Seeing*? "You mean Seve?"

Louis just raised an eyebrow.

"Okay. So no one else is beating down the door to date me. I guess you do mean Seve. It's just fun, Louis. Just… something casual."

Louis nodded. Rarely have I seen someone nod a "yes" when they so blatantly mean "no way." "He's new to Brighton, Max, but he's already got a reputation in the club."

No, I thought, I was *not* going to ask. "What reputation?"

"He likes being in charge. He doesn't take shit from anyone, especially the staff. His company pays bloody good money, but he expects long hours and no messing about. He cancels contracts with long-standing suppliers if they won't meet the Medina prices, and he's sacked a couple of dancers who don't get enough attention. He watches all the expenses, though he spends plenty of money on his car and his flat."

His flat? "His flat?"

Louis dismissed it with a graceful wave of his hand. "It's somewhere on Sussex Square. We all know how much those properties cost. He's rich and arrogant and obviously used to getting his own way."

Some people would wonder at what point that became a bad thing. "Is that what you've heard, or gossip?"

Louis had the grace to blush. "All right, so a lot of it's gossip, you know how the dancers are. We deal mainly with Angie, who makes the bookings—she was at the club before the Medina Group took it over. You know I've always wanted a spot, and the Medina contract pays great money. But when she called me up to offer it, I did think twice. There's something about the new management that gives me the heebie-jeebies."

I rolled my eyes at a phrase I hadn't heard from anyone except Louis since school days. "What sort of thing?"

Louis shrugged. "Nothing really. Just a more aggressive approach to business, I suppose, after the previous owners who—let's face it—never spent any money on the place at all. But I… well, I did ask Angie and some of the others about the new man."

"Checking up on me?"

He scowled. "Of course not, you silly arse."

Not on me, but on Seve. I softened my tone so he wouldn't think I was really angry. "I told you, it's okay."

Louis still didn't look like *he* thought it was. "He dates a lot. Plays the field, has plenty of offers. Doesn't see anyone more than a couple of times. There's the story about the boy band—"

"Heard it," I snapped. I wondered if Louis had picked up vibes about Seve fancying him, and just how much of Seve's playboy image was true.

"I'm just saying, he's not boyfriend material, Max. Just fucks and leaves."

And wasn't that just what Seve accused *me* of? I could be honest with myself—Louis wasn't telling me anything I didn't already know. Except, perhaps, the bit about the "couple of times" dating. Looked like I'd already blown that one out of the water. "I'm not after that, Louis. Hell, a few weeks ago, all the pair of you could talk about was me getting out more. Getting laid. And now you're recommending I lock myself in my room until Mr. Right—or Mr. *Something Better*—comes along?"

Louis frowned, his nose wrinkling. "Of course not. You're deliberately misunderstanding me. I'm just concerned for you."

"Thanks," I said, but he couldn't have missed the sarcasm.

He snorted, his cheeks flushed. "Point taken. I'll leave you to your obsession."

And he was right, wasn't he? Obsession was a fair description. I couldn't wait for the weekends to come along, so I'd started hanging out at the club during the week as well. I did Comedy Night and Electro-Pop Night and even a Salsa Night. I was greeted with a leery grin at the Girls On Top night, and so far I'd resisted the Come To Daddy Night. But it had been worth it. In all cases, Seve had appeared at the bar within an hour of my arrival.

I didn't know how to take that. Was he on duty every night, or did he spend all his leisure time there as well? Or were there some other kind of jungle drums that called him whenever I dropped in? I didn't—couldn't—believe that.

And after all, did I care? Each time, we'd exchange some empty talk that I could never remember properly afterward, then he'd take me somewhere. It might be out into the yard at the back of the club again, or in his car, or to the silent shell of a bankrupted shop around the back of Churchill Square. Anywhere, just so's we could fuck. I don't know how he knew where to go or where he got the keys to some places, but we always found somewhere. We took a B&B room a couple of times, but only to fuck, then leave in the dark. And we only went there in the first place because I complained about my arse being stripped and pounded in the pouring rain one too many times. Maybe he'd taken other men to these places in the past. I wasn't such an idiot I didn't consider it—but then he'd act as if a room was unfamiliar after all, and I reckoned I was the first.

It didn't matter, at least not while I was so *high* on him. Just like we were both high on the impulse and the risk involved. We weren't so desperate that we wanted to be caught—it wasn't that kind of recklessness. But the need for each other was always in our next breath, and we weren't going to wait for the feather bed to satisfy it. I was always bottom, but that was fine by me. The feel of him inside me, the desire that sprang from him like an electrical charge, the imprint of his hands on my body—it was the best I'd ever known. And we both liked it that way, it seemed.

"Max, are you listening?" Louis's voice cut in. "It's just such a change to find you out every night. You're drinking again. You seem…."

Different, he was going to say.

"…different, somehow."

"I used to drink and go clubbing. You know that."

"Yes, but that was before you left Brighton." Louis shrugged. "When you came back, you were so withdrawn. You said you wanted everything to change. You were angry about it, angry and fri—"

"Hey," I said softly, like a warning.

Louis paused, realizing my mood. "Okay. You're an adult now. You can do what you like. It's not for me to tell you who to see."

I smiled. "Is that you talking or one of your soap scripts?"

He laughed and we had a friends' hug. I may have hung on a bit longer than usual. But I was still going out tonight. I was going to find Seve and offer my body for him to use, and it was all I wanted at the moment.

"Max, you won't leave again, will you? Leave Brighton, I mean." Louis was a perceptive guy, and his question wasn't completely ingenuous. "Not without telling us?"

"No," I said, and I meant it. "I'm fine now. I'm seeing Seve and it's good, and I know what I'm doing." I meant that too. Maybe I hadn't at first, when it had been my physical desire and Seve's lust that had propelled me on. They were bloody strong instincts that I'd felt inside me all my life. Given in to them, and fought them too, with varying degrees of success. But I wasn't going to be sucked into a life I couldn't control. Not again; not in the same way.

"The sex… the lust. It's heavy stuff, Max."

"Yeah," I agreed with a grin. I knew that. I'd never had so much before—never felt so alive to it despite the sore arse, the scratches on my back and knees, and the aching limbs. "You jealous?"

Louis thumped me on the shoulder. "Stupid pillock."

I laughed. "You're going to have to trust me on this one, though." And I grabbed my jacket and left the flat.

CHAPTER 11

SEVE and I fucked in the park that night, around the back of the cricket pavilion. Not on the grass, because it was damp from a misty seaside evening and neither of us had a coat to lie on. And not slowly, either, because the police patrolled there at night. We dropped our jeans, and then Seve propped me up against the side of the pavilion so we were face to face. He hooked one of my legs up around his thigh and fucked me with quick, shallow strokes. It was fast and intense, and when I came, my gasp was a weird mix between a laugh and a cry.

We swiftly dressed again and leaned back against the wall for a while, gathering our breath. Despite the damp night, the weather had been good for a couple of days. Spring was handing over to the budding summer season, though with a slow mischief that was familiar to anyone who lived here. Tomorrow it could pour with rain again, I knew, so we'd made the most of the warm evening. I could hear the traffic in the distance along the main Eastern Road and a thread of distorted music from along the pier. A group of drunk young men passed on the far outskirts of the park. One looked over and yelled something obscene at us, but they continued on the same path. I watched until they turned a corner out of sight.

"You want to go back to the club and catch another drink?"

Seve shook his head. "No." His eyes were clouded as they often were after orgasm. He didn't look like he was concentrating on much, but his hand ran along my forearm, stroking me.

"So I'd better get back," I said. I was just trying to find something to say. My legs ached from holding my position earlier, but the rest of my body was strangely restless too. Seve sighed aloud. That was all, but it triggered me somehow. "What else should I do?" I snapped. "You bitch about me upping and leaving all the time, but what the fuck else is there to do?"

He stared at me, startled. His dark pupils were like liquid fire in the gray shadow of the pavilion. To my weary astonishment, I felt my cock stir in response to my desire to see that flame lit again.

"You're the one—"

"It's safest to be the first to say it, right?" I couldn't believe the bitterness in the words spilling out of me. "Before you tell me to piss off. Because that's all this is, isn't it? A fuck. I know that, I'm not stupid. I know the rules. And believe me, I'm the first to enjoy it. But that doesn't mean you get all of me."

"What the hell are you talking about?" Seve's voice was low and angry. "What rules?"

"You know." I wished I'd never started this, but the devil was in me tonight. "The rules that say we're free to fuck anyone—no strings. This is just fun. You said it yourself once—what we want is no interference, no one running our life for us."

Seve frowned. "I don't remember. I'm not sure I meant...."

"Doesn't matter, it's true."

He bit his lip. Saliva on the plump flesh glinted, a reflection of moonlight. "I never said it was anything different, Max."

"No, I know." My turn to sigh. *And I didn't ask, either.*

"I don't have a lot of time for myself, so I want to make the most of it. I am always busy with work." He didn't sound like he knew what to say next. I wondered if he had his staff give other exes the brush-off or if he just didn't turn up one night. Like I realized I'd been dreading ever since the first night I met him. "The family has expectations."

"Yeah, I know all about them." I snorted.

Seemed that was a trigger for him too. "What does that mean? You don't know anything about my business."

I really, *really* wanted to snap back. I opened my mouth but closed it again quickly. Some kind of self-preservation had kicked in at last.

"Or do you?" He grabbed my arm and turned me to face him. "Is that your problem?"

"Let go of me."

"I'm not the only one keeping to myself, am I?"

"What the fuck? Just let go, let it drop."

He did neither. "What do you know? What aren't you saying?"

His grip was very tight, and I didn't know whether the swell inside my gut was anger or fear. "I know very well what your family is capable of."

He let go so suddenly I stumbled on the slippery grass. "Is that why you hold back?"

"Hold back? Shit, how can you say—"

"Not in sex," he growled. "Dammit, you don't listen properly, do you? I mean, you hold back yourself. Something's stopping us—"

"Stopping us, what?"

He shook his head as if irritated he'd spoken out. "Just tell me what it is you think you know about my family. You cannot accuse us of something and not tell me what it is."

"And *you* can stop with the injured innocence. You're part of the management, remember? You're proud of being family."

He flushed. "Yes, I am. We have been successful. We *are* successful. I know people are jealous of that."

"I'm not jealous. I've got no stake in that."

"So what the hell's the matter? Tell me!"

"There's no point. That's not what we're about." I blamed Louis for disturbing my equilibrium tonight; blamed him and Jack for being a sickeningly happy couple; blamed Seve for making me want him. Blamed everyone but myself, like I should have done.

"So what *are* we about?" Seve said. His voice had lowered again and his eyes had narrowed.

"I'm going," I said. "I'll walk from here."

"Don't be ridiculous—"

"Don't tell me what to be or not!" I snapped. I turned and strode away.

He didn't follow.

I WALKED quickly but distractedly, thinking how I'd been a brat and an arse, and that was surely the end of me and Seve. My belly hurt and my eyes felt oddly sore. I probably shouldn't have taken the shortcut across the back of the county hospital, though it was a shorter route by a few minutes and there were usually people about, whatever the hour. But tonight was different.

As I rounded a corner of the perimeter fence, they stepped out from the shadows behind the huge recycling bins. Three of them, taller than me, twice as broad, in casual but dark-colored gear and wearing shades at night, which was a strong indication of the IQ accompanying them.

For a sudden shocking moment, I thought I recognized one of them, a man standing in shadow at the back of the group. Something about the set of his shoulders and his stocky build. But the context was all wrong. I couldn't recall seeing him in the Brighton streets— the strongest memory was a flash of a miserable life that I thought was long past. Nausea prickled the back of my throat at the thought. How could it be him? I was terrified at how easily it could all come rushing back, the fear and the anger that I'd tried so hard to keep at bay.

But I didn't have time to swap reminiscences. They were tough and they moved quickly for such big men. After a few ineffectual punches from me, they sideswiped me and I fell to my knees. A kick to my stomach and I doubled over, retching and clutching my guts, feeling as if they'd fall out without protection. I wondered how small I could roll myself to keep away from the kicks and the fists. I wondered if there was going to be any weapon involved. Another kick to my thigh laid me flat out on my face, and I yelled out that time. Pointless, really. I knew no one was coming to help me.

One of them—one I didn't recognize—knelt beside me. Without warning, he smashed his oversized fist into my throat. My breath burst out of me in shock and pain. "Back off," he grunted in my ear.

Back off from what? I only had a couple of quid in my wallet. I didn't have a jacket, and I'd never had any jewelry. What the fuck did they want?

"Keep your fuckin' fag hands off Mr. Nuñez." Another boot caught my ribs, landing squarely on a patch that was already bruised beyond sensation.

"Who says so?" I croaked.

"*He* does," the man said with a horrible barking laugh. He stood, took a step back, and I winced in anticipation for the next blow.

But it didn't land. They just turned and left me there. I heard their heavy receding footsteps on the cold ground, the vibration spiking through my cheek. Curled up in agony, my face in the dirt of a day's pedestrian traffic, I wondered what the fuck was going on. If Seve wanted to dump me, why didn't he just tell me he was tired of my skinny arse? Did I really need the message imprinted on my ribcage?

Why did he do this?

AND my God, did Louis make a fuss!

I didn't have the heart to tell him I'd broken a few bones before now, and the bruises weren't going to make or break any career aspirations as an underwear model. After a painful examination by

Louis's GP, I quietly neglected to follow up on the X-ray appointment, in case they asked too many questions about my *fall down the stairs*. After all, the doctor reckoned most of the damage was on the surface, and I'd be on my way back to normal after a few days of rest and copious painkillers.

Yeah, most of that happened. But not the "back to normal" bit.

It probably took me two days before I could roll myself easily out of bed, and another couple before I could jog up and down stairs and do all the other things you take for granted when you're fit and able. I had bruises on bruises. I reckoned a rib might have been cracked, but I assured Louis it was just a wrenched muscle. It'd heal on its own, and I didn't want any further fuss. The site said they'd keep my job for a while, but they needed me back sooner rather than later. I was keen to get back there too. I hadn't been with them long enough to have any entitlement to sick pay.

I moved about carefully and I slept a lot. I also brooded a lot. My nights were anguished and my dreams were wet and frustrated. When I woke in the dark with a heavy sweat on, there was no comfort in the memories of that cruel beating. I just wished I knew what the fuck was going on.

I REALLY didn't want to drop Jack and Louis off at Compulsion that next Saturday even though it was the trade-off for borrowing Jack's car to go to one of the three Vs' house for the evening. The girls had some problem with the landlord's plumbing, and I'd offered to help them out.

"It's on your way," Louis wheedled. "I can't walk far in these trousers."

"Can't you get a cab?"

"Why are you so upset about it?"

"I'm not fucking upset," I growled.

"Why are you growling, then?"

So the argument was lost and I drove them to the end of the street. Louis tumbled out of the car, resplendent in black satin sprayed-on trousers and a shirt that barely covered his nipples. He sashayed up the steps to the entrance, waving to a couple of friends arriving at the same time. Jack slid out of his seat to join him. I risked a glimpse at the club, weighing up the door monuments—two of them again, wide guys in heavy black suits and the ridiculous shades. I let out a breath. Not the heavies who'd attacked me. Not the man I thought I'd recognized. How could I have recognized someone I hadn't seen for a bloody long time, from another city, from miles away—from another *life*, for God's sake? I'd been hallucinating from fear.

I felt the pain returning, but it wasn't just my still-aching ribs. The sight of the club disturbed me. The pavement where Seve had stood, leaning insouciantly against his car. The memories of other times he'd driven us away from there, of other nights he'd been waiting for me. Memories of the dark yard, the stuffy storeroom. What was worse, something else was aching, and it disgusted me. I started to pull away from the curb.

"Max!" The call was peremptory, and I knew it was Seve.

Fuck. My heart raced and my cock throbbed. I cursed every nerve I possessed for betraying me like this. Why the hell was he here again? Why did he think it necessary to waste further time humiliating me? Most of all, I wondered why I couldn't have driven away that little bit faster. God knows, Jack's car had the acceleration. If I hadn't given way to the stupid memories....

Meanwhile, Seve strode quickly and easily to the car and placed his hand on the half-open window. I didn't think I should close it quickly and leave him fingerless, so I stopped the car. I should never have thought about his fingers at all... his fingers on my hips... his fingers at my mouth... his fingers sliding into me. I missed him. And badly.

"Max, where have you been?"

"I got your message," I said sharply. I could smell the tang of his cologne in my nostrils. My body reacted of its own free will, and I was immediately fiercely aroused. I hoped to God nothing gave me away. It was suddenly very important to me that Seve didn't realize the effect he still had on me. "There's nothing more to say, is there?"

"Message?"

"The postcard with a punch." I almost spat the words. "The warning off. Couldn't you have just left me a note behind the bar? Or tucked a tenner in my jeans and dispatched me back home?"

"What are you talking about?" His eyes darkened with even more anger. "A warning about what, Max? Who brought you a warning?"

It was a good act, I had to admit. "Three lumps of cretinous concrete like those heavies up there. Told me to *keep my fuckin' fag hands* off you. And as I don't welcome any more bruises and battered bones, I'm taking it to heart."

"They beat you?"

The tightness of his tone jarred on my nerves. No point in keeping up the charade, was there? I knew I wanted out of here. And fast. "I remember every kick," I said. "A few months ago I might have given them a better run for their money, but I'm obviously out of practice at taking on three guys twice my size. I don't need that kind of trouble, Seve, not even for you. There are safer men to see."

I was genuinely angry, but I knew my words were largely bravado. I didn't want other men, did I? He must have known that. And he knew I didn't want "safer," or I'd never have come anywhere near here again.

"I'll take care of it, Max."

"Sure you will." I suddenly felt more grief than anger. His hand was too close to mine, and his breath curled the hair on my neck. His existence made me vibrate with desire. *Fuck, no.* "Doesn't matter to me. I've got to go."

"You always go!" he growled. "You fuck and run—that's what I tried to tell you the other night. Why won't you give me time to sort things out? Tell me what's pissed you off. Let's talk about it."

I stared at him, startled. "But this is what you want, isn't it? You want to move on. It's okay by me—"

"Is it?"

I gaped. I wanted to say: Yes, of course, it's just fun, just fucking. "No," I said. "It's not." I didn't know what to make of this. He seemed genuinely disturbed and angry about the attack on me, but I didn't know what else was going on in his handsome, well-groomed head. I put my hand to his to push it away.

He grabbed me instead. "So come with me, Max. I want you, you know that. I told you I'll take care of what's happened. I'll make things good again."

No! His hand was strong over mine. He leaned in the window and his mouth ghosted its words at my ear. Half of my mind begged me to listen to him. Every instinctive inch of me tried to squeeze its way out from under the seat belt and flow against him. His lean, sensual body and his rich, acquisitive lips....

The other half of my mind—the bloody-minded, masochistic half—won out. "Get lost," I said coldly. "No one needs a fuck that badly. Or another beating. Find someone your family *does* approve of, if that's your problem."

I wrenched my arm away and he stumbled back. I saw shock flash brightly in his gorgeous eyes. Then I slammed my foot on the accelerator and the car lurched away from the curb. Difficult to concentrate on the wheel when your cock is hammering to be let out of your too-tight jeans and there's a strange, painful tightness in your throat.

I didn't do that corny old thing of looking back in the mirror as I drove off.

No, I didn't.

So maybe that was going to be the last time I saw him.

I still didn't.

CHAPTER 12

LOUIS had another of those looks on his face. When I was at my meanest, I wondered how the hell Jack coped with the exhausting range of emotions that Louis inflicted on us all. Then I'd watch Jack's calm, possessive hand on Louis's arse and I knew they had it sorted out between them. *I* was the one who had nothing sorted out with anyone, and I was the one who really needed help. It was long overdue.

"Tell us, Max," Jack said. They'd pulled the couch in the living room over to a couple of feet from the armchair, effectively forcing me to talk to them. It was late in the evening and I'd sat curled up in that chair ever since supper, with the remote control on my lap but the TV screen still blank and my book closed on the floor beside the chair, waiting hopelessly for attention.

"What do you mean?"

Louis opened his mouth to add his opinion, but Jack held up a hand to hush him. "Tell us what happened while you were away. There's something going on that I don't understand, and I suspect it's to do with that missing time."

I tried to shake my head but it just hurt. Everything hurt.

"I don't see how we can help you, Max, if you don't tell us everything."

"Don't need—"

"Yes, you do," Jack replied firmly. He had a full cup of steaming fruit tea in his other hand. He was in for the duration. *Bloody friends.* "You've been restless and low since you got beaten up."

"Hey, that's to be expec—"

"But it's not only to do with that. You haven't been out on your own since the attack, so you're obviously not seeing Seve anymore. You work extra shifts at work, you're knackered and hardly eating."

"You sleep badly too," Louis added. "You shout out in the night."

Fuck. "I'm sorry, guys...."

"No problem," Louis said, and he really did sound like it wasn't. "Just saying."

"I think it's depression," Jack said gently.

Something twisted in my chest. "That's crap." My voice was thin. I looked at their concerned faces, and in my mind, something shook loose. Feelings that I'd kept well buried began to stir. This time I wasn't sure I could keep the lid on them. My gut ached like those feelings were bleeding emotion inside my body.

"It's nothing to be ashamed of," Jack continued. "But I think it has roots back in the time before you met Seve, before the attack, before you came back here—"

"To hide," I said quickly, too loudly. They both stopped talking and stared at me. "That's what it was, you know. I'm a coward and a fuckup and I ran back here with my tail between my legs."

"Max—"

"I didn't have anywhere else to go," I continued, speaking swiftly to make sure they didn't stop me, didn't allow me the benefit of the doubt any longer. "I left Uni because I couldn't cope with it. I liked drinking and fucking and taking plenty of drugs, and I thought it'd go on forever. But I ran out of money and the course was coming to an end. I knew I'd be thrown out and all the friends I had were getting truly sick of me fucking them over—"

"Not all," Louis said, only half under his breath, his eyes both angry and sad.

"So I left and took all that baggage with me to London." *I ran away—the first time.* "I told you I was living with that moron Vince, but to be honest I already knew he was going to dump me. So I went out on my own, kept on the same way—drink, drugs, casual work. Plenty of action with men, some I liked, some I didn't, but they gave me money or supplies." Louis blinked a couple of extra times, but Jack's gaze was steady. "It all turned sour pretty bloody quickly, but I thought I could make it work if I kept going. I didn't have any other choice, did I?"

"Max," Jack said. "Take it slow."

I shook my head. I had to go on or I might never be brave enough again. "I wanted to be the great independent—be the *man.* Instead, I had no money, no food, couldn't hold down a job, got hit on whenever I tried to sleep on a park bench…."

Louis leaned over and touched my shoulder. It was surprisingly comforting.

"Then I got offered a job at a club near Soho. I'd exhausted everything else—pub work, office cleaning at night, runner for the Chinese restaurants. The club was a new renovation, but it wasn't exactly a regular job, you know? This man approached me and offered to find me a room and board if I did some errands for him. At first I just did some low-level running—some messages, a few packages."

"Packages?"

"Drugs, money—shit, I didn't know and I didn't care. The guy got me regular food and a bed in a local hostel with other casual workers." I edited over the following months as the trips got more frequent, the men I met more aggressive, the drop locations more dangerous. "It got to be a regular thing."

"Who was he?"

I shrugged. "They called him Peck, I never knew any other name. He worked for the club."

"You mean that was his day job?"

I stared Jack full in the face because I was pretty sure he'd understand without needing diagrams. "No, I mean he ran the drugs and the money *from* the club. They were behind it all. It was their racket. Apparently all the clubs in that group were known for it."

"This club...?" Louis looked like he was up to speed now as well.

"A Medina Group venue," I said bitterly.

We were all quiet for a moment. Louis glanced at Jack, but Jack was staring at me intently. "Max, tell me exactly what you did." Jack was no innocent and he always wanted the facts.

"I worked for Peck exclusively in the end. I ran the drugs out of the club. I knew the local contacts, the preferred dealers, the negotiated prices. He did the deals, but I was one of the most popular couriers."

"And?"

"And in return I got a room, food, protection. Yeah, and sometimes my own supply." It hurt to say it after all this time. "I had a smart mouth and fast moves, and Peck said he liked that. He told me the management liked that too."

And to be honest, it had been a heady and exciting time. I was someone important albeit in the strange, warped world of the street. The dealers looked at me with some respect, even if it was secondhand from Peck, who scared the shit out of them. I had a great time, especially when I was high—or at least, I thought I did. I slept around, went to some wild parties. I gave my hedonistic side free rein. It was what I'd always wanted, wasn't it? To do what I liked, to suffer no authority. I deserved it after the miserable months I'd spent when I first came to London. And many of the partners I had were like me— decent people but caught up in an indecent business. We might've stayed together longer in a different life. I might've found someone special.

Right.

"I knew it wasn't real, Louis." My friend's expression was stricken. "I knew it was wrong and I knew it wasn't going to last. I was bloody lucky I didn't catch anything or get seriously hurt. I just... didn't know any better at the time."

Jack broke in. "You say the management knew it was going on?"

I nodded. "They knew. They tolerated it. Dammit, they *controlled* it. Or so Peck always told me. And I don't think he was bright enough to have run things on that scale on his own. The Medina family were in charge."

"Shit." Louis sighed and looked into my eyes. "You poor stupid arse."

I smiled because it wasn't the kind of pity I despised, it was just Louis being there for me. It had *never* been a great time, I knew that now. And what was more, I knew it then.

Jack's quiet, strong voice brought me out of those thoughts. "And who was Stewart, Max? Where was he in all this?"

Here was somewhere I did *not* want to go, but I knew I had to. "He was something unusual, you know? He came around the parks at night. First I thought he was a pervert, then I reckoned he had some kind of death wish. Then he told me he'd been looking for someone in particular but gave up on that, got a job at the local youth center, and started looking out for other lost souls instead. People on the street hated do-gooders like him. Never did *them* any good. But Stewart was different."

"Tell us, Max."

I leaned back in the chair, briefly closing my eyes. "There was a group of kids I was friendly with. An odd bunch. All ages, all backgrounds. Some had been on the street for years. I'm not sure they'd have known what to do if they were offered anything else. They were all users." *All used up.* "Then Stewart comes along like some naïve knight in white armor, trying to help them."

I heard Louis make a small sound, but Jack hushed him again.

"He did too." Even I could hear the amazement in my voice. "Didn't tell them what to do, didn't try to scare or bully or shame. He was just there as a mate, and eventually they came to trust him. He got Joe into a clinic. Helped Luce get a job at some canteen. Got some medical help for others." How could I explain it? "He did things, didn't just talk about it."

"For all of them?"

"No, not all of them. That's a job too far." There was another brief silence.

"And what about you?"

"Yeah. He worked on me too." I opened my eyes and laughed, rather sharply. "Stewart wasn't a saint, you know. He'd let you know exactly what he thought. And what he thought of my job was that it was shit and I should stop it. Stop it and find something else." I shifted on the chair. "I, of course, told him it wasn't that fucking easy."

"Your friends…?" That was Louis, still trying to find some happy pixie dust in among the shit.

"They weren't friends, Louis. I had no real friends." When it came down to it, it was a life of complete and utter solitude. Full of sudden violence. Sickness, drug abuse. Pain. Cold, wet fucking misery. Honor among thieves? That was all crap. The first time I messed up with a delivery, Peck had me beaten up. Second time, I couldn't get out of bed for two days. I nearly starved until I got out for some food and drink. I didn't mess up a third time. "It wasn't easy because I couldn't see how to get off the roller coaster. I had no money but I wanted food and dope. Peck would give me all that but only as my earnings. The cycle continued."

Jack still seemed calm, but he clutched his cup like it was a lifeline. Louis had eased his way up closer to him on the couch.

"Stewart was your friend."

"Yeah. At least, Stewart was the nearest I got. I found out he *had* been looking for someone—a friend's runaway son—but the kid had scampered home at last and Stewart was going to move on. But when he saw some of the young people around Soho, he didn't turn that disgusted-but-blind eye to it all that other folks do. No—he wanted to do something about it." My mouth filled with the sour taste of regret. I should have protected him. I should have recognized the decency for what it was and treasured it, not taken it for granted. "We hung around together for weeks while Stewart was setting up his plans for the Refuge. He was in some kind of talks with the cops or with the social services. I didn't know the details, and if he'd told me, I'd have said it wouldn't change anything. But maybe it would. I'd been wrong plenty of times before. And gradually, I came to believe him on my own behalf. I still did my job, but I gave up the weed and pills."

Jack made a small noise of encouragement.

"Yeah," I said wryly. "It was hard at first, but luckily I considered food and drink more important than getting high, so I wasn't too far gone. And I started looking for ways to ease myself out of the business, hoping they wouldn't notice if and when I moved on. Stewart said he'd get me a proper legal job."

And we didn't go beyond friends. I think he was straight, though I never saw him with a girlfriend *or* boyfriend. But he never made a move on me—it wasn't like that with us. There were times I wished it had been, when I wanted to give something back for his attention and care. And what else did I have to offer?

"What happened then, Max?"

That night.... "He'd met me after work. I was doing some cash-in-hand cleaning at the club, and we were going to go back to Stewart's flat for coffee. I sometimes slept over on his couch, though we kept that between us." Yeah, I'd been hanging out with Stewart instead of walking the streets, fixing up appointments. Like the other hundred-odd nights that I'd been Mr. Fixit in Peck's world of peddling. Stewart and I were chatting and joking when I should have been out collecting the rest of the night's money, then crashing on my mattress and wondering when I could steal enough of the takings to buy a fare to somewhere—anywhere—Stewart was going. Then...

"This kid lurched out from nowhere. He had a knife." Stewart and I had been laughing at my clumsy attempts to do up his winter coat for him—he had his arms full of papers and files, and I was just glad to touch his warm body, his clean, comforting, civilized body, with my skinny fingers, trying to help him out in the cold night, to keep him warm. Then suddenly there was the flash of a blade, ice-white against the purple shadows. I instinctively twisted out of reach even as I turned to see who and what was coming.

"Stewart was knifed four times. One cut an artery, one half severed his neck. Blood everywhere." All over his new suit and that damn coat. All over the pavement; all over *me*. "He gargled a bit, but it all bubbled out so damn fast I couldn't believe it."

"Shit, Max!"

"I've seen someone overdose," I said. My voice sounded strained and alien. "And another kid die from the cold. In the morning, the life had just frozen away. She was a shell. And when I was new on the streets, I'd hear about kids who got run over because they were sleeping too close to the road. Shit happens and I knew that. But this was different."

"Of course it was." Louis looked very pale.

"There were rumors about Peck," I continued. "That once he killed a kid who argued with him one too many times. Strangled him with his bare hands. Apparently it didn't take long. And one of my group, Baz… the others told me he used to hassle Peck, wanting to be like him. Just stupid teenage hero worship. But Peck got annoyed and beat him really badly. Baz couldn't think straight after it, went a little mad." My heart seemed to be beating very fiercely. "I used to supply Baz just to keep him calm."

"And Stewart…?"

"I'd never seen anything like it. It was horrific. And by the time I'd started yelling for help, the blood was easing off to a steady flow. That got slower and slower, and I knew he was going. No last dying words or all that shit. Just shock and blood and mess." I turned away from my friends because I didn't want to see the disgust and horror I knew would be on their faces, but also because I couldn't trust the stinging in my eyes not to overspill into tears.

"Did you get a good look at who did it?" Jack's voice was low.

I chose not to answer that directly. "Everything was too fast, too wild. I could barely focus. I launched myself at the kid, got in a punch, but I doubt I did him any damage apart from a sore belly. Then he kicked me in the nuts and I wasn't a threat anymore."

"The police?"

My mind had drifted back to the sounds and smells of that night—the odd coppery tang of fresh blood, the distant *whoop* of an ambulance siren, the sputtering lights outside the club. My aching balls and the knot of pure fear in my throat. "The paramedics were really quick, you know, considering the neighborhood. But I could see they wouldn't be patching him up."

Louis winced at my harsh tone. He was the only guy I'd ever known who could *sob* and still look okay with it. Which he was doing right now.

Jack's eyes were wide and fierce, but it didn't seem his anger was directed at me. "What did the police do? What did you tell them?"

No straight answer from me, again. I could remember the tears on my face that night as if they were still there. "The wound—I just keep seeing the wound. Never seen anything like it." I rested my head against the back of the armchair and closed my eyes against the memory of such injustice. The way I'd felt then was still vividly, cruelly raw. The stirrings of hope in amongst the cynicism and the sagging self-esteem. I was going to change things, do it right this time. Someone wanted to help me and I had a friend. I was going to live up to what he wanted. But I never got the chance, did I?

"Max!" Jack's voice snapped me back to the present. "How did you get away from that? You're not telling me the whole truth."

"Jack! Take it easy." Louis turned to stare at his boyfriend.

I met Jack's gaze. "No, I'm not, you're right. I got away from that, Jack, because I ran. I saw the lights of the ambulance and heard the police sirens and I *ran away*." Silence from everyone else. "I had my tips from the club pot and a couple of Peck's dues I'd collected earlier in the day but hadn't yet passed on to him. There was enough to get a late coach out of London. But even by the time I got to Victoria, I wasn't sure where I was going. I just wanted *out*."

"You didn't wait for the police? You didn't tell them your story?"

I couldn't meet Jack's eyes. "I thought I'd be in too much shit myself. They might have suspected me—they might have asked me what exactly I'd been doing with him. In fact, what I'd been doing for the past year. They would have looked me up on the records." Where they wouldn't have found a whole lot of official information. So then would come the awkward questions. "I didn't dare stay around."

"So you came to us?"

"Please." I didn't know what else to say. "I just didn't know where else to go—what else to do. I got on the bus to Brighton and I called you. I know running out was a stupid thing to do. Cowardly. But when I saw he was dying, I persuaded myself I couldn't have helped anyway."

"And Stewart?"

"What?"

"Did he have relatives? A family?"

I stared at Jack, aghast. "I… he told me he was on his own, apart from a couple of distant cousins he never saw."

"But didn't it cross your mind that someone might need to know what happened, what you saw?"

No, it didn't. I buried my head in my hands. "And all I did was bring it back down here with me. Landed it all on you two. It's my fault."

Jack sighed. Louis leaped off the couch and came to kneel in front of me. He put a soothing hand on my neck. "You didn't kill him, Max. You panicked and you ran, but it was a mugging—pure chance. Of course it wasn't your fault."

I lifted my head to stare at him, and from the way he flinched, I knew that my expression still reflected the slide back to that world. My voice sounded weird, like someone else's. "You still don't have the full truth, though. You see, I did recognize the attacker—I *did* know him."

"What the hell?"

"It was Baz—Peck's pathetic little shadow. I knew he was damaged, but I never knew he was that violent. We'd kept him out of trouble for a long time, taking him around with us, trying to keep him away from Peck's shitty world. Not well enough, obviously."

"But you couldn't—"

"Haven't you been listening to me?" Now my voice was loud and angry. "I helped him get like that! He had no damn money, of course, but I'd share my supplies with him when he was desperate. I was the one who got him drugs, fed his habit, pushed him further and further toward the edge of madness until one day he obviously snapped for some reason—and Stewart was in the way. I might as well have put the fucking knife in his hand!"

That was it—I'd had enough confession for the night. I threw off their touch and the cloying air of their concern, and I lurched toward the door, holding out my hands to keep them away from me. Jack and Louis—great guys. Guys who'd found out their best friend had been a dealer and the worst kind of parasite. Tomorrow I'd face them. Tomorrow they'd tell me to move out. But tonight I had demons to keep me company instead.

"Max, wait!"

I paused in the doorway, though I didn't turn around.

"We'll sort something out," Jack urged. "You're different now, right?"

But that was the problem, wasn't it? I was trying to be... and I was failing.

"Have you spoken to Seve about this?" Louis asked quietly. "Told him what you know about the London club?"

"No," I said. Fear prickled at the back of my neck. "No point. You heard me say all the clubs were in on it—the whole Medina Group is run that way. And Seve's one of the family. He's part of it all."

"You don't know that for sure!"

"He's a Medina." I could hear the cynicism in my voice. "Of course I know for sure. He does what he likes." And I didn't want to get drawn back into that world again just because I couldn't keep my hands off him.

It was never going to be worth it.

CHAPTER 13

IT WAS eating away at me. *He* was. Seve. *Seve.* I dreamed him. Breathed him, heard him, tasted him. I woke up nights holding myself so tightly it hurt, and begging for it to be his hand on my cock, his fingers up inside me—

With a guilty pleasure, I listened to Jack and Louis making love at night downstairs.

I masturbated to thoughts of Seve, silently—a little ashamedly—but always *exquisitely.*

I was stupid and helpless and plain fucking angry.

I had to see him again.

IT WAS a Friday, a couple of days after I'd spoken to Jack and Louis about Stewart and the past year, a couple of days when I avoided them like I had some strange form of plague and didn't want them catching it off me. I came home from work about seven and went up to my room as usual to wash and change out of my overalls. But this time I took extra time in the shower and way too long wondering which polo shirt from my meager collection to put on. Then I grabbed a sandwich and left the house, all without catching sight of the others. All for the good, really. I had personal business to attend to.

I lingered for a long while outside Compulsion. There was a fine sheen of rain spattering on my shoulders and head, and I hadn't bothered to grab a coat. Damn, but I hated the rain. To me, it was the epitome of misery in its physical symptoms of cold and wet. At this early evening hour and with the looming gray clouds, the club looked half-deserted and totally harmless. There was no security on the door, just a weedy little management type. Even so, my ribs ached in memory.

Enough!

I marched up to the door and asked for Mr. Nuñez. I stood my ground when the Weed tried to tell me he didn't know if Mr. Nuñez was available. I made the most of my extra four inches to stare him down. I knew what to do with weeds, and it wasn't anything to do with gardening. Seve was there. I knew he would be.

Weed made some mumbled call into his radio, and I stood for another ten minutes, getting wetter. He pulled back into the relative shelter of the doorway, but I stayed out in the rain. Things had changed for me. For whole sections of time, I slipped in and out of another world—a far less comfortable one. A world where rain was the least of my troubles.

Seve came out a few minutes after that. He stared at me and I stared back, then he inclined his head in welcome like he often had before. He was dressed in a full suit today, obviously his working day look. He looked spectacular. It was probably designer—a soft, charcoal-gray fabric that hung from his broad shoulders with perfect elegance and hugged his narrow waist and hips. The plain white shirt shone with an expensive glare that I'd never found in the discount stores. His tie was subtly understated but probably silk. The damn clothes didn't matter, of course, because all I could think of was the body underneath.

"Max." His eyes had settled into a dark wariness. It had been a couple of weeks since we'd seen each other, since I'd pushed him away from Jack's car and driven away. A couple of weeks since we'd last fucked. I didn't want to recall any of these particular statistics.

"I think I know one of the men who attacked me, Seve." I could feel trails of water running down my collar as the rain got heavier.

Seve didn't answer. He seemed to be waiting for me to say more. His eyes were hooded.

"He's called Peck. I knew him in London. He's the lowest kind of scum, but then you probably know that. He's on your staff, isn't he?" What were the chances I'd meet up with the one guy in London I'd hoped never to see again? Was it luck or fate that I'd ended up frequenting another Medina venue—that my past would hang around me like the worst kind of storm cloud? And what were the chances Seve had the same kind of random luck? None, I reckoned. "Louis says maybe you don't know what goes on at your family's clubs. Maybe there's some other source for your smart car and expensive flat and your loyalty to your family business. But I know things about it, Seve. Firsthand. And I find it hard to believe that *you* don't."

Seve spoke at last. The rain was beginning to make sodden patches on his shoulders. "Max, you're talking nonsense. I don't understand you. I checked the staff here after you were attacked, and yes, I believe I remember a man called Peck. My uncle sent some support from the London club just a couple of months ago. I didn't know this man personally, I assure you, but I have sent all the staff that my uncle lent to me back to London with a report of their appalling behavior."

I was shivering, and not from the rain. Peck had been here, I'd been right. Coincidence, or a deliberate plan?

"I want us to talk, Max, but these accusations are bizarre. I never sent those men to attack you. I didn't know anything about it! And I don't like the way you talk about my family's business. My uncle runs a legitimate entertainment group. What else are you implying?"

There was a sharp edge to Seve's voice. Should I have been more cautious? Weed was hovering in the background, though Seve raised a hand and gestured for him to stay back. There were a few people about on the streets, but they were hidden under umbrellas and scurrying back home. I was alone and relatively unprotected. But I was also wet, bloody angry, and I wanted to hit the very man I wanted to caress. "I don't think it's me who should be answering questions, do you? That's not what I'm here for."

Seve tilted his head. "What *are* you here for, Max?"

And in that moment, I knew he had me. What the hell was it I wanted? Seve to confess that he knew Peck, that he'd sent him to see me off? The look in Seve's eyes was hungry for me, not angry that I hadn't taken the brutal hint. And did I expect him to admit the illegal activities that his uncle's business fronted so blatantly? Why should he, even if he knew? For my own edification? For some kind of revenge—or compassion for what I'd been through? Or… did I just want to see Seve again? *Crap*. It was all crap. He was right, I was in no position to accuse anyone about anything. I turned to leave.

"Wait!" Seve hurried down the steps to reach me. "Max, for God's sake, wait." There was a spark in his eyes, sharp like pain. "I don't understand you."

"So you once said." I sighed.

"Is it to do with this man Peck? I don't employ everyone personally, you know. They are my uncle's men."

"His men?"

Seve shrugged—the graceful, sensual movement that set off warning bells in my damp, shivering body. "They have worked for him for a long time. They are on the central payroll. They look after the family."

"Shit, Seve, it sounds like the mob."

He laughed scornfully. "Don't be so melodramatic! My uncle is just a businessman. It's necessary security for the club, and I suppose it's protection for me. Or so my uncle says." He frowned. "It's not what I want, Max. I don't need it and I tell my uncle so. And you should *never* have been threatened by any employee of ours. It's unforgivable. It won't happen again."

"Too fucking right it won't." I wished I sounded more righteous than petulant. "You know what Peck's into, Seve, back in London— you must do! And it's a hell of a lot more than *security*."

"I don't know anything about him. This is the only thing I know about." He waved a hand back toward the entrance to the club.

"Compulsion. This is the only thing I do. And it's just a nightclub. Nothing sinister."

I looked into his face, blinking against the rain, and for the first time, I saw his confidence waver. That superb, sexy arrogance that had attracted me in the first place. Was that how I wanted to see Seve?

"Why won't you listen to me, Max? I don't know anything else about it. What the hell else is bothering you?"

I backed away. I heard the squelch of a shallow puddle as I stepped into it, and Seve put out a hand to hold me, to help me. All I could see were his eyes. Bright and fevered, almost scared. What of? Of what I was saying—what I knew? Or that I was running away from him again? I knew I didn't want to. I knew I wanted him. *So, so much.*

"Don't go, Max. I don't want you to be scared off. It's the last thing I want. But I cannot accept your anger toward my family, not without some explanation. You must tell me what's troubling you."

"Why should I?"

His hand grasped my arm. Outwardly, I felt the wet fabric of my shirt clinging to my skin, but inside I sensed the heat of his body, flowing into mine.

"You also said once… the trouble you had wasn't worth it, not even for me. For *me*." His voice was low and husky. "No one has ever factored me into any decision like that before. No one has ever weighed me up against anything else."

I didn't know what to say. I didn't understand why he was so taken with a stupid comment of mine. I couldn't tear my gaze away from his hand on my arm, the skin looking gray under rivulets of rain.

"I want you, Max," he said. His face was close to me now. "I don't want any misunderstanding between us. And if you tell me everything, then I can protect you."

Protect me? The egotism left me speechless. Then I hit him. Or at least, I tried to. I reckoned I was better prepared this time, and Seve and I were more evenly matched. I'd been in fights during my life on the streets, though I doubted I'd ever be able to lay someone flat out. As it was, Seve dodged at the critical moment and his hand came up with astonishing speed to catch mine.

I heard a cry from behind him—probably the Weed, panicking. We leaned into each other, arms straining against each other's grip. I tried with my other arm to get purchase around Seve's waist. He gasped because I was obviously stronger than he'd imagined, but he stood firm. His free hand pressed against my shoulder, putting strain on my only recently recovered muscles.

And the rain continued to pour down on us.

It was all I could hear: *It won't happen again. I can protect you.* Seve—a pampered nephew, who had obviously never been crossed, never been refused anything. Who had wealth and power and people to watch over him. Who wanted me. Who didn't want me to leave him this evening. Who had no idea of my life and what I'd lived through in the past year.

"Please. Max!"

I was startled. I didn't think I'd ever heard Seve use that word in this context. Perhaps when I'd been at my most teasing with sucking him off or when I'd challenged him before he took me—held myself apart from him, even if it was only for brief, charged seconds. It had never been true begging; it was only ever a game. He knew I'd always surrender and be glad to do so. But this didn't feel like a game anymore. I felt the energy drain from my body. I'd not seen this side of Seve before—the desperate, almost clumsy touch, the plea in his vibrant voice. My face was chilled from the rain, the skin aching with tension, but I felt the soft heat of his mouth even before it touched me. He was damp all over as well, his face shining, his hair flattened to his head, and his beard and mustache slick with the trail of raindrops. I wanted to wipe them all away, and gently. I just wanted to touch him. To hold him that way. I accepted the kiss because—in all truth—it was my dearest wish.

My striking arm relaxed and I let him fold it down to my side. My other hand around his waist became enfolding rather than aggressive. I held him to me, wet cloth against sodden skin. I kissed him back fiercely, our tongues battling inside our mouths, when we'd been almost fighting with fists a moment ago.

"Relax, Max, please. I want you." We broke the kiss and Seve pressed his forehead against mine, breathing heavily. He didn't turn away, but I saw him gesture to one side, obviously letting the Weed know any danger was past. If it had ever been there at all. My body was throbbing with the sudden remembrance of what I'd been missing. Of his touch, his smell, his hold.

"Come to my flat."

"What?" Had I heard right? Was the noise of the hammering rain confusing me?

He scowled. His face was so close to mine that when he licked his tongue out of his mouth to catch the fall of drops from his nose, he licked at my lips as well. "I think there are things we need to talk about, things that don't need an audience."

"Just that?"

He grimaced. "And I want you, but this is not the place or time to do it, even I can see that. Even though I want to drop you to the pavement right now and fuck your tight arse into the wet concrete."

His breath was heavy and hitched. I think I just stared.

"Besides…." His laugh was tight. "I know how you hate the rain! Come with me, Max."

His voice was insidious, or maybe our short, passionate tussling had exhausted me. He tugged me with him around the corner of the building, where he'd parked his car in a convenient space. Perks of the management, I assumed. He kept his eyes on me all the time, as if he was afraid I'd run in the other direction. The arrogant smile was sliding back, like the first time he led me somewhere, and a possessive spark flared in his eyes. But there was that same hint of nerves that I saw earlier. He wasn't so sure of me, perhaps.

Was I sure of myself?

"…Max…?"

I realized I was clutching at his jacket, leaving creases that I knew the cleaners would struggle with. "Let's go," I said.

No one followed us. Weed must have scuttled back indoors, and I couldn't see any more of Seve's uncle's men to contend with. Seve eased me into the passenger seat, my boots pooling water all over the expensive upholstery. His hands lingered on me before he swung around to the driver's seat. I could have jumped out then, if I'd wanted to. Made my way home. Broken away from him.

But why the hell would I want to do that?

CHAPTER 14

OF COURSE I knew the area around Sussex Square. I'd just never got a dinner invitation there or, for that matter, any other invitation. It was another world from the cramped but cozy place that Louis and Jack had. Seve told me he had a top floor flat in one of the magnificent Georgian buildings between the Square and Marine Parade—I was sure the estate agents must have had a field day with the "fantastic sea views" and "access to private gardens." I was gawping from the minute we drew up in front of it. There was a shared entrance hall, and Seve strode through it with easy familiarity. I tagged along, wondering if anyone would ask to search my pockets.

The lift to the third floor was small, and although it was elegantly decorated, it had obviously been part of the original conversion. It shuddered to a slow and shaky start and I caught my balance, moving closer to Seve. His proximity made my skin prickle, and the suspense had been building all the way here. He'd tightened his hand on my leg as he drove, stroking fingertips between my thighs. I hadn't discouraged him; in fact, I was amazed we made it to his flat at all. I think he would've liked to have jumped me at the last set of lights, but they changed too quickly. Or perhaps I was too damn wet for him to get a proper hold.

I was wincing at the piped Muzak in the lift and admiring the carpeting that was better quality than the one in Louis and Jack's bedroom, when he pushed hard on my shoulders so that I dropped to my knees. I didn't get the chance to ask *how* slowly the lift moved because I was distracted by the rasp of his opening zip, and then my mouth was filled with his erect cock. I sucked very eagerly. Even though his trousers were damp from the rain, his skin was dry inside the smooth cloth of his boxers, and the soft, dark hairs at the top of his thighs brushed my chin. I licked fiercely at the ridges along his cock, dragging the sensitive tip in and out of my lips. He gasped and his hands grasped my hair. My knees trembled on the luxurious carpet.

I was surprised at how fast his excitement rose. He'd always shown great self-control, even at his most aroused, even as he fucked me some nights with the groans that told me he just couldn't wait any longer. But tonight, one hand tight in my hair and the other clamped flat against the velveteen-covered wall, he thrust with complete abandon. As the lift gave a quietly discreet "ping" and ground to a jerky halt on the third floor, his knees buckled slightly, he groaned, and his seed spewed out into my waiting mouth.

The doors opened. Thank God there was no one waiting to go down! And no pun intended. Seve thrust himself back into his trousers, then pulled me to my feet. I was overexcited myself. Threads of him were still in my mouth, and I was hard and aching inside my jeans. He dragged me out of the lift after him, then spun me hard against the wall of the corridor, panting and grinding his hips against my groin. I opened my mouth gladly for his tongue. He sucked on mine in return, tasting every nook and cranny inside my mouth. I was panting too by now, too eager to care about beard burn, and I'd have done it there and then if he'd wanted. Pulled down my jeans and let him fuck me hard against the wall, rocking more than a couple of the tasteful modern prints that hung there. They were looking down, I daresay, with artistic horror on our writhing bodies.

But he broke away at last, holding me at arm's length. "You're still wet."

I knew that. So was he. The dripping had reduced with every step, but our clothes had been soaked through and were clinging to our bodies. My hair wouldn't win any awards—I could feel the weight of it sticking to my neck and collar—and his suit looked like he'd bathed and then slept in it.

"You need to get your clothes off. You got anything on under those jeans, Max?"

For the last couple of times I'd met him, I'd worn no underwear. It had been both expedient and exciting, and the habit had stuck. He stared at my crotch now, and I knew *he* knew it too. I was as hard as a rock, my dick chafing against the denim of my jeans, just from a rushed blow-job in a rickety lift and a bruising kiss.

Seve didn't wait for any answer. He took my arm and tugged me away from the wall and toward a door down the corridor. I didn't know how many other flats were on this floor—obviously no one was common enough to stick a number on their front door or put their recycling out for collection—but all I'd seen was the lift and what I assumed was his front door. He pulled my head to him and nipped at my mouth, kissing and thrusting his tongue into me. When I grabbed at his shoulders to steady myself, he shrugged out of his suit jacket and started fumbling with the hem of my polo shirt. I bumped off the wall a couple of times, and when his hands slid into the waist of my jeans and started to tug them down, I nearly fell.

"Wait," I gasped, but then the wet denim had pooled around my ankles and I was hopping out of both boots and jeans, even as we reached the white wooden door. Surely this was his place? Couldn't he wait until we got inside? He pulled a key out of his trouser pocket and slid it into the lock, but he didn't immediately open the door. Instead, he turned and faced me, breathing heavily. His tie was crumpled and pulled loose from around his neck. Half his shirt buttons were open, and I could see the dusky skin gleaming with rain droplets.

"Get on your hands and knees, Max. Face back up the corridor."

And despite the bizarre nature of all this, I did it. I dropped to my knees on the corridor carpet and stared back up the way we'd come, back toward the lift. My arse was naked under my shirt and raised up toward him. My skin was cold and still damp, and I felt every goose bump individually. I cradled my cock for a second, then let it hang loose, heavy and warm between my thighs, throbbing with anticipatory lust. I didn't look around, but I reckoned I could feel his eyes on me.

There was a click behind me as he opened the door at last, and I heard the soft whisper of well-oiled wood on thick carpet. Now I looked back over my shoulder and saw him stepping back into his darkened hallway. He beckoned me in after him. "Still on your knees. Don't turn around."

I felt a fool, but an excited one. I clambered inelegantly back over the doorway, banging one foot on the frame, and then he brought me to a halt with his hand on my buttocks. I crouched there, half in and half out of the flat, seeing nothing except the coordinating carpet at my feet and, in the near distance, a tall terra-cotta pot of dried reeds and grasses placed artfully beside the closed door of the lift. And then Seve's other hand slipped between my sweaty thighs and tugged them further open. My cock bobbed, startled and dripping—and not with raindrops.

I sucked in a breath. "Whatever you want, Seve. Just get the fuck on and do it."

He did. I heard a gentle thump as he dropped to his knees behind me. Cloth rustled, and out of the corner of my eye, I saw his shirt thrown down on the floor beside me. The flesh of his bare arm was damp on my thighs as he stroked across my buttocks and down between them to tease at my opening. His fingers were cold. I think I clenched with the delighted shock—I certainly gave a yelp of pleasure—and he laughed softly.

Then I felt his hair tickle against my thigh, teasing my nerve ends, and his hot breath brushed my buttocks. I felt the almost indescribable thrill of his wet, fierce tongue licking around me, swiping across my entrance. I stopped clenching at once and relaxed. His tongue licked all around the hole, and then a single slippery finger slid in. It thrust playfully in and out of my opening while he followed its path with his tongue, dribbling saliva on my skin. Some of it trickled down my leg and some of it—*oh fuck*—he nudged inside me.

I held myself there—God knows how, when my legs and arms were shaking with the tension—as Seve slowly fucked me with his finger and his tongue. The door was ajar and my body was still halfway out in the corridor. If anyone had come out of the lift or turned the corner at the end of the hallway, they'd have seen me, half-naked and on my knees, with my discarded jeans in a heap on the floor beside me. I was shuddering with ecstasy, my head dipping up and down between my shaking shoulders, with nothing behind me but the hint of a shadow and a figure that might or might not have been clutching me around the waist and pushing me inexorably toward the brink of a consuming, wailing climax.

"So hot," Seve mumbled against my arse. His beard was rubbing up a small ridge on the crease of my leg. He grunted and nipped my buttock with sharp teeth. "You taste like soap. And *rain*."

It was the final straw. I lifted one straining arm off the floor and grasped my cock. A couple of tugs was all I'd need. Seve's finger went faster and harder into my arse and I bucked back against him, not caring if I hit him on the chin or not. The waves ran through me, my upper body arched, and I gulped down my yell as I came. Again and again, I spat seed out over my hand and my crumpled jeans. I couldn't feel Seve anymore; I couldn't hear anything. The only thing I was conscious of was the thrill through my own body and the retching of my cock as it gave it all up for me.

I fell to the floor on my elbows, unable to hold anything upright. Seve tugged me and my clothing inside, and the door slid to a merciful close behind me. But it seemed I still wasn't going to be given the guided tour. As I lay slumped against the discreetly patterned wallpaper in his hallway, he crawled over to me on his knees and pushed my legs apart again.

"Need you."

He was bare chested and with his trousers wide open at the fly. His cock reared out from his lap, well recovered from our antics in the lift. All I could do was nod. I needed him too. He hauled my legs up off the floor and over the crooks of his arms, then leaned forward and pressed his cock against my opening. I was wet from his saliva, but it felt like he'd prepared his cock as well—it was wearing a slicked condom and the aggressive heat that was the inimitable calling card of Seve himself.

I wriggled to get more comfortable, and perhaps he thought I was resisting.

"Don't fight me, Max." His voice was hoarse. "I know you want it. You want *me*."

Every passion I'd ever repressed was shrieking to be let out. And it was Seve who did that to me. Of course I fucking wanted him, but I didn't have to surrender quite that easily, did I? "I think you like a fight now and then." My voice was muffled, my chin pushed down onto my chest.

"I think that's just your idea of provocation."

"Yeah," I said. "You're damned right it is." I reached for him, gripping on to his shoulders for support. With a determined effort, I lifted my hips up onto his lap and down onto his cock, impaling myself. He gasped, but I was beyond gasping. I started to push down, drawing his dick up inside me. It was tight, awkward, painful—and fabulous. "Fuck me," I said through gritted teeth. "*Now!*"

I WOKE suddenly and in the dark, unable to remember where I was. Disorientated and startled, I sat bolt upright. A clean-smelling sheet slid down my body.

Then I remembered I was in Seve's flat. I remembered being fucked senseless by him the previous night, pounded against the wall and the floor until we'd both come again and then some. I remembered us moaning at each other, Seve keening as he held me tight around the waist. My own groans as I ran my hands over his smooth hair, letting its short strands trail between my fingers, reaching with my mouth to plunder his with my tongue again and again. Then we'd staggered to our feet with rueful grins and Seve fetched a clean pair of sweats for us both and a toweling robe for me to wear while my clothes dried. We went into his kitchen, where I had a beer and Seve had a glass of a thick red wine, and we realized we probably needed some food. He phoned up for takeaway Chinese, and somehow, between him hanging up the phone and me putting the menu down on the worktop, I found myself facedown across the kitchen table, the robe thrown aside, the sweats around my knees and my legs spread wide. There was the warmth of Seve's hips fitting snugly in between my thighs, the bright snap of another latex package, and excitement as he thrust into me. Excitement—and barely controllable laughter! The slim chrome legs of the table might have been fashionable, but they were ridiculously insubstantial. We rocked together fiercely, and they scraped across the glossy floor tiles in accompaniment. I nearly fell off more than once. Guess they don't make kitchen furniture fit for purpose—for ours, anyway.

By the time the delivery boy brought the Chinese food up, I was groaning loudly, clinging to the very edge of the table, and Seve was tensing for his climax. As he came, he dropped his head and marked my shoulder with his teeth—I felt the sudden sharp pain as he bit and sucked. In seconds I was hearing the angelic bells of my own next— and rather agonizing —climax, just as someone knocked on the door and called out something about spring rolls and fried rice.

I just about remembered the final staggering tumble into bed around midnight. More laughter as we reminisced about what we'd done, where we'd done it. And shared some more aerobic exercise before we finally slept. In a bed. *Seve's* bed. Together.

And now it was early dawn, or so it seemed to me. I blinked my eyes, getting used to the dim light, and took a good look around the room. There hadn't been much time last night to do anything except admire the size and sophistication of the flat. Now I was curious about the details of Seve's home. We'd turned off the lights in the hallway before we fell asleep, but the morning brightness was already seeping through the blinds of the bedroom window. I could see a clothes chest and a table and chair. Both were of pale wood, well polished. A huge flat-screen TV was mounted on the wall opposite the bed. The bed was covered with a crisp linen coverlet in an Aztec-style design, and there was a matching rug on the wooden floor. I nosed around some more. No pictures, no photos, no ornaments, no books. It was a little like a hotel room, but without the Gideon bible. A clock and telephone on his bedside table; a pile of used tissues and opened condom wrappers on mine. With a wry, private grin, I tipped my metaphorical hat to them, shifted in the bed, and then winced at my sore arse. Always being bottom wasn't necessarily the most comfortable long-term choice where Seve Nuñez was involved. I wondered if I'd ever dare to suggest anything else.

The room was cool like only good air-conditioning can make it, and the sheet over my legs was thin and soft. I turned to look at Seve sprawled across the bed on his belly, his sleeping head buried in the pillow beside me. Did I think he'd have left me sleeping and gone out on his own? I realized I had no idea what to expect in this new setting. It was a surprise to find him there, but a joy as well—so far, I hadn't seen much of his naked body except his mouth, hands and cock. He was truly gorgeous, as I knew he'd be—a broad back, with glinting spots of skin where sweat had pooled on the tight muscles. A light covering of hair on his shoulders, though not as much as on his chest. The most perfectly formed arse I'd ever seen on a man, and long, supple legs, coated thinly with darker hair. I knew how those legs could pin me down to the floor, how they could press between my thighs, spreading me just as he wanted. I sat there, staring, wishing he'd turn over so that I could get a full monty view.

He sighed and rolled over onto his back. *Thanks to the powers that be.* The front was perfect too. Dusky skin with the brush of hair across his pecs, framing large, dark nipples. I wanted to dip my head and lick at them. *Maybe later.* Great definition, like he worked out. I suspected there was a gym membership in his remuneration package. Bony hips and strong thighs; a sexy treasure trail over his belly and down to his groin. His resting cock nestled in a bed of curlier hair, flushed with that fresh, smooth sweetness that is morning wood.

And then he was awake and I was caught out.

"Hi, Max," he said sleepily. "Don't say you've got to go. You usually do."

I snorted and slipped back down in the bed. I knew now what he meant when he said I just fucked and ran. *It's my nervousness!* I wanted to say. *My need to make the decision to go before you make it for me. Before you tire of me.*

And maybe not that at all. Maybe some kind of self-preservation.

"You look great." He smiled, his gaze running over me. "Your hair's great." It had gotten seriously tousled as we rolled about in the hallway last night, and then I'd slept on it without a comb through. It was the one disadvantage of longer hair. Now Seve ran his fingers aimlessly through it, gently tugging out some of the tangles. "It feels great. All of you feels great. Want to fuck?" His hand was very warm and it was teasing between my legs, nudging my already eager boner with his knuckles.

I couldn't roll over against him fast enough.

CHAPTER 15

I FINALLY got up and dressed at about ten o'clock. My polo shirt was dry, though probably creased beyond recovery, and my jeans were stiff, but I managed to pull them on. The night before, I'd emptied my jeans pockets out on the side table—now I scooped up my phone, keys and wallet, loose change, and the red lighter with the Arsenal crest on it, and padded down the hallway in bare feet to find some coffee. I made a quick and quiet call to work to say I wouldn't be in until later in the day. I didn't like doing it, but I knew I wasn't going to make it across town in time to clock in this morning. I didn't often let them down—I was one of the most reliable contract workers they had. And even after the beating up, I'd gone back into work as soon as possible. I needed the money, but more than that, I wanted to do right by them.

I stood in the kitchen doorway and looked around. A bag of ground beans and a coffeemaker were two of the more familiar things I spotted. Otherwise it looked more like a showroom. Seve had all the latest gadgets—dishwasher, bread maker, food processor—but there was little evidence of cooking. And after I'd taken a nose around the fridge, not a lot of food, either. I found more bottled beers and only the basics: bread, cooked meat, and cheese. I supposed he ate out most of the time. The empty cartons from last night's Chinese meal were still piled up on the counter.

To be honest, I wasn't hungry, the taste and imprint of Seve's cock and tongue still vivid in my mouth. I poked at the settings on the coffeemaker for a while, trying to find points of contact with Louis's rather less sophisticated model, and eventually got it going. Then I went back to browsing around the cupboards while I waited for it to heat up. There were expensive-looking preserves, packets of dried pasta, bottles of oil with herbs suspended in them, and a couple of jars of something that looked like caviar. Definitely nothing I'd ever seen in my local supermarket. The coffee grounds had a Spanish name on the packet, and I nearly missed the sugar because it was a tin of solid brown crystals rather than the common granules I was used to. On the quest for milk, I examined an impressive store of red wine in a rack by the fridge. Some of them had names I'd only heard about in those celebrity dinner parties they show on reality TV.

Seve appeared in the doorway a few minutes later, smoothing his hair down, scratching his beard. Smart pair of sweats. Barefoot, no shirt. I wanted to jump him there and then.

"Not much for breakfast, Seve," I joked. "What do you offer guests?"

"I don't have guests," he replied.

I was going to laugh, but then I realized it wasn't a joke. I bit my tongue and placed a cup of coffee for him on the table. We sat down to drink. We both stared absentmindedly at the corner of the table where we'd fucked last night. I imagined I could see a stain from my come, but it was probably just spilled sauce from last night's takeaway.

"I want to know more about you, Seve," I said eventually.

He was quiet for another few seconds. When he replied, his voice was calm in that expressionless way he did so well. "That's not information I share easily, Max. You don't need to know anything else, really. You know what I do. What I like."

Not really, I thought, but that wasn't the topic for today. "I want you to tell me about Peck." I knew I was pushing my luck, but something was driving me on. "How long has he worked for your uncle?"

"Peck?" He shook his head slightly as if he didn't know what I was talking about. "Ah… him. I didn't know him, I told you. I don't hire all the men."

"How did Peck get to be working here? Do you know what he does for your uncle in London?"

"What?" His eyes were hooded again, and his hands shook slightly. I think I was upsetting him—the man I thought was always in control. "You mean his job? You mentioned this before. I had assumed security, though you're implying that's not the whole truth. But I don't need to know everything that goes on."

"Seve, don't you *ask*?"

"Ask what?"

I tried to work out if he was deliberately avoiding my questions or if he genuinely had no idea what I was talking about. "You must know what people say about the Medina Group—about the clubs. That they're a front."

"What the hell for?"

"Drugs. Money laundering." I took a quick breath. "They have a network of couriers, sometimes including kids."

"It's a lie." Seve's expression darkened. His fingers tightened around his cup.

"I don't know if the same things are going on at Compulsion—"

"They are not!"

I didn't let him distract me. "But you're either for or against it. You're either ignorant of it all or... you're part of the problem."

"Is this all to do with Peck—with that man? I told you I've sent him back to London. I recommended my uncle fire the men who attacked you."

I couldn't believe Seve thought that was all it took. "Do you think he's going to take any notice?" Peck had been in place at the London club for years before I even went there, or so I was told. He was well established and doing very nicely from it, thanks. That implied a working relationship with the Medinas that wasn't going to crumble just because a "friend" of Seve Nuñez had been awkwardly in the way.

"I'm in charge here. I supervise this club. I go my own way—"

"Not always."

He stared at me. "What are you talking about?"

"A few times when we've gone places in your car, we've been followed. Didn't you notice?"

Seve frowned. "You're paranoid. I don't understand why."

I knew I was right. "I think they're watching you, Seve. Either because they don't know which way you're going to go—or they're doing it with your blessing."

"What the hell?"

"You say you're in charge, Seve. You certainly seem to be, at the club. But I know what happens behind the scenes, and with the management's say-so. If that's happening at Compulsion too, maybe you think you need some protection. To stop anyone getting too close."

"What do you think is going on? That we're living out a Mafia thriller?" He stood up abruptly, pushing back his chair with a scrape. "This is unacceptable, Max. Why are you harassing my uncle's business like this? *My* business? This is my career and I'm totally committed to it. What has it to do with you?" He paused suddenly, as if a thought struck him. Damn same thought struck me at the same time, but it was too late to backtrack. "What *do* you know about it all, Max? You said you know what goes on behind the scenes."

"Seve." I began a feeble protest. Things were starting to go downhill. "I just know what sort of guys these are. Trust me on this."

He stared at me. I could see his chest heaving too much for normal breathing.

"Please," I said rather desperately. "I knew Peck before, you know? In London. Perhaps I never told you I spent some time there...."

"No. You didn't."

I peered at his angry face. Hadn't Peck told him? Maybe Peck never recognized me after all. Maybe it *was* all one huge weird coincidence. "He runs a racket out of the London club—your uncle's club. I don't know how or why Peck turned up here."

"But you believe it was to run the same kind of *racket?*"

I shrugged. It sounded pathetic in the face of Seve's confident ire. "I don't know."

"You have evidence of these things? You've seen them happening?"

"No, not here. But you're not likely to advertise it, are you—?" I knew at once I should have kept my mouth shut.

"But you've seen them in London? Tell me how that was, Max. Did you report this, either to my uncle or the police? No, I didn't think so. Your silence confirms that. So in what capacity did you see evidence of these events?"

Just for that moment, I heard the power that he must use with staff or people he wished to impress one way or another. His voice was as strong as always, but it also had a sharp vibrancy that made me want to do exactly what he said. To obey him. And not just in sexual matters, when I was already more than halfway willing.

"Sit down," I said. "Please." I waited until he did before continuing. "I worked for Peck, once. In London. And not on security."

"You were one of those couriers?" His voice was low but still sharp.

"Yeah. Well, I just did odd errands at first. I needed the money and he didn't ask for any references, you know? Then it just developed." It had been some weird kind of promotion. "There were a few of us on the regular rota. I got to know them well. Some of them were very young, Seve. Most of them were users."

"You too?"

I hesitated and flushed, which was an obvious answer to that one. "I haven't touched anything except alcohol since I moved back down here."

"Why did you come back in the first place? If you were doing so well in London—"

"That's not what I said!" My voice was loud and Seve flinched. "You think I liked having no money, being dumped, having nowhere to live? It was only going to be for a while. I know I let it get its hooks in me—I guess that happens to a lot of people. And not all of them can get out, you know?" I remembered the kids that Stewart couldn't help, the sad ones, the mad ones like Baz. I drew a deeper breath and tried to calm down. "It's all behind me now. You don't need to know how I got out, just that I'm damn glad I did, and I don't want to get drawn back down into that sewer again."

Seve hadn't moved throughout my explanation. Now he raised a hand, very slowly, as if to appease me. "It doesn't matter to me, Max. What you did, what you were. What you were into."

"Well, it fucking matters to *me*, okay? And it matters to your family, doesn't it? To your uncle. Because that's who I really worked for, Seve. That's who paid me, controlled me, directed me!" Seve was shaking his head, his eyes dark, but I didn't think I could stop now I'd started the tirade. "If your fucking uncle is into all that, why not here in Brighton too? New club, new manager, new market. Why else would Peck turn up on your payroll, doing what he's best at, running his own sordid little business on the side under perfect cover of a glamorous nightlife, with people who've had too much to drink and smoke, who've got money to invest in the cycle of dealing and creating addicts all over again?"

"Max, that's enough. Listen to me—"

"No, *you* listen to *me*!" I stood up. I was yelling now, God help any neighbors. "Where do you fit into all this? Tell me what's going on with this *family business*! Tell me something about *you*, something I can't fit on the side of a cereal box. How much do you know? How much do you get involved with? Why aren't you bothered? Or are you so fucking comfortable here that you don't question where the money comes from for it all?" Seve's mouth opened. He looked shocked, but I never gave him time to reply. I gripped the side of the table and leaned menacingly toward him. "Who hired Peck? Why? What were his instructions here? Did he tell you about his job in London?

Sharing his expertise, boasting about his success? Did he ever mention a man called Stewart Matthews?"

"That's *enough*, I said!" Seve stood too and grasped my wrist. He twisted it, and I yelped with the sudden pain. But it had the right effect—it shut me up and halted my growing hysteria. We stared at each other, panting. My hair had fallen forward on my forehead, and there was a trickle of sweat running down the side of my face from my hairline. My chest heaved with the agony of my memories and the fury I felt because they were returning. I wasn't even sure anymore if it was anything to do with Seve or not. I was absorbed in my own horror.

Maybe Seve saw my breath slowing. Maybe he felt my muscles relaxing. Whatever the reason, he let go of my wrist. I resisted the urge to wince and rub at the sore skin.

"I'm sorry." I wasn't sure if I wanted to be apologizing or even what I was apologizing for, but I found myself saying it. "You said I liked to talk, didn't you? It must be hell for you to cope with. Your guys obviously had it right after all—it's better I leave you the fuck alone."

He caught my arm, even as I drew away. He was gentler this time, though not much. "Stay!"

"Dammit, Seve, let me go."

He didn't. Instead, he drew me nearer to him. "You think I'm involved with this shit, don't you?"

"I don't know." And I *didn't*. I hoped not, but… I couldn't be sure. It was torture, and all the worse because it was self-inflicted.

"Yet you still came here with me. Still slept with me."

That was an easy one to answer. "I'm stupid."

Seve's expression was odd, unreadable. "No, never that," he said, softly.

"Then I don't know why," I said.

"I do. This is why." He leaned over and kissed me firmly.

I accepted it, my lips soaking up the moisture from him. The rush of emotion made me dizzy, and the flicker of desire in the pit of my stomach had been heightened by my passionate outburst. Despite my anger and confusion, I wanted nothing more than to thrust my tongue back into his mouth.

He pulled away first, leaving my lips quivering, searching for his, reaching shamelessly for him. "I'm a sucker for a good kisser, you mean?" My voice was shaky.

He shook his head like he was tired of my jokes. "I never met anyone like you, Max."

"Yeah, right."

"No, you'll listen to *me* now!" He gripped the back of his chair, and his voice was harsh. "That night at the club—when I first saw you. I wasn't looking for anyone, you know? I think I told you that. I was just looking out for the club. It's still early days in my job, and I want to do well. I have good staff but I often call in personally in the evening, at least for a while. I wasn't due to stay around that night. But then I changed my mind—because I saw *you*."

I was silent. It was a revelation, hearing him talk. Did I truly believe him?

"Yes, I know." He could see the doubt on my face. "You'd believe that I cruise my own club every weekend. That I pick up a different partner every night to fuck in some dim, silent backyard, with barely an exchange of names." It was a frighteningly accurate description of that night—of my original opinion of that night. "I won't deny it, Max. I don't hold back when I want something. Some*one*. And I am rarely refused. But that's not what I was seeking—not that night. Did you see me with anyone?"

"I… no."

"Believe me, I could have had company several times over." I believed it, because I'd been amazed that night that he was alone. That he'd beckoned to *me*. "I have always had choice, Max, plenty of choice and willing players for whatever game I suggest. But you appeared at the other end of the bar and that was it. I had to have *you*. I'd only meant to stay long enough to check how well the new lighting worked on the dance sets, and then I was due to go to a promotional party. Or come back here, which was looking more likely."

"You were bored?"

"I was," he replied, his voice level. Only the narrowed eyes gave away a hint of other emotion. "But you changed that. Something in you challenged me. It's not something I'm... *used* to. I wanted to know you. I wanted to find out about you."

"You wanted to fuck me."

"Yes." He wasn't fazed, whatever sarcasm I threw at him. "And you wanted me to, didn't you? I saw that in you, Max. But that's what attracted me—not just the desire in you but the passion barely held in check. The need. The self-control you must have, to act as a different person other than the one you sleep with at night."

"*Shit*," I whispered. I felt as if I'd been laid bare before him—and far more than physically.

"That's what appealed to me, Max. Your *passion*. I understand that too well. Don't pull away from me now. Don't let this strange obsession you have spoil things. Each time I see you, I feel... it's different." He shook his head, impatient with himself, I think, not me. "Remember how good we are—how much we pleasure each other. I... I don't have that from anyone else. I never have."

"No guests, Seve?" I looked around the beautiful but sparse flat. Anywhere rather than at those intense eyes. "No lovers?"

"Of course there have been lovers." He smiled wryly. "You didn't expect anything different, did you? But not since you—and not here. I like my sex fast, immediate, and sometimes dangerous. There's an added excitement to creative locations, don't you agree? But I do not invite people back here. At all."

There was something more here—we weren't just talking about lovers. There was little enough evidence of Seve's personal tastes and belongings in this flat, let alone the influences of anyone else. "You don't let people in."

"No, I don't. But I will for you. In fact, I'll do more than that. I'll fight for you, Max. I'll fight to have you for as long as I can."

His hand slid up under my shirt. I realized how close he'd come to me while we'd been talking. While I'd been listening, fascinated, to his deep, rich voice—talking about himself in a way I'd never heard before.

He nuzzled at my neck and ran a finger of his other hand inside my collar. "I can still see the bruises on you. Does it hurt?" There was a strange tone to his voice.

"I'm fine. They're healing," I replied. My throat constricted and I knew he was trying to distract me. The hand under my shirt slipped around my waist, his fingertips rough yet gentle at the same time. He wanted us to fuck again, I knew.

"I meant it, Max. I really don't care what you did before, what you've been. It's now that matters."

If only that were true. "I made mistakes. I'm not proud of it."

"You're brave to say so."

"No, I'm not." I shook my head, dislodging his lips at my ear. "No, Seve. Not... I don't want to."

He stilled and pulled his hand away. We both stood there for a moment, the only sounds in the kitchen our breath and the residual bubble of the boiled water in the coffeemaker.

"I'd better go," I said. "At the risk of being accused of leaving early." I offered a wry smile to take the sting away from my words, and Seve smiled back. But the pain and confusion in his eyes were unmistakable.

"I will look into it for you, Max," he said. "I promise you."

"Yeah, okay."

"No!" He tensed up, scowling at me, and for a moment I could imagine the fear that black look would instill in a recalcitrant employee. "You must believe me. I will look into my uncle's dealings, prove to you there is nothing untoward at Compulsion. I may…." He paused and restarted. "I will visit my mother."

"Your mother?"

"She will know if anything is wrong. She'll reassure me and therefore you as well. My family would never allow investment in the Medina Group to be shared with my father, who was only in the family by marriage, so the shareholding rests with Mama. She also retains control of the Nuñez business interests."

"She's still a Medina," I said and wished immediately I hadn't spoken it aloud.

His eyes had darkened. "No more talking," he said, and I could feel his breath, coarse on my cheek. As he turned away, his hip brushed against mine. His sweats were tented at the groin. But nothing was going to happen between us, I was sure of that. Not yet.

I retrieved my socks, which were scrunched up in two small piles by the front door. My boots were cold and still slightly damp, but I pulled them on regardless. Seve had followed me into the hallway, his arms held out from his sides as if he weren't quite sure what to do with them. As I straightened up, he nudged against me and slid a hand back around my waist. I didn't protest; in fact, I instinctively leaned into him. But when he ran his hand around to the front of my jeans and reached for the button, I flinched.

"Max...."

"No," I said. "No way." I laughed shakily. "My damn arse is so sore, I'll be walking into work like John Wayne. I don't want to have to explain that to my very lusty, very hetero mates, you know?"

It was another of my weak jokes, but Seve took note. That was another surprise. He lifted his hands off me and leaned in for a kiss instead. I wasn't going to begrudge him that, was I? It was a long, hard kiss, and his tongue delved deeply into my mouth. I could feel both our hearts hammering against my chest. Then he pulled his mouth away, trailing saliva as a thin silver thread between our lips.

"You taste so good, Max. I'm going to shower now. How about joining me?"

My head swam. What a vision that conjured up! I was mad to refuse him, my dick said. Get back to the flat, my head counseled.

Either way, I was a mess of thrill and panic. "I… no, Seve. I'm going."

He nodded and his cheeks looked pinker than before. "Max, you'll remember what I said, won't you?"

"Of course I bloody well will."

"I mean…." He seemed unsure too. "About me and you. I don't say that sort of thing every day, that… about meeting you. Wanting you."

"I know," I replied. "I understand." And I thought I did.

"Go, then. It's fine. I'll see you again soon."

I paused at the door. I felt I had to say something else, because I wasn't sure where I'd last left my confused, anguished thoughts. Somewhere inside the crotch of my jeans, and that wasn't necessarily the right place at the moment. "Seve, I *will* find out what's going on."

"So will I. Trust me."

Did I? His smile was tight and the glint in his eyes made my mouth dry. He was very assured, very calm. And so fucking handsome. "You…." This was going to sound bloody ridiculous. "Seve, you will be careful, won't you?"

He laughed. "You're being melodramatic again, Max. Of course I will! But can't you stay longer? Let's have another coffee." *Let's go back to bed*, came the subtext in the sparkling eyes.

I could feel my traitorous body responding to him again. I mustered up a grin, evaded his outstretched hand before it reached me, and I left the flat. He shut the door quietly behind me.

The lift crawled all the way down to the lobby. I imagined I could smell Seve's seed in the claustrophobic air of it—a heady, erotic memory. I strode out of the building as confidently as I could and made my way back down onto the promenade. My journey back on the bus wasn't going to be quite as comfortable as in Seve's car, but that was a good thing for me at the moment. I sat in a seat at the back for the few stops to Kemptown, just letting my mind empty. The town was filling with shoppers on one side of the road and holiday visitors on the seaward side. Delivery vans and courier bikes dodged around the bus on their way to and from local businesses. I'd withdrawn so far that I nearly missed the stop at the bottom of Jack and Louis's road but rang the bell at the last minute.

I stood looking up their road toward the flat I'd come to call home in the last six months. And then I started to climb the hill. After all, where the hell else did I have to go?

CHAPTER 16

I HEARD Jack and Louis coming back home just as I was trying to fit a final pair of tennis shoes into my bag. I'd washed, body and hair, and dressed in comfortable T-shirt and sweats. I'd called work, had a longer and more awkward conversation with my boss, and chatted with a couple of the other guys who were in the office. Then I'd packed up my pitiful wardrobe and a couple of personal items. I was sure Jack and Louis would let me come back and pick anything else up later.

The guys were earlier than usual—I'd expected to be gone by the time they both came back to the flat. Louis's work schedules were erratic unless he was on set, but Jack usually worked a full office-hours day. A glance at the clock told me it was only three in the afternoon. I took a deep breath. *No problem.* I probably owed them for some food this week, anyway, so it was better I settled up before I went. I wondered where I'd left my wallet, and patted around on the bed to find it.

"Max, what the hell are you doing?"

Fuck. Jack at his most assertive, standing in my doorway. Well, the soon-not-to-be-my-doorway. It'd be their spare room again, like it was before I came back and disturbed their life all over. "Don't make a fuss, Jack. I'll pay what housekeeping I owe, then I'm on my way. There's a room going at the same place as one of the guys at work; I can bed down there for the time being. I've taken the rest of the day off to get settled in. Eventually I want to look for my own place, but I can't afford it yet. If it's okay with you, I'll come back and collect anything else at the weekend. Or while you're at work, if you prefer."

"No, you bloody well won't." He looked shocked.

"Look, please, I know I deserve the abuse, but just let me go quietly—"

"Go?"

Now Louis was in the doorway as well. I'd have to be a damn shadow to get out between the pair of them. They had me trapped. Were they looking for some kind of fight?

"You can't go anywhere yet!" Louis cried. "The food's already on the table. And I only buy the sticky BBQ sauce ribs for you, neither of *us* likes them."

"For God's sake!" I flushed deeply. "I'm happy to be thrown out, but don't expect me to eat a hearty meal before I go. Stick the bloody things in a bag and I'll take them with me, if you're that anally retentive to care either way."

"What's he talking about?" Louis turned to Jack with genuine surprise on his face. "Thrown out?"

"We're having a late lunch, Max," Jack said. He seemed to be struggling to keep his voice steady. "All of us together. Did you forget? I swapped shifts with Martin at work so I could leave early."

Louis nodded vigorously. "Then we're all going to watch that new sci-fi film like we promised ourselves. Later on, the Vs are expecting us in town for a drink for their birthday. Or birthdays? I never know who or which is celebrating." Louis was gabbling, startled and bemused, but with me, not the Vs. "Where are *you* going?"

"He's not going anywhere," Jack said. His quiet, firm voice was back, the one I called his "practice" for his future day in court as an expert witness. He planted himself more squarely in the doorway and frowned at me. "You're not going anywhere, Max. Well, if you really want to, I'll listen to the reasons. But we're not throwing you out. Dammit, why would we do that? You're our friend. We like you here."

"Jack certainly does. He watches you in the shower, you know," Louis grumbled.

"Yes, I told you that, didn't I?" Despite the tension of the moment, Jack smiled mischievously back at him. "And don't you just *rise* to the bait every time." His fingers reached out and ghosted over Louis's groin.

"Bastard," Louis said fondly.

There was unambiguous, comfortably familiar lust in their expressions, and I envied them for their devotion—but they still weren't getting out of my way. "I lied to you," I said. I'd steeled myself to leave; I wasn't sure what was happening here. "You had no idea what shit I'd been up to in London, how I fucked up my life. You don't need the extra hassle. I need to get out of here and sort things out for myself."

"Shut the hell up, you stupid arse," Louis announced cheerfully. "We know who you are—of course we bloody well do—and we say that what's past is past. You're no different today than you were then." He narrowed his eyes, looking me up and down. "Well, a bit taller, and with muscle definition I can't, unfortunately, compete with." He ignored Jack's punch to his arm. "Just come and eat and keep us company through the film. Then if you don't want to come out with the Vs, you can come back here and put all those damn things back in the cupboard, then take an early night so's I can drag Jack to bed and screw his provocative little brains out."

"Not so little, you damn bimbo," Jack growled in response.

I stood there as they moved away from the door and back down to the living room, laughing and gasping dirty little promises that I doubted would wait to be honored until after the film. One of my tennis shoes was still dangling from my hand. I was more than a little stunned, and not just because I knew I'd probably have to move a few rows away from them in the cinema.

Jack reappeared halfway up the stairs, calling up to me. His expression was serious now. "We meant it, Max. We want you to stay. This is your home now."

"The things I've done—"

"Drop it," he said firmly but not unkindly. "Move on."

"The thing about running away when Stewart was killed…."

Jack nodded. "Okay, yes, we'll deal with that, I promise you. But we'll talk about the best way first."

I stared at him. I wasn't going to cry, you know? "Thanks, Jack. To you and Louis."

"Your life's good now. You're sound. In fact, you always were. We've just come different routes, Max. And we'll watch over each other, okay?"

"…but not in the shower!" came a mournful wail from the living room, and with a rueful grin, Jack turned to go back down.

AFTER I'd demolished the ribs with a—not unsurprisingly—healthy appetite, I took the plates out to the kitchen. Jack followed me while Louis darted off to their bedroom to struggle with the eternally thorny question of what to wear for an afternoon in a darkened cinema. Jack picked out some fruit from the bowl on the table, lingering by the counter as I ran hot water to wash up.

"I asked at work about Stewart," he said. He looked wary, as if he weren't sure if it would upset me.

"What do you mean?"

"About his death."

"His murder, you mean."

"Yes."

"You didn't…?" It was an instinctive response, and I flushed with shame.

Jack put his hand on my arm. "It's okay, I understand. And no, I didn't let anyone know why I was asking. Never mentioned you."

"What did you find out?" Jack had a bunch of contacts through work, in the police and occasionally the military too. He respected and looked after his sources, and in return, they sometimes helped him out with information.

"Not much. It's still an open case. I couldn't get many details because it's in the Met's jurisdiction and the police down here have limited access. They've been alerted, though, mainly because of the possible connection between the London club and Compulsion opening up down here. It seems the Met are looking for a young kid someone saw loitering in the vicinity on that night, but no luck in finding him so far."

Baz.... "Do they know about Peck? Is he implicated?"

Jack shook his head. "No one would tell me any more. I didn't like to mention his name in case someone asked how I knew him. There was less of a problem mentioning Stewart because the attack had been in the national papers, albeit briefly. They did let slip the Met suspects the attack was connected to their investigation into the drug trade around Soho."

I felt cold, though the flat was warm enough. "But Stewart was nothing to do with the drug trade."

"No, I know, Max. And no one said he was. But they think he probably got in the way. Apparently he was talking to the police about the situation with the kids. Perhaps someone reckoned he was meddling."

Was that what they called it? Saving some kids from tire-track arms and cold, sad little deaths? *Meddling*? "So maybe not just a mugging." I kept my voice very low. Was this really news to me? Hadn't I always suspected it myself?

"No, maybe not." Jack's voice was tentative. "You okay?"

"I don't know." And wasn't that the truth. "You say they're investigating the drug trade?"

"Yes." Jack bit his lower lip. "Look, I know you think the people in charge of the clubs—"

"The Medina family."

"Okay, yes, I know you think the Medinas are getting away with it, but the police aren't stupid. They'll have a watch on the clubs, and they probably have suspicions where it's all coming from."

"But Peck's still on the loose. No one's been caught for Stewart's murder."

"Max, give them a chance. Perhaps they don't have enough evidence yet to arrest anyone."

"You said they were looking into the connection between the clubs—"

"Only a possible connection. You don't know that the same's happening here—or that Seve's involved."

"I don't know he's *not*."

Jack's voice sharpened. "Listen to yourself, Max. You won't give anyone a chance, not even yourself."

"You don't believe me?"

Jack's hand tightened. "Of course I bloody do! Don't you dare turn this on me. And I don't know any different, not for certain. But if you're that sure you know who's behind it all…."

He didn't need to finish that accusation. I was the one who'd turned tail and run away from it all. I was the one who might have evidence that could help settle things, and I couldn't meet his eyes. "I'm sorry," I said. I didn't know what else to say. Sorry for the argument, sorry for the lies, sorry I wasn't brave enough yet to turn myself in. Sorry for *me*.

"There's always Crimestoppers," Jack said. "You can call in anonymously. Give your information over the phone."

"I will think about it," I said. "I promise."

"It's for your own peace of mind, Max, not mine." Jack sighed. "Is the kid they're after the same one you knew?"

"It sounds like it might be." Baz had been the most difficult to reach, the one with the least hope. My gang had tried to keep him protected from others and from himself, but who knew where he was now? And why the hell did I care, when he'd killed my friend and mentor? I had a sudden, vivid memory of Stewart, his voice, his smile, his arms full of those bloody files that he had to carry around with him almost all the time, just trying to keep up with his workload. And then the skinny body pushing up against us, the shock blindsiding me, the kid turning toward Stewart. The glint of a knife, the grunt of surprised pain....

"Max?"

I nodded to him. I couldn't trust words.

"Don't let it get to you again. You're building something for yourself here and now. I know life can be shit, but you can turn it around. You already have!"

After the night I'd told them about my time in London, Jack and Louis had never really quizzed me further. They'd never pushed me for details, never judged me. Just accepted it. After their initial suspicion, they'd never harassed me about Seve either. They were the good guys. "Okay," I said. The voice that came from my mouth was strange and echoed in the kitchen. "Sure. As if I'd want to lose myself back to that now, eh?"

As if....

IT HAD been just a week since I'd nearly left the flat. Things had settled back well between the three of us, and I'd finally convinced myself that the guys genuinely didn't despise me for my aberrant life over the last couple of years. I mean, *I* despised myself, but that was another matter.

And I hadn't seen Severino Nuñez since I left his flat in Sussex Square a week ago. I hadn't deliberately avoided going out, but I'd taken on some late shifts at the site to make up for the time I lost when I was off injured, plus Seve had said he was going to see his mother—I didn't know how far away she lived, or if he was back yet. Besides, I had plenty of things to think about on my own.

It was also Friday and Louis's birthday, always an excuse for a big celebration. Jack had a party planned for Saturday night, but tonight they'd invited the usual gang around for drinks. The evening went well, but my heart wasn't in it. I spent most of the time in the kitchen, dishing out drinks and keeping Bryan plied with food. Even the Vs didn't venture to tease me like they usually did. Must have been something in my expression.

I made my excuses relatively early and went up to my room, but I couldn't sleep. I listened as Bryan trotted back and forth to the kitchen, asking in an overloud voice where the cheese was. Then Harry stood in the hallway, belched really loudly, laughed, and left with a slam of the door. The Vs were singing as they left shortly after him. It sounded like selections from ABBA, but they hadn't quite mastered the harmonies. Last of all, there was a lot of clattering of crockery in the kitchen, then sniggering and stumbling into the wall as Jack and Louis made their way to bed.

They were the good guys, hadn't I always said? I didn't begrudge them a single second of their blissful, lust-filled love, and I hoped the rest of the immediate neighbors didn't either, because a couple of Louis's yells had a fine resonance that could probably be heard miles away. But when the thumping of their bed finally ceased and I was still restless, I got up and went downstairs to make a hot drink.

I sat in the semidarkness of the living room and watched my DVD of *The Lavender Hill Mob* on low sound and in all its black-and-white glory—always irresistible, whatever my mood—and I thanked whatever God there might be for my friends and their easy, supportive friendship, without which I'd have been lost. When I finished the drink and the end credits started to roll, I started to feel drowsy again… and, well, I couldn't help myself. I slid a warm hand into my sleep shorts and fondled my dick. To help me sleep, I reasoned. But if I were honest, it was to soothe the vision of Seve Nuñez that disturbed my every waking thought. It was affecting my sleep as well. Seven days since I'd last seen him. Seven nights….

I shut my eyes, seeing him in my mind, laid out in his bed beside me that morning—the naked, sleep-warmed skin, the dips and peaks of his back and buttocks. The supple movement of his body as the muscles bunched and lifted him up to lean over me. The wicked glint in his eye. The moist sheen on his lips as they nipped at my mouth, and the harsh knee between my thighs, pushing them apart. The smell of him—his cologne, his hair, his sweat, his flesh….

I started to pump myself a little harder. I ached from deep inside. I didn't know an ache could be so fucking deep. His vision smiled at me, eyes alight with desire. I imagined I could feel his soft dark hair on my face, and my free hand curled instinctively into a shape to grip his shoulder. His thighs were pressed on mine, the hairs on his legs tickling my balls. His voice murmured to me and his tongue licked seductively at my neck. I felt a twinge from the tooth marks in my shoulder, a souvenir of our last time together. I was panting and my hand flew up and down my cock. The agony cried for relief.

I licked the fingers of my free hand and slid it down under my arse, probing for my entrance. It felt hot and oversensitive as I slid a finger in. I teased as I stroked my cock, and I knew I wasn't going to last much longer. Seve—or his hallucination—was grinning at my desperation, relishing the fact he was responsible for my collapse. Seve's voice hissed crude words in my ear; Seve's hands were guiding my hands; Seve's cock was warm and thick and oozing precome on my thigh, and it was nudging at my hole, demanding to come in—

I came then, with a gulp and a quickly swallowed sob. My body arched up off the couch and the come pumped out of me and over my hand. My climax was so intense that the TV screen blurred in front of me and tears leaked out of the corners of my eyes. My limbs shook and I sank back down on the cushions. For several minutes I couldn't hear anything over the deafening hammering of my heart.

I was exhausted and physically sated for the moment. I didn't want to think about it any further. I mopped most of the mess off me with some of the paper napkins that were still scattered on the table. Then I pulled one of the throws off the armchair over me and slid into a few hours of oblivious sleep.

THE next morning, I was eating a bowl of cereal in the kitchen when Jack sidled in, looking tired and with his hair all over the place. His pajama bottoms were twisted awkwardly at one side and hung low on the hip, a strip of his dark skin peeking over the top. He yawned a greeting to me, hitched up his waistband, and groaned.

I grinned at him. "Hangover?"

He ignored me pointedly, which confirmed it. "You've remembered tonight's party?" he said.

"What about it?"

"Just wanted to check you're still coming. I mean, with it being at Compulsion."

"Of course I am," I replied. I concentrated on keeping my expression steady. "Did Louis get the dance contract?"

Jack's eyes brightened. "Yes. Great, isn't it? He's still keen on his acting, but this means he can earn some money here in Brighton in between TV bookings. He wants to see the guys at the club tonight, share the good news."

I moved along the counter and put my empty bowl in the sink. "So do you want a coffee, or is that one of those redundant questions?" I turned back, the coffee jar in my hand, to find him peering at me.

"You stayed on the couch last night, Max. Are you having trouble sleeping again?"

I'd forgotten to put the throw back in its place, obviously. "I'm fine. You're the one looks like something the cat dragged in."

He blushed and we laughed, though it made him wince. "Okay," he said. "Just wanted to check. If Seve's there tonight…."

"That's fine too," I said. I was proud of the way my voice sounded almost normal. "You taking Louis breakfast in bed?"

We bustled quietly about the kitchen, fixing orange juice, coffee, lightly browned toast, and plenty of honey for the birthday boy's favorite breakfast. I was fascinated and amused at Jack's devotion—I hadn't celebrated my birthday in any way for years.

Jack reached across the front of me to grab a spoon from the kitchen drawer. "So did you find anything useful at the Jubilee Library?"

"I… what?"

Jack smirked, no other word for it. "We often use the library, and I sent a research student down there yesterday. Suzie's a local girl, and she told me her friend Will who works there couldn't stop talking about the fit bloke who'd been in to browse through the newspaper section. Will—and Suzie—gave a very detailed description."

"Can't keep a secret from you, can I?" I didn't know if I was annoyed at being caught out or reassured that Jack had my back.

"It's only a visit to the library," Jack said. "Though I think Will is angling for something more."

I rolled my eyes. I vaguely remembered the man on the desk when I went in—tall, curly blond hair, helpful smile, eyes following me as I searched out newspaper articles over the last year.

"Did you find what you were looking for?" Jack was still nosing around, but he was treading carefully too.

"No. Well, I don't know. I just wanted to read some of the coverage on the Medina Group and London club culture in general. I thought there might be some cross-references between specific clubs and drug busts. Between the Medina Group and the way they've been branching out into clubs around the country."

"And?"

I shrugged. "Nothing much. There were definite accusations against the Medina club in Manchester for drug trade and violence. And alleged stories about London. But there was no coverage on Stewart's murder, or at least nothing that linked it to the club. The papers reported it as the death of a part-time youth worker, probably killed by one of the addicts who hang around that part of Soho."

Jack was watching me closely. "And that's roughly the story."

I nodded. "Roughly, yeah. But not the whole story." I sighed. "All the other reports I found just concentrated on the Medina financial results, mostly in import-export businesses."

"They couldn't necessarily report any connection even if they suspected it, Max. It'd be libelous unless the management had been charged with something."

"The police are—or were—interested in investigating the allegations. That's where the stories were left. You never get the full follow-up on these things in the press, do you?"

Jack made a sympathetic noise, but I think his attention was drifting.

"And, of course, there were plenty of features on Severino Nuñez," I said wryly. "Rock star charisma, bright graduate, promising businessman, poster boy for gay success. Brighton never had it so good, it seems." *Or he never had Brighton so good.*

"Has Seve said anything else about it? About the business in London?"

"I haven't seen him."

"Max…."

"I will do it, you know," I said abruptly.

Jack blinked. "What?"

"I'll go to the police with what I know. Personally, not anonymously. I owe Stewart that, at least. And not just about Stewart's murder but about the whole organization."

Jack's eyes narrowed. "What do you know about it?"

"More than I ever told anyone." I poured an orange juice and gulped it back, barely tasting it. "Not everything, of course. But after I got beaten up by Peck the first couple of times, I started to listen in, to keep my eyes open. I reckon I can remember almost all the courier routes, the names on packages, some of the regular visitors to the club—but to the office, not the bar."

"Jesus, Max." Jack's eyes were wide now. "You never said."

"I know. I didn't want to…." What? I didn't want them to know how much I'd collaborated in it all? How I'd pushed the memories far to the back of my mind in denial of what a coward I'd been? How much I still was?

There was silence for a long time. Then there came a call from Louis in their bedroom—he was getting hungry. For what, I didn't want to guess, but hopefully the toast that Jack had in his hand would suffice for the moment. It effectively broke the tension in the kitchen.

"Go," I said gently. "We can catch up later."

Jack looked conflicted. "You promise me, right? Don't do anything rash, Max. I've got some friends in the local force—let me introduce you to them. Yes, they'll be eager for any leads, I'm sure. But at least I know they'll treat you properly in return."

I stared at him. "It could open up all kinds of crap." *For me*, I meant.

Silence between us. Another wail from Louis in the background.

"It'll be okay," Jack said. "You were the victim. You were at risk and they used you. We'll make sure they understand that."

My nod was an automatic, physical gesture. Inside, I felt sick. I was in a shitload of trouble, yet I knew things had to change. I had to make things right, as far as I could.

"And what about Seve?" Jack asked gently.

He was giving both me and Seve the benefit of the doubt. "Perhaps I'll see him tonight at the club. I'll… yeah, I'll speak to him first."

Jack nodded. "Give him a chance to reassure you if he's not involved."

"He doesn't have much to support that, Jack. It's his family, his business. His choice."

"So are you," Jack said with a sudden burst of heat in his tone. "So are you, remember?"

CHAPTER 17

THE club was packed, even for a Saturday night, but we managed to grab a table when a group of partygoers left for another club. Louis looked fantastic in black latex and a scarlet vest, as outrageous as befitted the star of the celebration. Harry, Bob, and Bryan joined us, and other friends came across to wish Louis well, passing him drinks and joining in the gossip. The temperature rose, the crowds at the bar got tighter, and the music volume increased.

"Bloody head won't fit through the door after tonight," Jack growled, watching as his boyfriend air-kissed and hugged people, accepting total adulation as his due. Louis's face shone with pleasure. His hair showed white blond under the fluorescent lighting, especially vivid against his outfit. As he weaved across the floor, his slim, graceful frame danced around his friends like mercury unleashed. The lights flickered on his skin, a multicolored net that was never going to catch him. I knew Jack's complaint wasn't serious. Both of us knew they seemed to have found the perfect balance in their relationship; Jack was Louis's calm support.

That was nothing remotely like me and Seve. I wondered how I'd describe us together, or even if there *was* an "us." Sometimes it felt like we were two stags fighting for the same territory. Too evenly matched, and both of us too arrogant in our own way to allow the other much leeway. No future for us, I thought, and not for the first time. I filed the thought away in the mental folder marked "Denial."

Jack was dragged off by Louis to meet his new acquaintances, some of the dancers he'd be working with on a summer season special. They were all lithe, bright, restless things who made me feel clumsy, though a couple of them gave me more than a polite glance. On my way over to the bar, one of them—a striking young Ghanaian-looking man with fabulous long locks and straight muscled shoulders—broke away from Louis's chatter and took a step toward me, smiling.

"Max."

From behind me—Seve's voice. It was just a word, but in the low, sexy timbre that reverberated through my nerve endings, it was a statement in itself. What did he want? To ask where I'd been, why I hadn't been to the club for a week? Why I hadn't been to his flat? Though he must know I wouldn't venture there without invitation. I wouldn't want that dark look of his turned on me except in play, would I? I wondered if he knew I'd been looking into news stories about the Medina family's business, that Jack had been asking his friends in the police about the London club.

I didn't know whether to be welcoming, wary, or just turn tail and run for the door. I felt I'd been in that position for months, and not just with Seve. It was like being haunted. With a sick tug in my gut, I realized I'd never be free of my previous mistakes. All I'd done by running away was to bring the memories and the stigma back with me to Brighton. They seeped through my mind like rich red wine staining a white cloth. I was damaged goods, a mess. Meeting Seve had just been an additional—and cruel—coincidence.

The dancer was still looking at me, but my expression must have changed, because he frowned, then shrugged and turned away to rejoin his group of friends. I turned too, but in the other direction, pretty sure I was prepared for the physical impact of seeing Seve again.

More fool me.

I gazed into his face and my heartbeat hit the roof almost instantly. His eyes were wide and bright and he looked delighted to see me. His teeth gleamed white from the lights in the bar area, and he wore the same gold shirt that I'd first seen him in, with the silver chain around his neck. His skin looked flushed and healthy, and everything about him exuded confidence, control, and sexual charisma. He shone out from everyone else—there was no other way to describe it.

"Hi, Seve."

It sounded totally inadequate, but he gave the usual nod of his head in reply. His smile was tight, as if pleasure was trying to bubble out of him and he was reining it back in. I felt an answering excitement. Things changed every time I saw him: my feelings deepened in an alarming way. I didn't dare examine whether it was for good or bad, and perhaps it was the same for him.

"It's Louis's birthday," I said. There I was, stating the obvious, my tongue temporarily disconnected from wit. "We're celebrating."

"I can see." Seve moved along the bar toward me, revelers scattering around him like the parting of a human sea. I braced a hand on the counter, not sure what I was trying to steel myself against. He didn't touch me, but his smile grew as he reached my side. "The duty manager has already arranged things with your friend Mr. Wallis. We'll make it a night to remember for his dancer."

"Thanks."

"It's part of my job," he said dismissively. He didn't seem to have any other questions, like I'd expected. He stared at my lips as I spoke. I fought an irresistible desire to moisten them with a lick or two.

"I'll get you a drink," he said and raised a hand to call for one of the bar staff.

"Not for me," I said quickly. "I'm not drinking at the moment." I didn't add, *since this morning, actually*. I'd toasted Louis's birthday at home last night with a beer—Bryan's cocktail recipes inevitably led to both headache and indigestion—but after that, I'd called a halt. Things had to change, I reminded myself. Considering all the habits I might slip back into, drink was the first and easiest to address.

Seve raised an eyebrow. "Water, then?"

"Sure."

A passing female bartender reached for my glass, then caught sight of Seve beside me. She fumbled the glass and nearly dropped it. He snapped his fingers sharply and she grimaced at me.

"Sorry, sir."

"Get the water," Seve said very softly. His tone was icy, and she scurried off.

"No need for that," I said. "Just because you're in charge doesn't mean you have to be some kind of bully."

He blinked at me. Staff matters were obviously already far from his mind. "I missed you, Max."

"It's only been a few days." *Seven! Seven!* my body protested.

The chilled water arrived, a bottle for each of us. I watched as Seve was more polite in his thanks to the bartender this time. He pulled over two stools so that we could sit together at the bar, and although the music was loud, we were in the farthest spot from the speakers and could more or less hear each other talk. People pushed past us now and then, but the dance set had moved into the heavy numbers and flashing lights, and most of the clubgoers were out on the floor. Human voices yelled and laughed above the techno beat, which throbbed up through our seats. Sweat made the dancers' hair damp and their bare torsos glisten. People pressed and clung and caressed—they were all having a bloody good time. I wasn't sure if I was included in that.

Seve nudged my knee with his, regaining my attention. A shiver ran through my body as if a thread of electricity ran between us. "Will you come back with me to the flat, Max?"

"Now?"

"Yes, of course."

"No," I said. *Of course?* "I'm here with Louis and Jack. I'm not leaving right now."

Surprisingly, Seve nodded agreement. "You'll sit with me for the moment?"

"I... yes. Sure."

He cracked open the top of his bottle and took a large gulp. I watched the gentle throb of his throat and had to shift on my seat to ease my hardness.

"It's a good night," I said. "Plenty of business. The takings will be high."

Seve stared at me as if I wasn't the only one who thought I was spouting nonsense. "Yes, I think so. We're doing well. Where do you work, Max?"

How bizarre! It was arse about face, as they say. We'd been closer than two bugs in a rug, we'd fucked and argued and fucked again. Now we were talking as if it were a first date. We stared at each other for a moment, as if it had suddenly struck both of us at the same time. Then I grinned and he smiled back. The tension eased.

"I want to know about you," he said. "Not just what makes you moan. Not just how hard you like to be touched."

How could a room get so much hotter so quickly? "I work on the construction site around the back of Preston Park. They're building new homes and business premises. I'm not trained as a builder, but I'm a fast learner, and I do as many shifts as they offer. I'm hoping they'll take me on permanently at the end of this project." Seve was still looking expectantly at me. "Okay, other stuff. I was born here in Brighton and have been in the care system since I was orphaned at age seven. I don't talk much about it, but it was by no means the horror that some kids suffer. Nowadays I'm staying at Jack and Louis's flat in Kemptown, in their attic room." I glanced at Seve: he was concentrating on me very carefully. "I can drive but I've never been able to afford a car. I take size eleven shoes and have an awkwardly high instep. I like old black-and-white movies, both comedy and drama. I listen to rock music but I'm not a great fan of live gigs. I'm a crap cook, I can play very basic guitar, and I can assemble flatpack furniture like a professional. I hate mayonnaise and pineapple juice, and my favorite pizza topping is pepperoni. When I was very young, I fell out of a tree at the children's home and scarred the back of my thigh—"

"I've seen it," Seve interrupted. His eyes were even brighter.

I laughed. Despite the noise and the weird situation, I felt more relaxed with him than ever before. "Your turn."

"Me?" He looked startled. "You know about me."

"No, I don't."

He looked genuinely disturbed. "I don't know what to say."

"Pretend I'm a journalist," I said, not without some bitterness. "Pretend it's for a gossip mag."

He frowned. "I do not tell them everything, Max. Only what they want to hear. Only about the club." When I didn't reply, he shrugged. For a brief moment, the music's volume dipped and the beat shifted to something slower. His voice was perfectly clear. "I don't know what to say to you."

I decided to go easy on him. "Tell me some fun things, like I did. I know where you live, I know what you do. What films do you watch, what music do you like? You know the kind of stuff I mean. Best sport, dream car, fantasy holiday, favorite T-shirt."

This time he laughed. "I don't think I've had the same kind of fun as you have, Max."

"You've traveled, though? Seems to me your accent isn't just London or Spain."

He nodded. "I was born in Madrid, where my father worked as an engineer. But he was American, so we traveled between the USA and Europe for most of my life. He was in much demand for international projects. I expect I have picked up many speech patterns over the years."

"Must have been exciting."

He made a strange grimace. "Not as much as you think. I have been to many schools, transferred to and from several colleges. Friends aren't...." He cleared his throat, and perhaps not just because the music was throbbing in our eardrums again. "It's difficult to maintain friendships when there's so little continuity. I learned to adapt to wherever I was. When Papa died, we returned permanently to Europe and Mama introduced me to the family business."

I found myself gripping my bottle of water more tightly. "And you've been there ever since."

He didn't answer directly, but he seemed to be entering into the spirit of the conversation. "It has shaped the whole of my adult life, I suppose you'd say. I have little leisure time outside the club. I buy my clothes from designer catalogues and my daily living needs are provided for me, including my car and my flat." Suddenly, the reflection in his eyes sparked with something like resentment. "I used to swim a great deal, I was in the top team at one college. I used to read a lot of science fiction. I enjoyed making my own tapas dishes." It was all in the past tense. "And amazing though it may seem, I also like pepperoni best."

A laugh burst out of me. When he snaked a hand behind my neck, I leaned forward into the kiss. His skin felt warm and his cheeks were very flushed. We didn't speak at all for a few long, languid moments. Goose pimples ran up my spine and my jeans got tighter around my crotch, but there was also something else at play—something more relaxed, more sensual. It felt like we were taking our time for a change. When we finally broke apart, it wasn't because of the bartender's raised eyebrows or the wolf whistle in my ear from further along the bar. It was because we chose to.

"I've been to see Mama," Seve said slowly. His head was still forward, his breath against my ear. "I have told her of the concerns about my uncle and our clubs. She assured me he has nothing to do with gangs and the drug trade." He made the idea sound as unlikely as interplanetary travel. "He's just a businessman. You must take my word for that."

I must, must I? It was a cruel and unpleasant reminder that Seve and I had far more between us than a foot of bar counter. I wanted to believe him, I really did. Was it possible that I was wrong? That he wasn't that naïve? That he wasn't blinded—or not so blinded—by family loyalty?

I wanted to believe—didn't I say that? But it was a world I'd been burrowed into for a long time, and I knew who and what had been involved. There was nothing I could see that would stop it happening here. I stared back at Seve. I thought I was so sharp, but now I'd never felt duller. I didn't know where the hell I was going with this. With *us*.

Seve's tone was firm. "Step away from it, Max. You came to see me like I came to see you. That's what matters. But we can't talk properly here. Let's leave." He slid a hand up my thigh and squeezed none too gently.

Yes, of course I wanted to leave with him, go somewhere with him. I had eyes only for him. My mouth opened in reply. "No," I said. "It's Louis's night and I'm here as his friend and guest. Maybe we can get together later." Oh, how cool I thought I sounded. So bloody laid-back. Seve smiled like he was imagining me *laid back*, and his hand tightened on my leg. My dick strained inside my jeans. I had to find a looser, more comfortable pair.

Then his mobile rang in his pocket. He let go of me and slipped off his stool, turning his back to me as he answered the call. I took a long, almost sly look at those shoulders I now knew had been broadened by swimming, the tight arse that had been muscled by strong legs kicking through the water.

"I have to take a business call," he said, turning back to face me. "For… it's confidential."

I wrenched my gaze back up to his face. "Sure."

He didn't move away, though, and I couldn't identify his expression. "I meant what I said about us, Max. We cannot talk here. Will you meet me later? I will be free from here in an hour or so."

"Sure," I repeated. "If I'm still here." I didn't mean it to sound snappy, but Seve's eyes narrowed.

"Be here," he said. "Please." Our eyes met. Then he turned and strode through the bar area and back out toward the exit.

WHEN I got back to our table, Jack was with Bryan, who was chomping through a pile of nachos in a plastic bowl. I assumed the others were all dancing or with friends elsewhere. I noticed several bottles of champagne on the table, already opened. "From the management," Jack said with a wry grin. "Severino Nuñez stopped by. He says all Louis's drinks are free for the night."

I nodded. Reached for a glass, then remembered I wasn't drinking.

"Want some?" Bryan thrust his bowl under my nose, but bar snacks were the farthest thing from my mind.

Jack passed me a sealed bottle of water, reading my expression more accurately. "You okay?" he asked. Or rather, he mouthed it, because Louis had somehow wrangled his way into the DJ box and was choosing all his best—and loudest—favorites. "Did Seve find you? He looked disappointed you weren't here when he came over. Wanted to know where you were."

I took a long swig of the fresh water. "Yeah. He found me."

Jack looked at me more carefully. "You talked to him?"

I didn't want to get into this, not now, not here. I smiled back at Jack and pretended I was having more trouble hearing than I actually was. "Might go and get some air," I mouthed. I needed to find somewhere I could think more clearly, without the beat of the music vibrating through the soles of my feet, without the tang of alcohol in the air making my mouth salivate, without Jack's well-meaning questions, without… the imprint of Seve's hand on my thigh and his breath in my ear. I turned to make my way out of the bar, but Jack caught my arm.

"He left you a message, Max."

"Sorry?"

There was a confused moment when Jack and Bryan both scrabbled in the pocket of their jeans.

"Who's got it?"

"Did you pick it up off the table?"

Finally Jack pulled out a folded piece of white paper and Bryan shrugged, returning his attention to the cheesy dregs of his snack. Jack passed me the note, a paper napkin from the bar. Above the Medina Group logo was scrawled "Meet me in the yard, Seve."

"Did Seve give you this?"

Jack shook his head. "A girl from the bar just brought it over with a fresh bottle of bubbly."

I peered at the note. Maybe he'd finished his business call earlier than expected, though I didn't know why he hadn't come over personally. I realized I had no idea what his handwriting looked like. Dammit, the list of things I didn't know about him got longer by the minute. But I wanted that to change and I thought he did too.

"Max?" Jack looked like he wanted to say something else.

"I'll just be a while," I said. "Back soon." The excitement at seeing Seve again was already thrumming through my veins in a completely different beat to the dance music. Jack let go of my arm and Bryan nodded to me. I grabbed my bottle of water and made my way in the opposite direction—across the dance floor. Louis was over by the music desk, dancing and laughing and sweating; his hair was damp and clinging to his cheeks. I waved at him but I wasn't sure he saw me. I weaved through and beyond the dancers and over to the back exit.

There was a security guy near the door. He turned as I passed, watching me, but as before, no one stopped me. I pushed on the door and it opened easily. I stepped out into the cool night air.

CHAPTER 18

THE first shock was that Seve wasn't there. Second shock was that Peck *was*.

At the same time, I felt a sick kind of relief. I was proved right—he was still around and he was *here*, at Compulsion. I'd correctly identified him when I was ambushed in the park on my way home. He was probably the one following Seve—following *us*. Then the relief gave way to more sensible but colder fear. Hadn't Seve said Peck had gone back to London?

The door swung quietly shut behind me, the noise of the club cut off as if by a sharp knife. I glanced around to see if Peck had his thugs with him, but he seemed to be alone. He just stood there, looking at me. He was smoking but the cigarette had barely burned down—he'd only been here for a short while.

"Not keen on the club, Max? Far as I remember, you used to like the company. And the booze too." He was surprisingly well-spoken, though his words had the truncated consonants of a familiar London accent. He was shorter than I was but much heavier. His thick muscled limbs gave him a slow waddle when he walked, but I knew from bitter experience how fast he could move when he had to—and how hard his fists were. He was dressed in a sober black suit with a thick Crombie-style overcoat. No security badge on his lapel, but I assumed he didn't need it. No one would mistake that hulk for one of the dancers.

"I'm not drinking," I said.

He raised his eyebrows. "Using?"

"That neither."

He laughed. It was obvious he didn't believe a word of it. "I realized it was you in the park that night. Didn't put two and two together when I heard the boss's kid was fucking someone new. But something made me join the others that night, and I'm glad I did." His smile was a sneer. "Always good to meet old friends, right?"

"So that's your idea of Saturday night fun? Beating up random guys?"

He laughed again. "Alvaro Medina doesn't like his kid seeing anyone too seriously, you know? And I agree. It's bad for our business. The kid's been…." He waved his hand as if searching for the right word. "Distracted, since you two started screwing."

What the hell? "So he told you to attack me?" I remembered Alvaro Medina was the name of Seve's uncle.

Peck shrugged, his coat shifting on his wide shoulders. "Just a polite warning, that's all. He's happy for me to take the initiative when it's needed."

Holy fuck. Peck was running his own show down here just as much as he did in London. "Seve's an adult. He can do what he damn well likes."

Peck rolled his eyes exaggeratedly, as if he wasn't even going to grace that with a reply. "You were never shy about the screwing, were you, Max? Plenty of times I found you in the khazi with your jeans around your ankles and some faggot on his knees with his face in your crotch. Or vice bloody versa." Peck grimaced with distaste. "Fucking disgusting, if you ask me. But you never did ask me, did you? Went your own way. Thought you knew best."

"Fuck off, Peck." I was amazed I kept my voice steady. "We've got nothing to say to each other."

"You think?" He took a single step toward me and I felt my gut somersault. "I think we've got some unfinished business, Max. You left halfway through a job. You left without giving any bloody notice at all."

I knew where the catch to the door was—I could dart back in if I moved quickly. But I didn't think I could move at all at that moment: my legs seemed rooted to the spot. The memories of London all came flooding back, sharp, painful and ugly. An angry, sordid time. A cruel time, with Peck as supervisor of it all.

He dropped the cigarette and ground it out under his boot. "Why'd you leave, Max?" His voice was deceptively calm. "Why'd you run like some scared fucking rabbit?"

"Pension scheme wasn't good enough," I muttered. "Why do you care?"

"Because no one *runs*, Max. Not from me. Not until I fucking *tell* them to."

I couldn't think of any more snappy replies. Peck's nasal breathing and my own harsh gulps were the most prominent sounds. The noise of the seafront traffic in the background was no more than a hum, and the rest of the world seemed very far away. Peck's hands hung loosely at his sides, and I assumed he wasn't armed. We weren't in one of those ultra-violent London gangster movies, were we? This was real life. But that could still be just as shocking. And this was a confrontation I knew I'd been running from.

"It's over," I said and took a step back toward the door. "I've got nothing to do with that shit anymore."

"Yeah?" Peck clasped his hands together and cracked a couple of knuckles. Maybe I *was* in one of those movies after all. "That's not for you to say."

"It is—"

"Not!" Peck growled, shocking me further. "You were one of mine, Max, and I needed you there. Now, if you're expecting me to find you a place here instead—"

"What? No!" It was my turn to snap. "I quit, Peck. Totally. I'm out of the whole mess."

He frowned at me. "Yeah, right. It doesn't work that way. You still need it, Max. The money, the fun, the hits."

No. "No!" My protest was hoarse and loud in the quiet yard. I couldn't help seeing how vulnerable I was, yet I couldn't let this drop. "That's not me anymore. In London, back here… it's not me."

"Just words." There was a tight edge to Peck's voice. "I said you had a smart fucking mouth, didn't I?"

"What you just said…." My head ached and I knew I should be running, not blabbing from that smart mouth of mine. "Asking me if I want a place here instead. What are you doing here?"

"*Out of the whole mess,*" he mimicked my higher voice. "That's what you said. Change your mind?"

"Tell me," I said urgently. "Are you planning on running the same racket here in Brighton? Is that why you're here? So the Medinas can expand their business?"

"You should know. You're *fucking* one of them. Don't you perverts have pillow talk?"

I ignored the homophobia. I knew Peck wasn't going to discover equal opportunity tolerance any time soon. "Seve oversees the club, that's all."

Peck laughed again, and really damn loud. "He's the main man, Max. He's *family.* Mr. Medina has high hopes for him. Why else do you think I have to keep parasites like you away from him?"

I can't have kept my expression as clear as I'd hoped, because he laughed again.

"So there *is* pillow talk. Fuck me. You dirty bastards. So are you the bitch, Max? Are you the one takes him up the arse?"

"For fuck's sake. That crap never worked on me before, Peck, what makes you think it will now?"

He peered at me. "Can't believe your boyfriend hasn't told you all about the plans. He was up in London earlier this week, didn't you know? Seeing his uncle. Happy families, catching up."

I felt genuinely nauseous. I really didn't want to throw up in front of Peck, but I had to swallow hard to keep down the bile. "Just fuck off. I'm going. I quit then, and I'm not interested now."

"Sharp mouth," he repeated, then paused as if thinking something over. "Loose tongue too?"

There was a sudden pregnant silence between us. And then I realized what he was really after. He didn't want me to work for him again; he wasn't even looking for a punching bag for his gay bashing, though I was sure he'd make an exception for me. No, he wanted to find out if I was a danger to him—if I'd reported it all. If I'd turned Honest Citizen. He didn't know I'd just kept my head down and hid. Or rather, I had until now.

"You were there that night, weren't you?"

"What the fuck?"

I shook my head impatiently. He knew exactly what I meant. Astonishingly, I found myself moving toward him and my hands balling into fists. No way would I come out of it with all my limbs intact if I went head to head with Peck. My body just seemed to be running ahead of my common sense. "Baz was working for you, wasn't he? Maybe he still is. Did you send him after Stewart?"

"Who the fuck's Stewart?" But awareness was flickering in his small eyes. "One of your pathetic bum buddies?"

I knew in that instant that Peck had definitely been behind the attack on Stewart. "He was stirring up trouble, wasn't he? So you got rid of him."

Peck shrugged again. "No fucking idea what you're going on about. But I've got no time for tossers who are in the way. Who threaten me and mine." He snapped his fingers as if to illustrate how easily he'd deal with that. He didn't need to say more. One snap… one knife… one fatal wound. I bit back a groan.

Peck had been watching my approach with narrowed eyes. "You tempted to do something rash, Max? You want me to make a better job of it than last time?" His eyes glinted. "You think I ought to take out that loose tongue for good?"

"I didn't go to the police," I said. "But I will."

"Yeah? You think they'll believe a word you say?"

I wasn't going to tell him what I knew, what evidence I might have. My silence frustrated him.

"What are you, after all? A courier, a dealer, a user. A street kid, a dosser. You'll be in the shit before they even question anyone else. You think Mr. Medina won't protect his own? He has plenty of fancy-arse lawyers for just this reason."

I shrugged. I was trying to show a hell of a lot of confidence I didn't really have.

Peck bit his lower lip. His knuckles were whitening. "And so what if you take that insane little fucker down with you. I couldn't give a shit. He's becoming more trouble than he's worth."

So Baz *was* still around. Deranged, dangerous little Baz. For a moment, hope flared in me. I could take him to the cops, get him to confess to killing Stewart. To tell them about Peck. I had no doubt that Baz knew even more of what went on than I did. Then I remembered the kid's weird darting eyes and fractured speech, and I knew it wasn't going to happen.

Peck rolled his shoulders and widened his stance. He leaned forward, and his grin at me was more of a snarl. Things were decidedly colder out here now. I'd played my only card and probably too early and too rashly. But then I'd never been any good at poker.

Time to move.

I took three loping steps backward and threw myself at the exit door, expecting the momentum to push me on through the opening doorway and into the warm, suffocating safety of the club. But the lock never moved. My right side thudded heavily against the door, and it never shifted a bloody inch. Instead, the leap knocked the breath out of me and I sank clumsily to my knees on the cold ground, crumpling down like a broken toy. My whole body was jarred, every nerve shocked.

I could hear Peck laughing behind me. "Got new security arrangements now, Max. All private doors lock from the inside. Health and Safety regulations, you know."

I wheezed painfully and lurched up onto my knees. My right arm was numb and the rest of my body was shaking with a healthy side order of fear. Louis would be bloody disappointed if I spoilt his birthday party by ending up dead in a backyard.

Peck crouched down a few feet from me, near enough so I could see him but just outside my reach. "Feel better for that little drama? I'd love to stay for an encore, but I've got more important things to do. I've explained the important facts to you, so you know what's in your best interests. Keep your mouth shut and stay away from the Medinas. If you can't manage that…." He held out his hands, palms upward. "I'll have to come back and visit you again, won't I? A proper little Friends Reunited it'll be."

He stood, towering over me. He nudged at me with his boot— just trying out the feel of it, I guess—then he reached over and tapped three times on the door. It opened from the inside and the music blared out.

"Get the fuck out of here, Max. And stay out of our business. You talk like some kind of gangster movie, but things are professional nowadays, you know. Mr. Medina's got standards and strategies and proper business advisors. And a loyal family too." He leaned down, and his spit dribbled onto my cheek. "And no sniveling arse bandit is going to bother me. Got it?"

One last kick, and I nodded that I'd got it. He stepped over me and walked into the club. I heard him laughing until the door snapped shut again.

Things were *really* cold out here tonight.

CHAPTER 19

IT WAS nearly 1:00 a.m. and I was at the Sussex Square house where Seve's flat was, pressing every damned buzzer on the entry intercom that I could find. My body was still shaken from the impact of the door at the club, which had resurrected the barely recovered pain in my ribs. Fuck, I thought, it's only pain. Of more importance were the fear—and the anger.

After Peck left me, I'd taken some time to regain my breath. Then I tried out his stupid secret knock and they let me stagger back inside. The first thing I did was look for Seve, but there was no sign of him. Instead, I'd found a deliriously, drunkenly euphoric Louis and a happily distracted Jack. They did ask where I'd been, but I didn't think my experience would add any value, so I brushed off the questions. The music throbbed through the floor, the drink flowed, and the partygoers were committed until dawn. I managed to prop myself against the table long enough to mime along to "Happy Birthday" when they all sang to Louis, but I couldn't take much more. Assuming that Seve had left the building, I just snuck myself away.

I'd had enough. The legacy of my former life was thick like mud in my mind and more or less as filthy. Unless I did something about it, it looked like I was destined to have it with me forever. It had already followed me to my new life like an albatross around my neck, spoiled the recovery I was trying to make, and—worst of all—was now irretrievably linked to the man I loved.

I'd been sitting at the back of the number 14 night bus on its route back toward town from the marina when that particular epiphany struck me. Love... what the hell was that, appearing suddenly in my vocabulary? I rolled the word around on my mind's tongue. Tried to ignore it. Never been there before. Not something I'd been looking for. But whether I liked it or not, I suspected there was no other description for the way I felt. More emotional than lust, more intimate than friendship. Disturbingly unfamiliar, yet mixed with an almost obsessive desire to know more. And that was all there, whether Seve gave a fuck in return or not. Had the impact with the door knocked my brain off-line as well?

If a couple of girls hadn't lurched up in front of me, yelling and giggling they'd missed their stop, I might have missed mine too. But I limped off the bus at Sussex Square, and here I was now, at Seve's place and determined to see him. He *must* have come back here. That was after protesting his innocence—after begging to meet me later. And after one of his uncle's staff threatened me yet again, kicked the hell out of my existing injuries, and humiliated me about my former life. No, I wasn't in the best of moods.

There was no answer on his button, but eventually someone in one of the other flats buzzed the front door open. I could only hope they hadn't called the police at the same time. And as I stumbled into the hallway, I heard the lift arrive with a rattle and wheeze and Seve stepped out to face me. He was dressed in the sweats I'd seen him in before, with a thin denim shirt. He looked as if he'd recently showered and washed his hair and was settling down to finish the night at home. Quietly, with little fuss. And definitely not with a semihysterical lover whose clothes were looking the worse for wear and whose body was aching with several new and exciting bruises.

"Max?" He looked tense now I saw him up close. "I was in the shower. I only caught the end of your buzz but I came straight down. What are you doing here?"

"You left the club."

He winced at my abrupt tone. "Yes. But you know that. You told me not to look for you later, and as I had finished my business, I came home."

"I told you…?" I stared at him.

"The bartender said you had left a message. The girl who served us earlier. I was annoyed…." He paused as if anger was rising up again and he was trying to damp it down. "But I couldn't see you anywhere. I assumed you had already left the club."

He'd regained control. But I knew him better than that, even after such short acquaintance. I saw the jitter in his dark pupils—the slight shiver to his lip. He was mad and wary with it.

"Same girl," I said with a sigh. "Makes me think her heart's not really in that job."

"What are you talking about?"

The bartender had played us both, hadn't she? Presumably she was answering to Peck, not to Compulsion. Passing on messages to meet Peck's needs, not ours. "Can I come up to the flat?"

Seve still looked bemused. "Do you expect to?"

I stepped up close and grabbed his wrist. It was down by his side so there was no awkward jarring, but I made sure he knew how tight my grip could be. "Yes, I do. I think I deserve a better reception than Peck gave me in the backyard tonight."

"I never meant… wait, what do you mean? Are you hurt?" There was real panic in his eyes. But he hadn't protested at hearing Peck's name.

"Take me upstairs," I insisted. "I may not be able to stand here much longer. We'll talk there."

"YOU knew Peck was on the payroll!" I growled the words at Seve. We sat on opposite sides of the living room, each of us on one of the deep leather-covered couches. He'd opened two bottles of water and placed them on the low table between us, but I hadn't touched mine so far. "You *knew* he was still around. And everything I was talking about, everything that happened to me in London, at a club owned by your family, under their control—you knew it was real. You knew I was *right*. However much you try to hide behind your job and this single fucking club, it's all in *your* family's name!"

"For God's sake, Max, calm down."

"Don't deny it, Seve! Credit me with some intelligence. Okay, so I've been really stupid so far—"

"No!" he snapped back at me. "I've said before, you are not stupid and I don't believe you ever were."

"Misguided, then. Bloody naïve." That sounded almost as bad. "But not anymore, you hear?"

Seve steepled his hands on his chin and seemed to consider his reply very carefully before he spoke. "Have you told anyone else about this?"

About what? I wanted to shout at him. *About being beaten up by thugs, about being threatened by a lump of shit who once strangled a kid for being insolent? About running drugs for the illegal rackets that your uncle runs out of the Medina clubs? About suspecting you're involved, that you've been playing me along just like that bartender…?*

I wiped my eyes with my sleeve; I was bloody tired of it all. "No. Not yet. I've never told anyone the full extent of what I know—what I did. I've been too fucking ashamed of my own past to own up to the present. Isn't that pathetic? But then Peck will have reported back to you by now to tell you that. I'm sure he's told you I'm not a critical risk—not just yet."

Seve's expression was cautious. "Peck hasn't contacted me at all. I don't expect him to."

"But you obviously know he's still around. Still checking on both of us."

Seve was silent.

"Look. Whatever you do…." My voice was shaky. "Stop the lies, please. Stop trying to fool me, to hide what you're doing, what *you* know. I need the truth from you, Seve. Just… stop."

There was another too-long, too-painful silence.

"I said once I wanted to protect you, Max," Seve said.

"And I tried to punch your lights out."

He grimaced. "Yes. That definitely needs work."

My laugh barked out, but I bit it off quickly. "I don't need protecting."

He shook his head, his eyes angry. "I know. That doesn't stop me wanting to do it."

All I could do was stare at him.

"Max, I've kept you out of things because you don't deserve to be *in*. I swear that I did not lie to you—that I did not know about the problems in our other clubs or my uncle's involvement." He flushed. "You must understand that I found it hard to believe your allegations against the knowledge and experience of my own family, especially when you are—"

"Just a casual fuck."

"—barely known to me!" he snapped. "Do not speak for me, Max! I intend to do that myself."

I swallowed hard and nodded. "Okay."

He sat back in the couch, but he didn't look fully relaxed. "I wanted to find out for myself. Since you first spoke to me about it, I've been looking into the organization. I have a certain freedom, being part of the family. I have used it to look at the books and records of the clubs. I have checked out the notes from meetings—the e-mail correspondence between my uncle's management."

I was back to staring at him. Was this true? He'd been some kind of spy, all this time I thought he was Mr. Playboy and living off the Medina ill-gotten gains?

He must have mistaken my astonishment, because he flushed again. "I know. If there is anything amiss, it's not likely they will write it all down for me to find. And perhaps I have been clumsy. As far as I knew, Peck had been recalled to London. I complained bitterly to my uncle about the threats to you, and he assured me that was the end of the matter."

"But you saw your uncle this week," I said. "When you told *me* you were going to appeal to your mother."

Seve shook his head again, but gently. "I saw them both, Max. I am not lying to you, just as you asked me not to. It would be strange if I visited London and didn't see both of them. They have been the most influential people in my life since my father died."

"Did you…?"

"I did not speak to my uncle about the rumors. We compared notes about the clubs' business, and he updated me on the latest group marketing campaigns. That's all. Before I confront him, I would like to investigate his business deals more closely, and if there is corruption, see what I can do to make things right."

"I think Peck is working here on his own," I said. "Whatever your uncle has done or is involved with, he should be bloody careful of what's going on in his name. It won't be long before Peck steps over the line and the whole damn thing spirals out of control."

"I'm not sure he would thank you for your concern," Seve said with a wry smile.

I frowned. "The police are still investigating the drugs racket. They'll catch up sometime."

"This isn't easy for me, you'll understand. Perhaps it would be better to wait for that, if and when it happens." Seve took a swig of his water and dropped his head back on the couch cushion.

"Better for who, Seve?"

"For my family." His eyes narrowed. "For you." Yeah, he knew trouble for the Medinas would bring trouble for me too.

"What was the call you took tonight at the club?" I said.

"I'm sorry?"

"You took a phone call while we were at the bar. You had to leave straight away." He'd looked… *odd*. "Was it from Peck?"

"No, of course not. Like I said, I have not had any contact with him. Max, I told you—"

"I know," I interrupted. It took a while tonight for things to sink into my battered brain. "You're not lying. I'm sorry. Give me time to cool down, okay?"

For a moment, we were both silent. Seve put his bottle of water back on the table and leaned forward on his seat, his hands clasped in his lap, his gaze on me. "Max, there's more I must tell you. I did see my uncle, we did talk about the club. But he also told me that they want me to take a more active role in the Medina Group. They want to promote me to the board of directors—involve me in the overall management of the clubs."

"A more active role?" My breath caught in my chest. My old life and my new were overlapping even more quickly than I could have imagined.

"I haven't been able to tell you," he continued. "I'm not even sure how I feel about it myself. Not yet. I've needed time to think this through, do you understand?"

I nodded.

"If I hadn't met you, there would have been no question. I am loyal to my family, and I am also ambitious. The chance of joining the Group management is exciting to me."

"But now you know what else it entails?"

He glanced sharply at me. "You have more proof?"

My gaze fell. "Not yet."

"Even so, it's enough to make me cautious. I take your allegations seriously, you see." He nodded slowly. "You're still suspicious of me?"

"I don't know," I said honestly.

"Tonight's call at the club was from one of my uncle's assistants. To ask for my response."

"Which was?"

He worried at his lower lip, the thick flesh easing out between his white teeth. "I have asked for more time to decide. But I will say no if it's proved we have been involved in anything illegal."

"No temptation to take your cut?"

His gaze met mine, dark and determined. "Of course not."

Had I really misjudged him so much? I'd been stupid all round, it seemed. "Do you think he knows why you're delaying your answer?"

Seve shrugged. "I don't know. My uncle says there's a fine line between profit and profiteering. I thought it was a family joke." He gave a short, harsh laugh. "But maybe that has been his strategy for all these years. Mama has always insisted on the importance of family, but she's never really been close to him. He disapproved of her marriage to my father, for one thing. And he didn't think she should have inherited so many shares in the Group in her own name. Things have been uneasy for many years." He sighed. "I have not paid enough or the right attention."

"You and me both," I said.

Seve settled back in the couch again, his gaze still on me. "Peck had spoken to my uncle too," he said. "About us."

The casual *us* sent a chill down my back. I didn't know if it was delight or horror. "What did he say?"

"He told my uncle I was seeing someone regularly. *Too* regularly. That was bound to irritate Uncle Alvaro, who not only insists my liking for men is a mere phase of sexual experimentation before I marry but who believes a man should live and breathe his work alone."

I recalled Peck cornering me in the backyard, warning me off. I wondered if he'd told Uncle Alvaro about our London connection too. Maybe not, if Peck was trying to boost his reputation with his boss. He wouldn't like to admit he let a courier out of his grasp—and one who was now intimate with a member of the Medina family. *Messy.*

Seve's eyes flashed. "I told him it was no business of his who I dated."

There was that *us* implication again. The chill was feeling increasingly like delight. "And your mother? What did she say?"

He stared at me, his eyes dark and deep. "She understood."

I watched him sitting there, apparently calm. He'd flung his arm over the back of the couch, and his denim shirt was open to the top of his breast, showing the hairs on his chest. I remembered every line of muscle and bone of that chest. I'd kissed it—I'd caressed it. It had crushed itself against me as he fucked me, *took* me, my legs clasped around him, our tongues thrusting into each other's mouths. I felt nauseous again, and the devil in me wanted to shatter his composure. "That's not enough, though, is it? Why did you let us go on?" His gaze snapped up to me, startled. "There was only ever going to be trouble, Seve. Better to have dumped me quickly and kept your relationship with the club purely business. Better to have diverted all these fucking awkward questions and my sordid past, and found another fuckbuddy. Why, Seve?"

I'd unintentionally hit a trigger again. He sat up suddenly, his eyes blazing and his hands gripped into fists, his legs tensed as if he was ready to leap up—or thump me. "Why the hell do you think, Max? I'll tell you why! Because I *wanted* you, and then I had you, and it was a thousand times more exhilarating than I'd ever imagined. I didn't want to give that up!" As I gaped at him, he rushed on. "You met me on equal terms, unlike the sycophants who meet me through my family or the girls and men who enjoy my body as a way to attach to my money."

"You're not telling me you haven't taken advantage—"

"*Please.* I know, I've had fun, I'm not denying that. There was always satisfaction—but only for a moment. No one has ever given me more, Max! But you give as much as you take. You're honest with your desire. I never felt that you surrendered to me, only that you willingly participated. We enjoyed each other, and I didn't see that we needed anything else. I trust you, Max." He stopped, his mouth half-open, his expression stricken. "I cannot find enough words. I want you. I don't want any other."

My head struggled to work around the twist in my heart. "No, believe me, your words are fine, Seve." *Shockingly fine.* "I just never knew you felt... as strongly as this. You could have said something."

"Of course I could." There was misery in his voice. "But I never have. I don't act that way, Max."

"But you're doing it now."

"Yes. Well… trying, perhaps. For you. To try to make you understand me. I *need* you to understand me."

What *I* needed was to kiss him—to touch his skin, to absorb his warmth. My desire was both torture and thrill: a hunger that always teetered somewhere between striking and seducing. I suspected it was the same for him. It had been that way with us from the start, hadn't it? Fierce and frustrating and fabulous. But I'd never heard him speak this way about personal feelings. About *me*. I wasn't sure it was any protestation of love—I mocked my own ridiculous feelings in that department. But it was something more than indifference. Dammit, much more. I let the warm, tentative hope trickle a little way into my heart, still afraid it'd bring disaster and disappointment in its wake.

I was tired and hurt and unusually vulnerable. But that seemed to be my default status nowadays. I didn't move away when Seve reached out to pull me closer. "Seve. It's not over yet."

He sighed into my ear, his lips brushing the lobe. "I know. But we're free from it for tonight, maybe?"

"You said you trust me."

"Shouldn't I?" He brushed the hair back from my neck, and I found myself leaning into the caress.

"Peck knows," I said. "He knows I have information on the club. On the drugs and the… on other things. I should go to the police with it."

Seve stilled. "Yes, you should." He turned his head to look into my eyes, his expression wary again. "That's the right thing to do."

I laughed rather harshly. "Who knows what's right and wrong at the moment? I wish I fucking well did."

His phone rang again, a muted, generic ringtone. Seve cursed.

"Answer it," I said.

He pulled it out of his sweats pocket, glanced at the caller ID, then canceled the call. "No. It's only Mama. I'll call her back later." He tossed the phone onto the table.

"I can leave."

"Shit, Max!" The bitterness was startling. "Don't you ever listen? Or do you just not hear? Tell me—why did you come here tonight?"

I tried to think it over carefully, but then just let instinct take over. "To see you," I said. At heart, it was the raw truth. "To be with you."

He nodded and drew in a sharp breath. "Why do you want that?"

I knew only too well, but I was scared to say. "Forget it."

"No," he said, quickly and sternly. "I won't forget it. *We* won't forget it. But if you have to go…."

"No." It was my turn to say it. I slipped off the couch to kneel at his feet, and kissed him swiftly but firmly. "We're free from it for tonight, right?"

CHAPTER 20

IT HAD been a surreal night, and I was confused about everything that was going on—what I suspected, what I knew, and all the other crap that I didn't. But I'd never felt in any danger from Seve himself. I wanted to see behind Seve's distress, to learn more about him. Meanwhile, the solace we both sought was a familiar one.

"Come and sit with me, Max." Seve peeled his shirt off over his head, exposing his bare chest. The living room was lit by a tall uplighter on the floor by the couch, and its muted light made the beads of sweat at his throat glisten. It made me want to lick them off. I sat up beside him on the same couch and he started opening the buttons of my shirt. I helped him push it off my shoulders and soon I was half-naked too. He tangled his fingers in my hair and I bent my head to his. We began a kiss that was tentative to start with, then as fevered as always. He tasted of warm saliva and cool water. The combination was delicious, though it didn't seem exotic enough for him tonight. He slipped his other hand inside my jeans, over my arse. His palm caressed the dip at the bottom of my spine until his strong finger snuck down between my cheeks, searching for the welcoming pucker.

Except that I didn't feel totally welcoming. Yeah, he'd said things to me that had really shaken me up—that had excited me in ways I hadn't expected or hoped for. And he'd sounded totally sincere. But I was still cautious, even if my instincts were telling me to get over myself and run with it. I wanted a truth that I could rely on. There were small flames of rebellion inside me that weren't extinguished yet, not enough for me to be able to roll over and let him in, physically and otherwise. Not that easily.

I lifted my lips from his, just to make it clear. "Not tonight. Not yet."

Just as earlier in the club he'd accepted my refusal to leave with him, he calmly accepted my reluctance to fuck too. He must have known that he could have easily talked me around, but he didn't try. Instead, he pulled my head back down to his and the kissing continued, but he was more careful. More respectful, as if he wasn't sure how much I wanted. He slid his hand back out of my jeans, and placed it on my groin instead. He started to rub me. The denim was a barrier between our flesh, but his fingertips played a firm little tune up and down my dick. And it was really, *really* good.

"Let me do this, at least, Max."

He flipped the button of my jeans and tugged down the zip. I was back in boxers, for all the protection they gave me. He peeled the waistband gently over my hot, oversensitive tip, then pulled me down on the cushion beside him.

"Ouch."

He stopped, his expression turning to worry. "You're injured? I forgot…."

"It's okay," I said. I shifted to favor the side Peck had kicked. "Let me empty my pockets before I stab myself on something." I pulled out my wallet and phone, my door key, the crumpled envelope from a birthday card one of the Vs had brought Louis, a couple of pound coins, and the red lighter. I tumbled them all on the coffee table beside the couch.

Seve looked at the pile. "I have never seen you smoke."

I shrugged. "I don't. It's a… souvenir. From a friend." I'd borrowed it from Stewart one night to help a friend get their one-ring gas hob going. When I offered it back, he'd waved it away with a smile. *Keep it*, he'd said. *Easy for me to buy another one next week.* Then there'd never been a *next week*—not for him, anyway.

"Max?" The word was almost a sigh as Seve ran his hand gently down my arm.

"I'm fine," I said firmly. I turned back and leaned into him again. "Don't treat me like an invalid."

He didn't. When he took hold of my dick again, he wasn't as gentle and the friction was more intense. His strokes were strong and exciting, and he knew exactly where to torment me—how to make me shiver. He tugged the skin over my swelling shaft, teasing out the precome and smoothing it all over the tip so that his hand moved more easily.

I whimpered. Every sweep of his hand dragged the ache in my groin with it, and my hips jerked upward to meet him. My nerves were stretched so tautly I winced every time he varied his touch. He paused at the base of my cock, kneading my balls gently with the pad of his palm. His thumb caressed the hairs, uncurling them with a tug, then letting them bounce back into place. And all the time he stroked me firmly and demandingly, squeezing me toward a climax that I knew was going to be so fucking poignant it was going to be painful.

When he pulled down the waist of his sweats and tugged one of my flailing hands toward his own cock, I grasped it eagerly. I started to pump it in time with his movements. He gave his own soft groan as I worked the flesh up and down.

"This is mad," I gasped, though I wasn't exactly sure what I meant. That it was bloody uncomfortable, scrunched up on the couch? That I should just give up and go to bed with him and let him fuck my arse like my body so obviously wanted? That I shouldn't be here at all? He tightened his grip and I yelped with pleasure. That last one just wasn't an issue.

"No. This is good." Seve's smile was tight as, like me, he fought to postpone the inevitable ecstasy. He rolled against me, his breath harsh and shortening rapidly. Although the couch was a generous size, we were still awkwardly crushed together, but he never lost control of his hand, of *me*. We lay face-to-face, still fully clothed from the waist down except for our escaped pricks, and we jerked each other off like teenagers discovering each other and not yet prepared or experienced enough to go further. It took longer to come than I'd expected, though I'd been aroused so quickly—but that was part of the joy. We savored each other and the feel and touch of each other's flesh, and it was very, very *fucking* good.

"Make as much noise you like," Seve hissed in my ear. "No one will hear us."

How did he know that was what I wanted? I was panting and swallowing moans in the back of my throat. I'd had to be quiet in some of the astonishing places we found to fuck, and I'd assumed that applied even to this private but pretty exclusive flat of his. But now I let go. I gave a loud, echoing yell, and my body arched up off the cushion as the climax racked through me. It was a brilliant, gasping relief to let the noise out, to express the shuddering pleasure that burst up through my cock, spewing hot and sticky come all over my stomach and Seve's supple fingers. The world swam out of focus around me, and I clutched the arm of the couch, trying to anchor myself.

"Uh... Max... *so good.*" Seve's voice was ragged as he shifted against me. His cock gave a sharp throb and I squeezed him one more time. He gave an impressively fierce yell of his own and jolted against me so that we both nearly rolled off the couch. Come spurted from his cock, his head pressed down hard on my shoulder, and I could feel the shudder rippling through him. I folded my arms around his chest and held him as he jerked and twitched. I could feel the thick gloopy stuff being squashed and spread all over our stomachs. We'd be well and truly messy together.

We lay for a minute or two, silent except for our heavy breath, and that slowed after a while. Seve didn't pull away from my embrace, but I stirred awkwardly underneath him. "I need a shower."

"Take one." His voice was soft. "There's plenty of hot water. Stay with me tonight."

His face was close to mine, and I stared at the soft swelling of his lips where we'd kissed, where we'd snapped at each other's tongue as the climaxes approached. He nuzzled my ear, his eyelashes brushing my temple. I knew what he wanted.

"I'll stay, Seve. But just a shower. Just a bed. Nothing else tonight."

He sat up stiffly, pulling his sweats back up around his waist. A smile tugged at the corners of his mouth. "I know. I heard you." He got up off the couch, stretching the muscles of his shoulders in the graceful way he had. "You know the way to the bathroom, right?"

IT WAS an expensive shower with a booster pump, and the steaming water came out fierce and scalding hot, just as I liked it. It felt like a guilty pleasure, enjoying the fast-flowing water and good soap. Pampering my aching body, reveling in the sensual delight of touching everywhere for a perfectly good and yet purely selfish reason.

I stood for a long time, checking out any new bruises, pleased to find I wasn't seriously damaged from my new hobby of throwing myself at locked doors. I washed my hair a couple of times, running my fingers through the kinks. Streams of hot water ran down my back, fast and furious, and I luxuriated in it. How good it'd be to wash the whole damn lot away! The present confusion and the whole of the miserable past. The loss of my friendships and my innocence. The missed opportunities—the sense of constant failure. Perhaps that was exactly what I was trying to do. I rubbed harshly at my skin so that it began to burn with sensation. I washed out the smell of Seve and his leather couch, of Peck's cigarette ash, of the club, of the bleak backyard....

I felt Seve there, in the room, seconds before I turned and saw him. I was in searingly hot water, but goose bumps scattered across my body. He'd drawn aside the shower curtain, and clouds of steam floated gently out over the whole room. He stood there, watching me, tall and still and completely nude. Steam condensed on his shoulders and chest and made his cropped hair look blacker and sleeker.

"Max." His eyes were bright like a fox's in the moonlight, and his gaze ran from my legs up my naked, dripping torso to my face.

They lingered there. Perhaps there was a question in his eyes—perhaps it was just lust.

"Not tonight, Seve."

"I know. I just want to watch you."

I looked down at his cock, which was thick and erect again. Jutting high and swollen, reaching for me. Free of its confines, it sprang out from the curly black nest of hair. Seve sucked in his stomach with a tight breath. He really wanted me.

"You want to take care of that, Seve?"

"What do you mean?"

I smiled. A trail of water ran down my cheek, and I licked it into my mouth. "Let me watch as well. Do it for me, Seve. Touch yourself."

There was that same look on his face, like the first time I'd sucked him off and swallowed his come. Was this something he'd never done? Yet I knew how he liked to watch me jerking myself off. Seve still had a lot to learn, it seemed. I leaned back against the tiles of the shower cubicle and turned the water flow down. The dribble of water continued to run down over my skin, but now it caressed my growing erection. Seve's naked body was a sight for sore eyes. I wrapped a hand lazily around myself and gestured for him to continue.

He was staring at my cock and he licked his lips. *Yeah*, I thought. Perhaps that'd be next. "Do it, Seve. Don't touch me—touch yourself. I want to see it."

He paused only a moment, as if he weighed up his appetite for it. And he obviously found he was hungry enough. He took a step back, leaned his hips against the washbasin and tugged gently at his cock, freeing some sticky hairs. I could see his shiver—I could see how much he wanted satisfaction. For a second or two, he looked hesitant, but then he curled his hand around his cock and began to stroke himself.

I gave a moan and his gaze darted up to my face. His eyes were only half-focused. He spread his fingers and started to run them up and down his cock. There was no sound except for the musical trickle of water from the shower, and Seve's low panting. The soles of my feet squeaked on the tiles as I sought for better purchase to support myself.

"Is this what you want, Max?" His gaze was now fastened on my groin as I fondled my dick. I couldn't have held back on pain of hideous torture—the sight of Seve was too exciting. His free hand gripped the edge of the basin, the knuckles whitening. His lips were slightly parted, moist with his saliva, and his mustache looked damp on his top lip. All the time I watched, his hips moved against his hand. The muscles of his arm tightened and relaxed; the definition of his chest and abdomen flexed sharply as he rolled his palm around his cock with a deep, familiar deliberation.

"Yeah. That's just what I want." I could feel the terrible, tortuous ache of need coiling in my groin again. He was gorgeous— he was a work of art. He was doing this for *me*.

"You want more, Max?" The words came out on a series of staggered breaths. Seve took his free hand away from the basin and slid it down behind his back. "*I* want more."

I blinked some stray water out of my eyes. "You got toys?"

Seve gave a thin smile. "Not here." The inference was *I'm not moving right now*.

I took a deep breath. "So you know what to do."

He nodded. "And you will watch."

I stared, fascinated, as he wriggled his arse and reached his hand down between his cheeks. I couldn't see, of course, but I had a bloody good imagination. He leaned forward, his buttocks still balanced against the basin and his other hand firmly around his cock. He winced very briefly. The muscles of his lower arm flexed as he probed into himself.

"*Shit.*" I realized how quickly a tease could turn into playing with fire. I wasn't really aware of how tightly I was clutching my cock—only of the sudden desire to start pumping. I braced my legs so my footing was more secure in the tray of swirling water, then leaned against the shower wall and thrust into my hand in earnest. My other hand helped support me, until I gave in to temptation and moved it around my hip to reach my buttocks. I sucked in a breath and brushed a fingertip over my entrance. The sensation made my cock jerk and my skin shiver with need.

Seve moaned and his eyes closed briefly. I wondered how many fingers he had inside him. How often he did this to himself. Whether he'd let me do it to him—and *soon*! Then his eyes flashed open again and I could see new sweat on his brow. His hips were rolling steadily between the pressure of his hand at the front and his fingers at the back.

"Is this what you want?" he repeated. The atmosphere seemed a hell of a lot steamier in here than it had been fifteen minutes earlier. His cock strained up out of his fist, the fierce red tip shining, damp from precome and the water vapor in the room. The tendons on his hand were raised, the veins purplish.

"Come for me, baby," I said raggedly. I dipped the very end of my finger into my hole, letting it be sucked into the soft heat. "Are you close?"

"*Damn* close." His eyes were glazing over, even as he stared back at me.

"So, come."

He did. His eyes widened, his mouth opened in a soundless cry, and he thrust back against the fingers up his arse. He gave a couple more strokes to his cock and it jerked inside his grip. The tip swelled, then the seed spilled out the top and over his hand. His fingers clamped on tightly like they'd become part of the stiff column of flesh, and the arm hugging his arse went rigid. Through it all, his gaze was on me, his dilated pupils fixed on my face. It was the most exciting thing I'd ever seen.

"Seve...." I never finished any coherent sentence. My cock thickened in my fist and my belly clenched instinctively. My wet hair fell over my eyes and my vision was misted, but I could see Seve staring back at me, smiling wearily and fondling his softening cock. Then I yelled and together we watched the come burst out of me and splatter onto the tiles of the shower floor.

IT TOOK me a longer time than usual to dry myself and gather my wits. My muscles ached, both from the earlier bruising and from the excitement in the bathroom. I glanced in the mirror and winced at the tangled mess of my hair that'd need some serious combing in the morning. But I'd rarely felt so deliciously exhausted. The light was dimmed when I went into Seve's bedroom, and I didn't bother putting my boxers back on. No point in being coy now. Seve was already in bed, lying on his side, propped up on a hand. Watching the doorway—waiting for me. There was a sheet over him, but it left very little to the imagination.

"Come to bed, Max."

I slid in beside him. It was a shock of delight to feel his fresh, cool skin against mine again. I almost groaned when I felt my cock give a little hiccup of hopeful lust. Whatever I wanted of Seve, I didn't think I'd be up to much more tonight.

And—surprisingly—Seve seemed just as relaxed about it. I could feel the life returning to his cock as well, nudging at my stomach under the sheet. But he didn't make another move on me. For a while, all he did was kiss me and stroke gently at my skin. I began to relax. I was ready for a bloody long sleep, which meant I'd probably have to cry off the overtime I'd half promised over this weekend, despite needing the double-time pay. Seve was bad for my employment record.

"So…," he said. "*Baby?*"

I flushed. "It was in the heat of the moment," I protested. "It didn't mean anything, okay?"

He chuckled. "I don't mind. At times like that… call me what you like."

I tried to drift off to sleep, but obviously not hard enough. My mind returned to our earlier conversation. "Seve? What will happen to you if the police catch up with your uncle?"

"Hmm?" He sounded half-asleep already. "I'll be fine. I'm not involved, right? Mama will handle it."

"Your mother?"

He yawned, his jaw pressing on my shoulder. "If I find any evidence, she says she'll take it to the board. They won't dare to ignore her. She's a Medina."

True, but she was also only one person. For some reason, I wasn't as reassured as Seve obviously was. "*I* have evidence, Seve."

Seve's fingertips stroked aimlessly down my arm. "Then you must meet my mother!" He chuckled again, but tiredly. "Talk about it tomorrow, Max. We'll work it out tomorrow. Decide what to do, who to see. Okay?"

I lay still, thinking.

Seve continued, "This man Peck... I don't want you to come up against him again. You mustn't put yourself at risk. I don't want anything to hurt you. I want you in my bed again. I want you in my bed every night." His voice was lower now, and it lulled me in a warm, comfortable way, like hot chocolate on its way down my throat.

"I have my own bloody bed," I said. It just sounded childish.

Seve made a sharp tsk noise. "I don't want to own you, Max. For God's sake, isn't there a middle ground? I don't know how to say it... I've never said...."

And I didn't want to hear—not at that moment. There was something else attracting my attention. The sound of a door lock being cracked open was unmistakable. To me, that is, who'd broken into a few deserted buildings in my time as a squatter. But I'd never entered an occupied one. I sat up in the bed.

"Max?"

I put a hand to Seve's mouth, warning him to be silent. He understood immediately and nodded. I listened for a few seconds more and couldn't hear anything. But that didn't mean things were okay.

"Stay here," I whispered. I slid off the side of the bed, groping for my jeans. I didn't want to face a burglar—or any other threat— stark naked.

Seve mouthed, "What is it?"

There was a sudden rattle from the kitchen, as if someone had knocked over a crockery mug on the counter.

"Stay here!" I couldn't get enough urgency into a whisper without alerting the intruder. "Call 999. There's someone else in the flat." From the hopeless way Seve cast his eyes around the room, I realized he didn't have a phone or a mobile nearby. And where was *my* mobile? On the table beside the empty water bottle and the other contents of my jeans pocket, in the living room where we'd sat and made out earlier tonight. I'd never been to Boy Scouts, but I should have been better prepared for any trouble.

Go and take a look, Max. I moved as quietly as possible to the bedroom door and peered into the hallway. The lights were off, and it took me a moment to get my bearings in the dark. There was no sight or sound of movement from the kitchen, but the door was wide open. I was sure we'd closed it behind us on our way to the bathroom and bed. A dim light from inside the room lit the doorway. It was probably from the streetlights outside, filtering through the kitchen blind. I took a few more steps down the hall.

An alien aroma seeped into my nostrils—not the remnants of whatever Seve had eaten for supper or the scent of soap and water from the shower. This was much less appetizing. It made me gag, like the fetid smell of rotting vegetables or very stale body odor. Or maybe both laced together. I was alarmed by the instinctive memories it conjured up: the smells of damp pavement, metal, and blood—the gut-churning feelings of misery and pain. I inched myself around the kitchen door frame, starting to sneak into the room.

There was a sudden draft of cold air and the door slammed into me, knocking me off-balance and forward into the room. I saw a shadow moving in front of the cupboards, a glint of metal. I knew I had to get away, but my shoulder was throbbing again, and everything I did seemed to be in slow motion. While I was still processing the shock, small strong hands shoved me against the wall, and I found myself trapped there, recoiling from a ten-inch open blade at my throat.

Staring into the mad dilated eyes of a kid I knew only too well.

CHAPTER 21

I STOOD totally still. My heart was beating fiercely and I could feel my legs start to shake. When I swallowed reflexively, the edge of the blade nicked my earlobe. A small trail of warm blood ran down my neck, tickling my skin.

My captor stared up at me. I'd always been half a foot taller than him.

"Baz," I whispered. I couldn't get anything stronger out of my mouth at that moment. "Baz, don't do this."

"Max?" Baz's squeaky voice was familiar but also new: a strange, reedy twist of its natural state. Drugs, I reckoned. Some bastard had tweaked him up to the eyeballs. His pupils looked way too large and there was sweat on his top lip, but his hand was steady. I didn't know whether that was good or bad luck for me. I'd never known Baz's age, and everyone called him a kid because he was short and skinny, but the sly look in his eyes tonight suggested he was older than I'd thought and with far more experience than an ordinary youth would ever have. His face was grubby and he wore dark clothes, including pull-on black boots. No belt, no laces. When I'd known him, we barely trusted him out on his own—it looked like that was still the case. He stank of sweat and the cloying damp-leaf smell of weed. His hair stuck up on one side of his head like he'd slept awkwardly on it, and there was a motley selection of bruises and scars on the forearm pressed against my scapula. I remembered how I'd punched him when he killed Stewart. I wished—for the millionth time in my life—that I'd done a hell of a lot more damage.

"Yeah, Baz. It's me. Look… can you take this fucking knife away? Way too sharp for shaving, right?"

He didn't laugh or move. Me and my pathetic jokes, but I was having enough trouble just talking. And now I saw he had another blade in his other hand. It was shorter, but serrated like a hunting knife. He held it out to the side, and I knew that he had the doorway covered—my only exit. Baz may have been a real pothead and sometimes barely able to piss without help, but his control of weapons was impressively robust.

"Can't do that, Max." He peered up at me. "I've gotta job t' do. Goin' t' be paid an' everythin'. He asked f' me, specially."

It had to be Peck he was talking about. His twisted hero worship still seemed to be in place. "Sure, Baz, I understand." I tried to sound like I did. "But it doesn't have to be like this, does it? I'm just on a friendly visit here and then I'm off home. In fact, I'm on my way right now. Why don't you come with me? We can get an early breakfast at the café, or I've got beer and bacon sandwiches back at my place. We'll chat about the old days in London. Whatever you like."

I knew it wasn't working. Baz had always operated on another planet. His eyes remained fixed on my face, his arm holding me hostage to his knife. He didn't look like a guy to be distracted, not even by an old mate.

"I din' know you'd be there, Max. Y'know. That night."

"What?" I thought I heard a rustling noise in the hallway outside, but I'd told Seve to stay put. I don't know why I ever imagined he'd take any bloody notice.

"In town." Baz's voice had a wheeze behind it. "That night. Wiv' the do-gooder bloke. Din' know *you'd* be there."

Shit. I really didn't want to think about that night again. Not now, and not when I was under threat of getting my throat cut. This was obviously a favorite weapon of Baz's. I tried to muster up a reassuring smile, I really did. It just wasn't happening naturally at that moment. "Sure, I understand." I didn't know whether to be pleased about Baz's need to chat to me. On the one hand, it might give me time to think up some escape strategy. On the other hand, it might just put off the evil hour. I was afraid that I'd disgrace myself—that I'd cry in the face of death, or piss myself.

I remembered the sight of the blade going into Stewart. It had been so fast, so unexpected—I'd no memory of any fear at the time. Just anger and a consuming flood of horror, like immersion in a freezing bath, like the world suddenly snapped into negative. Now I wanted to shake my head, to clear the paralysis that shock can bring. I didn't dare actually do it.

"He told me t' get rid o' trouble," Baz went on. The blade stayed put, but it had loosened from my throat so I could take a quick swallow. Baz's mouth was trembling a little, some saliva trailing out of one side. "Told me the man from the social was goin' t' the cops. They'd put me away. Din' want that, did I?"

"He wasn't from the social, Baz. Stewart wasn't from the government at all. He just wanted to help us. Who told you he was going to put you away? Peck? Did Peck tell you Stewart had to go?" I was shocked to find how emotionally difficult it was to say Stewart's name. His face flashed through my mind in various settings—frowning at me, laughing, playing football, lying dead on his back on the cold ground. He'd be thrilled if I went the same way as he did, wouldn't he? Really thrilled that I'd learned so well from the experience... *not.*

Baz shuddered but his hand on the knife never wavered. "He told me if I did it, things'd be okay. He's goin' t' look after me, Max. Goin' t' sort it all out, everythin' I need. But people want t' stop him. They want it all f' th'selves."

"That's not true, Baz." I knew this was probably a hopeless cause, but I had to try to talk him round. "Peck's not telling you the truth. Yes, you need some help, but he's not the man to give it. He's just using you, Baz."

Baz was either too high on drugs or just didn't understand what I was saying. "Mr. Peck talks f' me, that's what he says. No one else gives a fuck. If I help him wiv' his problems, he'll protec' me— gimme a proper job. Wiv' him."

I heard an indrawn breath in the hallway. The shadow by the kitchen door seemed to shift. Was Seve trying to creep up on us? "Baz, just give me the knife."

Baz frowned. For the first time, I saw his doped gaze waver. I'd often been in charge of keeping him in order. Baz always wanted to know where he stood, what to do, and where he fit in, even if he didn't always follow guidance. I was hoping old habits died hard. I moved my weight onto the balls of my feet. I might have to dodge suddenly, and my reflexes weren't what they used to be.

"Nah, Max," Baz said slowly. I could imagine the rusty cogs of his mind grinding around. "Not happenin'."

I surreptitiously placed my palms flat against the wall behind me. Maybe I could surprise him—launch myself at him. "Let's go and find Peck." I just needed another inch or so to maneuver out from under the blade. "I'll explain it all to him. He'll be really pleased with you, you know."

Then his head snapped up like it was on a spring. He grunted and tightened his grip on the knife. My precious inch of potential escape was lost; the gap between me and the blade narrowed. I froze. So—luckily—did he. He slid it along my jaw line and up to my cheek. It felt cold and hot on my skin, all at the same time. Just an illusion, I guessed. I wasn't really thinking clearly.

Baz chewed at his lower lip. It looked chapped and sore. "Dun' be s' fuckin' stupid, Max." His voice had deepened. He was no longer whining—he sounded older even than me. "You dun' tell me what t' do anymore, do y'? *He* does. And I do wha' I'm told, and so I'll be okay. That's wha' *you* oughtta do 's well. Then I wouldn' have t' be here, would I?"

I missed the logic of this, but I wasn't about to argue with him. At the corner of my vision, I saw a blurred movement in the kitchen doorway, and I tried desperately not to let the sudden awareness show in my face. Seve was strong and fast. If he could catch Baz's hand, twist the knife away... dammit, we were two strong adults, we could—

It didn't happen that way, because although Seve was fast, Baz was faster. Baz had slipped the blade across and away from my cheek and barreled into Seve before I could gasp a warning. Before I even felt the cold metal leaving my warm skin; before I registered the long thin slice on my face that was already starting to ooze a drop of warm blood. Somehow Baz had heard Seve approaching.

The speed of Baz's reaction ambushed Seve and knocked him off-balance. It looked like he'd been reaching for Baz, trying to grab Baz's arms, but now he stumbled and fell against me. He was naked apart from his sweats, and his arms flailed as he tried to right himself. We both crashed back against the kitchen counter. I clumsily banged my leg on the edge of the metal vegetable rack, and I saw Seve thud against the door of the fridge. It bounced open, spilling a sliver of light across the room for a second before it slammed back shut.

Baz followed us across the room but he moved jerkily. He darted forward, the serrated knife in his hand flashed dully, and Seve cried out in pain. In the dim light I saw blood welling on his arm, shining black drops. Then Baz gave me another surprisingly strong push and Seve and I ended up almost in each other's arms, jammed against the edge of the counter between the fridge and the waist-high wine rack.

Baz had the large knife aimed back at my throat. He wasn't touching me anymore, but he had a knife in each hand and was well within stabbing range. His eyes were shining and he had to cover us both, but he knew he had the advantage. He was still moving erratically, but he never once strayed close enough for us to grab at him first. Native cunning, I assumed.

"Stupid, stupid!" he hissed. "Look at y' both, no clothes, no knife, big 'n clumsy an' *stupid*. You can't catch me! Max knows that, dun' he? I can do my job an' be away before y' know it."

"I caught you once," I snapped back. "Not so fast then, were you?" Beside me, I felt Seve tense.

Baz blinked hard as if trying to assimilate the memory of me hitting him. "You weren' meant t' be there. Jus' the do-gooder. It was goin' t' be real quick. I like a knife, y'see. It's clean 'n quiet, an' you can get real *close.*"

I glanced briefly at Seve, sure my desperation showed on my face. He had a hand over his cut arm, trying to stem the blood. I wanted to apologize; I wanted to protect him from this. *Not again* beat through my veins in the rhythm of my heartbeat. *It can't happen again.*

Baz caught my look. He stared between us curiously. "You both faggots, then?"

Seve tensed again, but I touched his shoulder, trying to calm him. It had never been more than a casual insult from Baz—I'm not sure he knew anything about gay men, though he knew that's what I was. "Faggot" was just a noun in his very limited vocabulary. It was what Peck often called me, so that's what Baz used.

"Yes," Seve said, his voice startling me. He wouldn't catch my eye. "We are. What about you?"

It was my turn to tense up. "Seve—"

Baz sniggered. "No way."

Seve smiled as if unperturbed, still looking straight at Baz. "Aren't you just a little curious? Wouldn't you like to see what it is we do? What *Max* does?"

Where the hell was he going with this? Baz had never shown any sexual interest in anyone, as far as I knew.

Baz tipped his head to the side. "What the fuck y' mean? I'm not puttin' the knife down, y'know. Still got my job t' do."

Seve shrugged. I was so close to him I could feel his skin and the shiver that ran through him. "So have a bit of fun before you kill us both. Give me one last chance to touch him. He feels really good. And you can watch. Would you like that?"

Baz had an unhealthy devotion to Peck, of course. He'd always seemed to like me too. But how could Seve know if that was what turned him on? This was a strange strategy of Seve's, and I didn't think I was reassured by it. Not reassured *at all*.

"You're a fuckin' pervert," Baz said conversationally. He flexed his wrist so that the large knife caught a glimmer of light from outside. "Y' like that snuff stuff 'n all?"

"Maybe," Seve replied. His voice was low, calm, and almost seductive. "We can talk about that another time. But Max is gorgeous, isn't he? Got a great body... you can see that, can't you?" Still that soft, lulling tone. "You can keep hold of the knives. We won't be any trouble. Just give me one last touch."

Baz stared at him like he was genuinely disgusted, but there was a flicker of curiosity in his eyes too. "Guess if he takes it up th' arse, he deserves everythin' he gets, eh?"

"Guess so," Seve said. Very, *very* softly.

And Baz seemed to relax—only slightly, but enough for the knife to dip down from pointing at my throat. He leaned back against the kitchen table opposite us, still only a few feet away. "Come on, then. Do it."

"*What?*" I suppose I hadn't thought through what might happen next.

"Drop your jeans," Seve murmured in my ear. He tugged me sideways to stand in front of him, his hand holding me around the waist, both of us facing Baz. "Show him what you've got to offer."

Baz was flushed and his eyes blazed, scary companions to the knife blades. I was suddenly afraid that we'd pushed him further along the wrong path. I twisted my head to shoot a look at Seve, trying to say without words, *What the fuck are you doing*? He glanced at me with a steady gaze and I was none the wiser. So I turned back to face the front and, with fumbling fingers, I slid my jeans down my legs and stepped out of them so I was naked again. The air in the kitchen was cool on my skin.

Baz sniggered again. "Not much goin' on there, Mr. Pervert. He looks pretty fuckin' small."

"So would you, Baz, if you were waiting for some lunatic to cut your throat!" I snapped back. Seve pressed my arm as if in warning, but Baz didn't seem to care about my anger.

"Just do somethin'. Gonna see if it's fun f' me or not."

Seve leaned forward against my back, his breath on my neck. I felt pretty bloody vulnerable. I assumed he had some kind of plan. Though if it involved us actually having sex, he was going to be way out of luck. Like Baz so succinctly put it, I was totally shriveled. And any other orifice was tightly clenched as well. Fear does that to a man, you know.

Baz let himself down slowly onto one of the kitchen chairs. It skittered on the tiled floor and one of its legs settled on my discarded jeans. Guess he was getting a ringside seat: the condemned man has his last grope. *Bizarre*. His grip on the long knife was as good as ever, and his eyes were animal bright. I had no reason to believe he wouldn't move as fast as before, if and when he needed, and I didn't want that knife any nearer either of us. He was surprisingly strong too. Maybe between us, we could have taken him, but not without someone getting cut. And I'd seen the effects of that once, and once too often.

"Look, Baz, why don't we—"

"Y' talk *shit*!" Baz's voice had risen again. "That's all y' ever did, Max. Talk 'n smoke 'n tell me what I din' do. No more talkin' anymore, okay?" He turned his gaze to Seve. "Show me."

I felt Seve's hand on my buttocks. He caressed me soothingly. Was this going to be the last time he touched me like this?

"You feel good, Max." His voice was soft, maybe not only for Baz's benefit. "Lean back. Let me touch you."

I did what I was told. My mind was whirling. Seve held my back against him so I had to look at Baz, at his blinking, putrid, suddenly lewd little eyes. I had to look at the glint of the blade in his hand, listen to his ragged wheezing. If I weren't so petrified, I'd have thrown up in his lap. Seve tugged me closer, our bodies blocking Baz's view of the counter behind us. I cursed Seve's minimalist taste in furniture because I couldn't see anything around us I could use as a weapon.

Seve gave a soft groan behind me. I was shocked to feel his dick swelled inside his sweats. How could he get aroused with a wavering blade held inches from his body and the threat of possible death? He hitched down his waistband and rubbed his cock up between the cheeks of my arse. We were both damp with sweat, but thank God he didn't try to push inside. I didn't fancy being dry-fucked just before I was murdered. But it seemed he didn't have that in mind, anyway. He moaned quietly and gave a few thrusts of his hips, as if he were moving inside me. It was an act. But to what point?

"Is he good, then?" came Baz's reedy little voice. "Dun' look like he's enjoyin' it."

"He's very good," Seve said. There was a strained edge to his voice. "And of course he's enjoying it. Aren't you, Max?" He slid a hand down my belly to my groin and circled my dick with his palm. He started to stroke it. Baz followed the movement, apparently fascinated. Seve nuzzled into the crook of my neck and whispered to me, "Give him a show, for fuck's sake. Then when I give you the sign, duck down."

"Huh?" I grunted and tried to turn it into a moan of pleasure. Seve continued his pantomime, and I thrust back toward him, twisting an expression onto my face as if I was being well and truly fucked.

"I like you naked," he murmured in my ear. "No clothes between us."

Baz leaned forward in his chair to hear better. His expression was an odd mixture of repulsion and prurience. The serrated knife lay in his lap, and his grip on the other had eased as well. The chair creaked underneath him.

"Right?" Seve whispered to me.

I nodded. I understood now.

"Can't see much," Baz whined. "That all y' fuckin' do?" He gazed at my cock, nestled in Seve's fist—at my thrusting hips, as Seve rolled his behind me. Baz was just that little bit entranced. Just that little bit distracted.

One of Seve's fingernails pressed sharply into my hip, and I took it as my signal. I leaned forward, pulled swiftly out of Seve's loosening grip, and dropped to my knees. Baz snarled, his instinctive suspicion awakening. No more sordid entertainment for him; he was all business, jerking up the blade and aiming it straight at my neck. He was less than a foot away from me and I was a kneeling, naked target. He couldn't miss. I imagined I could already feel the slice across my nerve endings, feel the shock of mortal pain.

And then my mind settled, a chill running through my whole body. *No clothes between us*, Seve had said. I scrabbled for my discarded jeans and yanked them toward me, wrenching them out from under the leg of the kitchen chair—another example of Seve's fashionable but ridiculously flimsy furniture. The chair tilted awkwardly, and with a shout of anger, Baz began to topple back. At the same time, Seve stepped forward in front of me, swung something out from behind his back, and brought it down on Baz's head, *hard*. I didn't know what it was until I heard the smash of glass and smelled the sudden rush of alcohol. One of the wine bottles from the rack behind him!

Baz continued to fall, the chair slipping out from under him. Liquid ran down his face, dark trails in the half light, drops falling from his nose and chin. He still gripped the knives, but his limbs were uncoordinated. His mouth was open, and he looked nothing more than startled. On his way down, he collided heavily with the table and finally slumped to the floor, sprawled between two of the table legs in a spreading pool that could have been red wine and could just as well have been blood. His fists opened like limp buds and the knives clattered out onto the kitchen tiles.

Silence. All I could hear was my own harsh breathing. My legs were shaking so hard I couldn't stand. I scrambled on hands and knees back to the relative safety beside the kitchen cupboards. I just wanted to get beyond Baz's reach, even though he wasn't moving now. It was difficult to avoid the smashed glass, and I nearly put my hand on a large shard. It rocked back and forth, the torn label flapping wetly. As far as I could see, it had a fancy Spanish name on it with a big Roman numeral; its concave surface was covered in dust.

"Fuck, Seve." My voice was very hoarse. "That wasn't an expensive one, was it?"

Seve knelt beside me, his hand on my shoulder. He'd pulled his sweats back up around his waist. "Are you okay?"

I didn't know how to answer that. "We need to get dressed." My mouth opened and words came out, but I couldn't take much responsibility for them. "We need to get shoes on. Clear up this mess."

Seve ran his hand gently over my head as a parent might try to console a scared child. He stood up and carefully made his way to the light switch. The light came on with a flood of fluorescent white that made me wince. All around us, the floor was covered with shattered glass and spilled wine. Baz lay motionless on the cold, wet, too-shiny floor tiles.

Seve glanced at me. If he'd meant to smile, I had to tell him it looked a hell of a lot more like a grimace. He stepped gingerly around the carnage and crouched over Baz, placing his fingers on Baz's neck. He made a small sound of exhalation.

I clasped my jeans to my chest, ignoring the fact both legs were soaked with booze. "We must call an ambulance."

"He's dead, Max." Seve said it calmly, but I could see his shoulders shaking.

"Dead?" Don't you just hate those people in films who repeat the bad news like a parrot?

"He must have hit his head on the corner of the table. It was an unlucky blow—for him, anyway."

"But...." I had no idea what to say. "That wasn't meant to happen."

Seve sighed. "Max, the kid was insane. This is for the best. He was going to kill you."

"Well," I said. "That's where you're wrong."

"What?" Seve looked both angry and amazed. "Don't tell me now you care a fuck about a manic, murderous little—"

"It wasn't me he was sent to kill," I said. "I'm not saying he wasn't going to slit both our throats when he found us together, but he was surprised to find me here."

"What the hell are you saying?"

"You," I said. "I reckon he was here for *you*."

CHAPTER 22

SEVE prised my jeans out of my hands and found me a pair of his sweats and a sweater to wear. I couldn't seem to stop shivering, though the flat wasn't cold. When I pulled the sweater on, the neckline caught on my cheek, and blood from one of my cuts smeared the luxurious wool. Seve never even flinched.

He dragged a sheet off his bed and rolled Baz's body up in it. The parcel looked like an obscene mix of shroud and cocoon. There was surprisingly little blood, so I assumed the blow to the head had hit a pressure point rather than cut him open. I didn't think too closely about the logistics. We pushed him against the wall by the door and started clearing up the mess on the floor. As I mopped tiles and swept up more slivers of glass than I'd ever have imagined would come from just one bottle, it didn't seem too weird to have Baz's body lying in the room with us. But then I think I was still in shock.

Seve changed out of his blood-spattered sweats and dressed in jeans and a polo shirt. I bound up his arm with a bandage from his medicine cabinet, and in return, he washed the shallow cuts in my cheek and neck. It was a quiet time between us, and I found it oddly touching. Then I twisted back the ends of my hair with an elastic band and went to settle myself in the living room. I needed recovery time. Seve offered to make a hot drink—compared to me, he didn't seem too bothered about working in the kitchen alongside his uninvited guest.

Half an hour later, I was still huddled on the couch. The cashmere sweater was fabulously soft and doing its job in warming me up, but I had my hands gripped around a second mug of hot, sweet tea and I was still shaky. Seve was pacing the room.

"That was a bloody good move, Seve. The thing with the wine bottle. Feeling me up, distracting him…."

"It was obvious." Looked like Seve had regained his natural arrogance. "I could see the way he looked at you."

"What?"

"Not sexual," Seve said impatiently. "A kind of devotion. Anything involving you would have been a distraction to him. I used that to gain some time."

"He'd still have killed me."

"Yes," Seve said. "He'd still have killed you. When you heard him break in, why did you tell me to keep out of the way?"

"Huh?"

"What the hell were you going to do, Max?"

I shrugged. Damned if I knew. I was certainly no action hero. "I just wanted to stop anyone getting to you, I suppose. This is your home, your… sanctuary."

"You think I'm vulnerable? You think you can take on lunatic intruders by yourself?"

"Well, we can all see how that went," I said dryly.

"You wanted to protect *me*," he said slowly. It sounded like he couldn't understand the concept. Not sure I could myself.

"I wanted to talk him out of it. I thought I could."

"He was too far gone. It was in his eyes."

"I know." I was thankful Seve didn't tell me how rash I'd been, though I'd told myself plenty of times in the last half hour. "We should call the police."

"Not yet. Let me think, Max. What the hell makes you think he came for me?"

I worried my lower lip. "Peck sent him, I'm sure. Yeah, Peck's starting to think I'm a threat because of what I know about the London operations, so I'm sure he wants me out of the way. But you said you've been nosing around the business yourself and haven't been as careful as you could have. He'd want to warn you off too. And then Baz...." Seve glanced at me, so my voice must have sounded as odd to him as it did to me. "He was surprised to see me here. He was almost apologetic about killing Stewart... in front of me."

"I can't believe it. I *won't* believe it! Peck has nothing to do with the central office functions, so he wouldn't have known I was nosing around, as you say. That would mean...."

"Your uncle must have told him." *Instructed him.*

"Uncle would not...." Seve's words dried up.

"Maybe Peck didn't mean to kill you. Maybe he sent Baz just to scare you off. But Baz was never controllable."

Seve shook his head as if trying to clear a tangle of disturbing thoughts. He didn't turn to face me when he spoke next. "Who's Stewart?"

"Huh?"

"You said Baz killed Stewart. And you've... said his name before. In your sleep." Seve seemed to be forcing each word out between his teeth. "Did you know him in London?"

"Seve," I said slowly. Dear God, we'd only spent two nights together, and it was as much of a minefield as our waking hours. "This is really not the time."

"For what?"

His brow was creased in a frown, and I felt a strange, exhilarating rush of care for him. "For inquisition."

But he didn't let go. I imagined that was never Seve's forte. "It's his lighter, isn't it? A souvenir, you said."

I nodded.

"Was he your lover?"

If I hadn't been fighting off a stress headache, I'd have rolled my eyes. "He was a friend, not a boyfriend. He was a counselor, helping the kids on the streets." Helping *me*. "But I believe your uncle thought Stewart was messing with the club's courier runs, and wanted him gone."

"Was he like me?"

This was so *not* like Seve that I laughed out loud. "Are you really wearing the jealous hat, Seve? I can't believe it!"

He looked dogged. "Would you have stayed in London? If Stewart hadn't been killed?"

The inference was *stayed in London with Stewart*. I was too weary to argue. "I expect so."

"I repeat, was he like me?"

"What are you saying, Seve?" Was he asking me to stay with *him*? Be with him like I'd wanted to be with Stewart? I would have treasured Stewart's friendship all my life; I would have stayed as close to him as I was allowed. I would have followed his principles until they were my own.

What were Seve's principles, compared to that?

"I spent too long in that world, Seve," I said. I was definitely still in shock, and so I was treading very carefully along this thin, cracking ice that was our conversation. We'd just killed someone, hadn't we? In self-defense, maybe, but we'd both contributed to his death. Seve had hit him with the bottle, but I'd been just as keen to see him dead. I remembered Baz leaning over me as I knelt on the floor, shifting the knife in his hand to a better grip. I remembered the ice in Seve's tone as he tempted him to watch us. I didn't know if I felt grateful for being saved or resentful at being manipulated. I didn't know *what* I felt. "I've been there. Baz's world. Peck's world. Your uncle's world, for that matter. But I got out, you see. And I don't want to be sucked back in."

He stared at me. There were dark circles under his eyes that I'd not noticed before. "You needn't be."

"We *need* to call the police, Seve. Get this all sorted out."

"Soon."

I sighed. He was reluctant and—to be brutally honest—so was I. There'd be questions. Suspicion. And then more questions. Seve sat down heavily on the couch beside me and reached for the bottle of water I'd left there the previous night. He took a long swallow, then passed it to me. I drank too, then handed it back. In my befuddled state, it seemed one of the most intimate things we'd ever done together.

When his phone rang, we both jumped. I glanced at the clock. It was barely 5:00 a.m. Who'd be calling Seve at this hour of the morning? He picked it up from the table where we'd left our stuff the night before. He glanced once at me as if considering whether to take the call away from me, but he stayed put. I could hear the high, excited pitch of the caller, not giving him much opportunity to reply. And I saw the way his face paled.

"Who is it?" I hissed.

Seve's eyes didn't meet mine. "I understand. Of course I do, *mamá*. Soon, I promise you. Let me call you back." He disconnected.

"Tell me," I said.

"It was Mama. She's been trying to call me since last night. Since I went to see her about the club, she's been looking into my uncle's business. And yesterday...."

"What?" I could see his eyes were full of shock.

"She was burgled. Nothing was taken, but the house was ransacked. And she's received several anonymous calls. Someone has been in her house, is accessing her life, is harassing her."

"Your uncle? Peck, working on his behalf?" God forbid, not *Baz*, even if he wouldn't be doing anyone any harm now.

"I don't know, but she believes my uncle has initiated it. Enough evidence was in the records to make her suspicious of my uncle's finances—there's a trail of potential money laundering. She had made an appointment to see him tomorrow, but now...."

"She should get away from him," I said urgently. "Get her somewhere safe. Then she can pass the investigation to people who know what they're looking for. Who are qualified to take the risks."

Seve looked at me. His expression was strange, as if he were happy and sad at the same time. "But that is exactly what I must do, Max. You're right. Go to her and protect her. Between us, we have enough to go to the police. But until they can protect her by arresting my uncle and anyone else who is involved, I'm the only help she has." He blinked hard. "I must go to her as soon as possible."

"Of course you must."

"Max, you don't realize...."

"What?"

He sounded exhausted. "She has already fled to her home. In Madrid. I must go to her there."

I stared at him for a long moment. The look on his face was awesome; it was soft and hard and bitter all at the same time. It reached right through me to something far beyond. It was a look of angry challenge and also a look of defeat.

"What are you really saying? What about...?" I struggled to say it. "About Baz?"

He reached over and ran his hand behind my neck. It was as if he wanted to pull me in for a kiss, but all he did was stroke my skin. "Leave it to me, Max. Leave it all to me. Let me and Mama clear up this mess. I promise you that we will. It'll all be okay. My uncle will be exposed and arrested. We'll all be safe."

I didn't want to stare at him—I didn't want to lose my righteous anger into the dark, vibrant depths of his eyes. What I *wanted* was to see my face reflected in them as I did when we were held close. I wanted to see that hint of nervousness, the softening of the arrogance that had been gradually disclosed to me over the last few weeks. I wanted that truth, at least. "You want me to keep quiet about this? To let you dash off to Spain and leave me here, with some kind of promise that it'll *all be okay*?"

"It will, Max. I do not promise lightly. Mama is scared, but she's honest and determined. But I need to be able to join her in Spain. I need a few days to plan things with her."

"What happens to Baz's body in the meantime? You'll leave it propped up in your kitchen between the dishwasher and the fucking fridge?"

He winced. "Of course not. I will… arrange things."

"And me? What will you arrange for me?"

His grip tightened. "You will not be at risk. I will not allow it. Just give me this time, Max. Let me do this. And then I'll be back. Trust me."

I wanted to shout, *Why the hell should I?* But I wasn't a kid anymore. Even if what happened tonight had been outside my control, I'd put myself in this situation. The choices I'd made, the paths I'd taken—they'd led me here. A thread of cold understanding had sprung up inside me, growing like a shoot out of a seed—one of those you grow on a school windowsill in a jar, you know? All green and new and slightly amazing. I resurrected a long-buried memory—we'd all grown one of those seeds when we were kids in school. Mine had shriveled away from neglect. Jack's had grown steadily and modestly until we planted it outside. Louis's had lain dormant for the longest time, then burst up six inches overnight and sprouted a flower or whatever. He'd been the talk of the class for days. I tried to get him to admit he'd dosed it with some secret fertilizer, but he never confessed.

I was rambling in my mind. I missed my friends. I wished I had their help now. "I just can't believe the way you talk about it, Seve. You told me once I was too melodramatic, but you… I don't think I know you at all. Aren't you scared of anything?"

"Of course I am." His hand slipped away from my neck and he pulled back on the couch. "I'm scared of *you*."

"Me?" *What the hell?*

"Of the look on your face now," he whispered raggedly. His eyes were wide with what looked like genuine fear. "Of your withdrawal from me. Of *losing* you."

I HAULED myself up from the soft luxury of the couch and went over to the window. I opened a couple of inches of the blind and the morning light flooded in, careless of either material obstruction or human angst. It spilled a thin pale band across the carpet and Seve's bare feet, then dappled on the couch cushion beside him. His hands were clenched tightly, his body tense. He was holding back from following me—touching me. I was sure he wanted to use his desire to influence me. That had always been his way in the past. *Our* way. Why would I expect him to change overnight? Or myself to change, for that matter. Because I'd felt the same arrogance for so long now that it'd become as much *me* as my skin. "I am as I am," I boasted to anyone who'd listen—maybe not directly, maybe not intentionally. But it was there in everything I did and said. I carried my baggage like a prize while all it did was drag my arms to the floor like I was a fucking gorilla.

But things—and people—*did* change, didn't they? Whether it was deliberate or not, welcome or not. We all had baggage from the day we were born. And as we limped along in life, lumps of experience bounced off us like tiny meteors, and we gathered even more. But how far did you let it drag back your progress into the future?

"You've kept me at bay as well, Max," Seve spoke quietly.

I spun around to look at him. "What?"

"You haven't told me everything about you. From your friend's murder to your reluctance to allow me time to make things good between us."

"No," I said sharply.

"I think that you *want* it to be all about the sex. I admit, it was for me at first. But we have moved on from that, haven't we? Don't you think we can be together, just as ourselves? *For* ourselves?"

I turned back to the window, stunned. Was he right? Had I seen him as the one always in control, whereas I'd been just as guilty of calling the shots? Topping from the bottom, Louis would call it. He was one of the worst offenders, so he should know. Hours ago, I was bandying around words like "love" to describe the draw I felt toward Seve, the fascination, the hollowness of not being with him. But had I ever let him know about that? Why was I hiding it? To be realistic—or to protect myself?

"I don't know," I said. Seemed my vocabulary had deserted me along with my wits. I wanted him to touch me, now, and to touch him back. Didn't know how to say yes. Didn't know whether to say no.

Seve sighed. "I see."

"No," I said. The distress had eased, but I knew the mess remained. My head was still throbbing. "I don't think you do. I'm just trying to say that this isn't exactly what I want, Seve."

He raised a thin eyebrow. "What *do* you want, Max? Would you want to go back to the time before you met me?"

It felt like a hole had opened up at the bottom of my gut, just at the thought. "Yes, I would," I said, brutally honest. "I was starting out all over again—a new life, good friends. I was going to make something good of it all." Seve's face was still pale. I could see the sweat drops on his forehead. I knew how salty-sweet they'd taste. I threw my head back in frustration. "But, shit—I can't ever *do* that, can I? Not now! Meeting you has turned the whole fucking show up on its arse. I'm different now, and it's because you've changed me. I can't remember a time that anyone disturbed me so much, that I was ever so absorbed in someone." *That I was ever so alive!*

"Not even Stewart?" he asked softly. Like he was ashamed to say it but had to. Like his possessiveness was a habit he couldn't break just yet.

I felt the need to talk swelling inside me—the need to tell him how I felt. Was it now or never? Caution got hurled to the winds.

"That was my old life, Seve. He was a really good friend and I'll never forget him, but I came back here to move on." I heard Seve suck in a breath, though he didn't speak. "But it was a sham, I think—my *new life*. It was never going to work like that, not long-term. Do you remember, you once said that I loved the risk and the spontaneity as much as you did? That was honest, even if I didn't think so at the time. You've made me realize I was just hiding it all inside. Just hiding my true nature—that *passion* in me you talked about. I thought it was the only way to make my new start, to mold the new me. To keep it all buttoned up, to repress my desires. After all, those were the feelings that always got me into trouble."

"Max," he whispered. He stood up slowly.

"But then I met you," I hurried on, "and it all just burst out! So wild that I thought I'd lost control. It felt fucking *good*, but I didn't welcome it, and I've been fighting against it even as I leaped right in with both feet. And although I feel like shit right now, I know I'm more comfortable in my skin than I have been for a long time. I've let you drag it all out of me—all the things I thought I wanted buried. When really, I needed to think of a different way to control them."

"But that's good?" he said.

"Yes. And no." I sighed. Just *be together as ourselves*, he'd said. As if we knew each other well enough already—as if it wouldn't take a hell of a lot more work to make that happen. Yet... it was what I wanted. "I want more, you know? Not just more sneaking about in corners and fucking, though that's been so damn exciting I have trouble walking straight at times, just thinking about it all."

Seve's smile was wary.

"But more of you," I whispered. The deep whirlpool of his eyes caught and held me and churned up every sense beyond sense. "I want to sit and hold you and talk to you. Play cards with you and make meals together. I want to watch a film with you and argue about the casting and the plot holes afterward. I want to take you back to meet the guys and maybe go out for a drink together—just sometimes, because Louis's social expectations can be a little overwhelming for long periods of time." I ran my eyes over his body—the smooth, softly heaving chest. The muscles clenched along his upper arms. The tasty little hollows between his neck and his collarbone. The juicy, lush pads of his earlobes. "I want more sex with you, Seve, but I want to do it without condoms, if we can. Fantastic and impulsive sex is way more than fine, but I want to be around you long enough so we can check it out. And…." I shrugged, suddenly flushing. "I think I'd like to try top with you, just once in a while. That thought kind of nags at me at night. Basically, I want it all. And not just doing it, but to talk about it, and to laugh and bitch about our day, and to plan a weekend, and to sit in sometimes and be bored together, and… *fuck*." All sorts of things that I'd never realized, that I'd never allowed myself to think about.

He let out a small gasp that brought my attention back to him. He was swaying slightly, and his expression was pure astonishment. I was breathing heavily with the rush of words, and when he put out a hand to steady both of us, I let it rest on my shoulder.

For a soft, silent moment, we leaned into each other. Nothing more than a hand on a shoulder, the warmth of a palm on my knotted muscles. A fingertip's gentleness ghosting across the taut skin of my neck. He was like a breath seeping into my pores. They opened for him. *I* opened for him. My hands came up from my sides, and they slid underneath his arms, and I let him gather me into him. His torso was warm under my touch, and my chin rested gently against his chest. He held me there and we breathed together.

I'd told him, hadn't I? About the love thing. Not in so many words, but… I'd be eternally grateful I had.

CHAPTER 23

EVENTUALLY Seve drew us both down to sit on the couch. I felt shaky and maybe he did too. "You must know how much I want you, Max."

I know, I know. I nodded to him.

"No," he murmured in my ear as if I'd said it aloud. "Not just the sex. I also want all that you said. I think that the sex has distracted us from the start. But you are a disturbance beyond that."

"Is that how you see me?" I laughed, but it didn't sound quite right.

His hands tightened on me, perhaps to stop me drawing away. "I've always been used to being in control, Max. I've always had what I wanted, been praised and groomed for success. It is what I do—it is what I *am*! But now... I'm adrift. I have been for as long as I've known you. The ropes slipped their knots that very first time, though I'd never have admitted it. That first time, when the danger was no longer entirely in my hands... I kept saying to myself—I do not do that. I do not get involved, I do not stay around."

"I thought that was my line," I said quietly.

"It was like an addiction," Seve said, ignoring me. His eyes sparkled, though his expression was very serious. "I was consumed with the need to have you again. To hold you, to fuck you—just to *see* you again. I watched you with your friends, only waiting for when you could be with me. I watched you laugh, and walk to me, and argue with me, and *touch me* where I didn't mean you to."

I couldn't recognize the Seve I knew. Or—let's face it—thought I knew. Strange, intimate words were tumbling out of him into my ear and my neck, and the breath was warm, so it must be real, mustn't it? The hands on my waist were the ones that had lifted me on and off the kitchen table. The lips that brushed my cheek were the ones that had kissed me and teased at my nipples under the sheets in the dark. It was Seve—and it wasn't. But how welcome it was!

The low voice thrilled as always, but it was less than steady. "You've taught me many things, Max. Whether you meant to or not, and whether I was willing to learn or not. I'm learning not just to be angry, which you'll understand I've had plenty practice with. But also to be desperate, to be *unsure*... to question myself. To open my mouth to talk, not just to demand." He sighed. "It is my turn to say what I want, yes? I want *you*." His lips whispered over my forehead, and I felt my face turning up to him. "I want to be inside you. Every night. I want your hair loose and tangled against my neck. I want your hands teasing at my thighs. I want your generous mouth over my cock, sucking me, laughing, licking me."

He was almost kissing me—*almost*. There were a couple of millimeters of hot, charged breath between our mouths. I wanted him so badly that I felt as if my heart had stopped and my body was tapping its watch, waiting for reconnection.

"When I eat, I want you. When I walk, I want you. When I smile, when I dress, when I wash—I want you. When I *breathe*...."

"*Shit*." I groaned. "When you learn to talk, you talk, you know?"

He ignored me. Or rather, he kissed me. Just with his lips—firm, moist lips that pressed his need into mine and breathed his desire through my body. I kissed back, and I took it further. I pressed my tongue to the sides of his mouth, and I lapped at him until he opened his lips for me to slide in. Who was in control now? *No-fucking-one.* He tasted of tension and anger and sweet, sweet lust, but underneath it all he tasted of Seve. Pure man. Pure proud, arrogant, newly lyrical man.

"What does it mean, Max?" he murmured.

I drew back, licking at the delicious taste of his saliva that lingered on my tongue. I trailed a hand on his chest because I couldn't resist the warmth of his body anymore. "This is the best thing I've ever had, Seve."

"So…."

"And maybe the worst as well."

He paused. "Isn't that what we've been saying? It needn't be. We can just do what we want."

I gave a rueful smile. "I can't do impulse any more, Seve. Look where it's got me."

"You *did*. You came to me, from the start."

"Yeah." And damn, it was great! "But now I'm fucked, in all senses of the word. It'll take me months to get over it again." It was, perhaps, another of my feeble jokes. Or perhaps I really meant it.

"Why do you need to?"

He didn't understand, of course. "What do you think, Seve? Don't you see where we are this morning? There's a dead man in the kitchen and a maniac with a power complex out there, threatening both you and your mother. I know I need to go to the cops with what I know, yet I'm holding back because I'm afraid of getting you into trouble, when all I want is to see you safe and alive. I'm fucking *worn out* with turning it all over in my head and finding just more things to sort out. You think we can just roll back into bed and carry on as before?"

"What do you want, then?" he asked, with more than a note of frustration. "If you go to the police now, we'll both be wrapped up in this mess from the minute we walk in the door of the station. Mama will be left in danger and your past will be dragged up for all to see. I don't want that either."

"I know." I put my fingers to his face and traced the worry line across his forehead. His breath huffed against my wrist. Then his face changed. He seemed to draw himself up, and the cool mask slipped efficiently back over his features. He was, again, the Seve Nuñez I had met that first time: the man who had nodded to me, oh so slightly, and lifted a glass in invitation. The man who controlled Compulsion. Who controlled a lot of things. But not me.

And he knew it.

"You said you wanted to get out of this life, Max. Perhaps I do too." I realized he wasn't looking for my agreement or even my sympathy. He was just stating his case. "I want the chance to be different, now I've met you. Isn't that what you wanted for yourself?"

"I… yes, I guess so."

"I want out, Max."

God, it sounded so simple, the articulate words, the confident tone. Seve was a man who'd rarely been refused anything in his life. A man with his personal charisma might well make anything happen. "Seve, do you think it'd be that easy? How would you do it? Become Mr. Ordinary, like me. Without your job, your family support, your money. And nothing's settled yet. There are too many things coming out in the open now. It's gone way beyond just *us*."

"You don't want me to change, not even when I want to be with you?" He stared at me, bemused. He held out his hand, and I raised mine to match it. I spread my fingers and reached for his. Five fingertips touched five others and pressed gently together. It was an electric feeling—the current ran swiftly and shockingly through my veins. Our fingers slid slowly down and interlocked. His palm was sweaty.

"Seve, I want to be with you as well."

"But—?"

I hushed him with my fingers on his lips. Rich, beautiful, appetizing lips. "But that's not going to happen for us, is it?" I whispered. "Not the way things are. Not after last night."

I WENT into the kitchen for another bottle of water. I felt more resilient now. The room smelled of tea and cleaning products, and there was no evidence that anyone had been working in there at all this morning. Except for the bundle rolled up in a sheet against the far wall. It wasn't Baz any more, but it had once been a man. It reminded me of Stewart's death.

I knew now that it wasn't my fault that Stewart died. He was still dead, of course, and it was still fucking painful to think of him. But some of the terrible guilt had eased. I'd been part of the world that had killed him, but it hadn't been my hand that harmed him. It hadn't been my order that sent Baz to kill him—it hadn't been my negligence that led any of us to that spot that night. Stewart's conversation was clear in my mind, his complaints, his amusement. His world-weary wisdom and his unassuming friendship. His desire to help others, and not in some insincere, sanctimonious way. His steady belief that I could be better.

And I knew very clearly now what my way should be.

WHEN I came back into the living room, Seve was standing by the couch. He looked steadier on his feet now. Actually, he looked damn gorgeous as ever. The polo shirt was slinky and was probably really expensive. It gave him the impression of being respectably dressed, and yet I could see the movement of his muscles under the cloth and the hint of erect nipples that made him look erotically half-naked. He'd run a hand through his hair, and it stood up spikily on his scalp. He displayed a casual elegance that I'd never seen anyone else do so well. I'd told him how I felt about him—and he'd returned the compliment. I didn't think he was going to lie to me anymore. Part of me didn't mind either way. I had my truth. And anyway, what did it matter now?

I drew a deep breath but I wasn't afraid. Just needed to bring things back under control. "I'm going to the cops, Seve."

A flash in those hooded eyes. He'd obviously been thinking things through as well, while I was out of the room. "Yes." He inclined his head in that way he had.

Bloody man, I thought. Now is *not* the time to return to monosyllabic conversation. This was difficult enough as it was. "I want to tell them about London. I want to get myself clear of that shit, at least. And I want someone to be accountable for the drugs and for... Stewart. Okay, so they'll probably charge me for something— the courier job or leaving the scene that night. I have no idea how much trouble I'll be in. But that time was nothing to do with you. I don't want you dragged down with it." Was that selfish or naive of me? Was that even possible? "Yet with all that's happened this morning...."

He pursed his lips. I leaned involuntarily toward them. He looked like he'd been making decisions as well. "What happened this morning is *my* problem, Max."

"What?"

"I feel the same way for you—that I do not want you responsible for something that is not to do with you."

"But we both—"

He made a sharp tut noise that silenced me. "This man came to my flat to threaten me because of my family's business. My family— my problem. So you must not be involved with it."

"I can't do that!"

He continued regardless. "Give me a few hours before you call the police. Just give me the rest of the day to arrange things."

There was that phrase again—*arrange*. "What about the body?"

"It'll be found," he said. "Just not here."

"And Peck?"

"I said I'll arrange things. Mama has many friends still here." His eyes met mine, and the dark chasms were hiding both fear and decision. "You will not be incriminated, Max, not from anything that happened here. I hope that I will not be either. But I cannot afford to be mixed up in it at the moment. I must keep Mama safe. Peck can do too much damage, and with my uncle unchecked, our entire business is vulnerable. My uncle is a shrewd and clever man—I am afraid we will all take our turn as the scapegoat. I need to be away from here to try and salvage what I can. We must act immediately—to put an end to the threat hanging over all of us." His pupils widened. "Over you too, Max."

A chill spread slowly across my body. "Is it your turn to run, Seve?"

His eyes flashed. "I will do what I have to. I must leave as soon as possible. I haven't initiated this, but if I can help put things right, whatever it takes, I will. Many of my family will. We're not all in it for the money, Max."

I held up a hand in apology, though I'd never said or meant that. I wondered if he'd have a job and the expensive flat and car or a family business at all when he came back. Didn't they freeze assets when businesses were under investigation? Was that as important to Seve as being pursued by Peck and his death wish?

Or perhaps he wasn't coming back at all.

Fuck.

"They'll call you in. They may arrest you."

"The police? On what charge?" He shook his head. "I don't think so, even if and when I provide the information they need. I am not involved at a high enough level in the business, you see. I'll be just a whistleblower: a pawn in their eyes." And from the frown on his face, in his eyes too. "They will want my uncle and his network, which Mama and I will give them. And they still want Stewart's murderer. You'll make sure they have that as well."

"Even if it costs me."

"I think they will see you as a hero, Max, not a villain. But I do not know for certain. I don't wish that trouble on you. If I could help…."

I nodded. I knew. But this was for me alone to work out.

"And if they do come after me… well, Mama has her own network on the continent. I won't be easy to find."

The chill washed over me again. "If they can't find you, Seve, neither will I. Will I?"

He stared at me. "No, you won't."

The ache inside me was like a wound.

"But you misunderstand, Max." He stepped forward, and although I tensed, I let him take hold of me again. "I assumed... I cannot leave you here if you think Peck is still looking for you."

"Hey. I'll be okay. Once he finds Baz has gone, he'll think twice. And I'll stick close to the guys, no one will get close to me if I don't want them to. And the gang at the site are pretty useful as bodyguards too." I wasn't sure if I was joking or not, to be honest, but Seve looked stricken.

"No, Max. I mean... come and join me as soon as you can. I want you to come with me to Spain."

People describe some of the defining moments of their lives as the hardest thing they've ever faced, don't they? The most painful decision they've ever made; the most heart-wrenching choice they've ever taken. It's just shit, really, isn't it? To be in that position.

"No, Seve."

His hands, tight on me. His knee brushing mine. The whole smell of him, the remembered taste. "You don't mean that."

"I do. I must stay here."

"Explain this to me," he said in a clipped tone. His accent had become more pronounced with his emotion. "What do you really mean? That it will be some time before you can come? The wait is not important."

It seemed very easy now to explain. To put into words the way that *I* was going to be now. "It's my promise, Seve, you see. My promise to myself and to Stewart."

"He is dead, Max."

I dismissed that with a shake of my head. "I'm still following his advice, Seve. I'm going to accept the past and then move on, but properly this time. I'll accept the great friends that I have—I'll treasure them. I'll let them help me with all those issues, all my *baggage*. I'll accept...." I met his eyes. "Accept new relationships, if they come along." I'd wanted to live up to what Stewart wanted—what he thought I was capable of. What he said I deserved. But I'd been taking the line of least resistance for too long now: pitching below standard, doing only enough to get by. Trying not to be noticed. But I'd dragged the past around with me regardless. I hadn't seen how anyone could ever forget it. I couldn't seem to forget it myself.

"I'm going to make this change wholeheartedly." My voice was jarringly brittle in the quiet room. "I'm going to make my own choices and ask myself exactly what I want, and I'll live it properly. Set the slate clean. Start again with some more realistic goals. And they'll be mine and they'll be honest. I'll build up some respect for myself at last."

He stood like a statue. Only the hitch of his breath and the pulse in his throat showed me that he was listening to every word.

"It's… a lot of it is due to *you,* Seve, you know? Meeting you—finding you." And that's what was making this so bad. So fucking *bad.* "I want this new me, Seve. I like it! But this is my place now, and I have to stay here to do things properly—to start growing up. Even though I know what this means to… us."

The air in the room was tight with tension. Dust motes spun in the ray of sun through the window. I heard a motorbike pass outside; a church bell tolled slowly in the background. When Seve spoke, the sound rippled around me like I was in some kind of deprivation tank; I could barely make out coherent words. I hadn't realized how tightly I was holding on to my senses.

"I won't lie to you anymore, Max."

"Sure, I know."

He was trying to tell me something again, with his eyes. I could only see misery, and it was depressing me beyond anything else. "So I'll stay here with you."

"No!" My voice had risen, which startled us both. "That's not going to work either, is it? There's your mother. The business. What *you* need to do."

Our eyes must have reflected the same anguish, the same realization. It was stalemate for the moment.

"No, of course not," he whispered.

"Good." I sounded shaky, even on the single word.

"But... if you had asked...."

I sighed. "Yeah."

He took a deep breath as if it pained him. "When everything has been concluded, I will come back here."

I swallowed hard and moved away from him. His hands gripped more tightly for a second, hanging on to my arms. Then he let me loose. "That's great, Seve. If that's what you want. But don't do it for me." He winced as if I'd hit him. "I don't *want* us to go separate ways," I said. "But I need to get my own head straight. I think... it's better if I have some time on my own." There'd been another death, another crime. Seve and I just had too much baggage. It was heavy, and it was complex, and if we didn't move on, it was going to bury us both. This was the best way to come clean. To start afresh.

At that moment, I was totally sure of it.

Seve made a strange, soft whimpering sound that I'd never heard from him before. He moved suddenly, pressing up against me again, clumsily as if his limbs were no longer under his control. I thought I should probably run—really fast, and in the opposite direction—but I didn't. I didn't want to. He clasped me to him, shifting his body against me, and his hand brushed against my cheek.

"I must go, Seve."

"Of course." His voice was deep and rough, and it washed over me like a too-hot shower on a cold day. Pure, unadulterated, painful pleasure. "I must go too. I need to make some calls, then pack a bag and order a cab to Gatwick. Just... a little more time?"

He kissed me again then. He reached an arm around my back, and I folded into him like melted chocolate. His mouth was firm and demanding, and I was happy to surrender to it. We were warm, and the taste of him was poignantly sweet. I wrapped my arms around his neck and traced the pattern of his cropped hair at the nape, trying to commit it to memory with my fingertips. He rested his hand on my head, wrapping strands of my hair around his fingers and tugging almost playfully, directing my mouth against his whenever it tried to shift away elsewhere. Our tongues were very fierce and very hungry. I slid my hand up underneath his shirt. He felt rich and exotic, and the flesh was smooth under my touch. I ran my fingers around to his back and then down to his waist. He drew in a breath and pressed his body closer to mine. I had to wriggle to rest my swelling cock against the side of his rather than full on.

"Yes?" he murmured. His hips moved very slightly, but he knew I'd realize what they were asking.

I moved back, adjusting myself to the side again. "No."

He smiled sadly, not offended nor surprised. "Sure." He did his own investigation, his own memory game. He ran his lips down my neck until I thought I had no more blood left in my body except the amount that was racing to my groin area. He traced the profile of my face and ran his hands down my sides and hips. He would have run them around to my arse and up my inner thighs if I hadn't stopped him. A man can only stand so much sensory ecstasy.

"I'll miss this. Touching you, Max."

"Arguing with me," I whispered. Lame fucking joke.

"Yes," he agreed. "That too."

Neither of us mentioned the *maybe never again* option, but I'm sure we both thought it. He placed a single finger on my mouth and ran it gently from one side to the other. When it lingered there a little longer, I slipped my tongue out to moisten my lips, and I kissed the tip of it. He shuddered. And then he left the room. I heard him striding up the hallway toward the bedroom.

Shaken, my eyes stinging, I stuffed my wallet and possessions into my pockets and let myself out of the flat.

CHAPTER 24

LIFE goes on, as they say. Six months later a lot of things had changed—and a lot of them had stayed the same. I was still living with Jack and Louis and doing more than my fair share of washing up. It was as if I thought I had to build up my credit status, though they never said anything like that. I was still working at the construction site, but I'd reduced my shifts because I was looking into a change of career. More of that later.

I couldn't remember much of my exit from Seve's building that day, or the walk back up the promenade, or how I decided eventually which café to stop in. I couldn't have said what was driving me right then—my anger, my determination, my fear... or my heartache. But as soon as I'd settled with a large latte, I pulled out my phone. It was time to turn into Mr. Honest Citizen.

The relief was immense when Jack answered. I would have been happy to talk to either of them at the flat, but Jack was... something else. I'd been hoping he hadn't yet left for work.

"Max? Are you okay?" Thank God for his practical streak.

"No. But I'm not hurt. Jack...."

"Yes?"

"You know you said you had friends in the police who'd listen to me. Who'd treat me properly?"

He drew in a sharp breath. He'd known how things were. "You want me to give them your number? When do you—?"

"Any time is okay. Thanks. And Jack?"

"Yes?"

I tried not to sound too pathetic. "Are you working this morning? Have you got time for a coffee?"

He gave a soft chuckle. "That'd be good. Tell me where you are and I'll be there as soon as I can make it."

He arrived half an hour later. He'd taken the morning off anyway—Louis had an audition at the London TV studio later in the day and had begged a lift to the station. I'd been sitting in the café, silently, my coffee growing cold, my fingers touching the soft wool of Seve's sweater every now and then. I was glad he hadn't asked for it back, not least because it was probably the only thing reassuring the waitress I wasn't a tramp settling in to stink out the café for the day. Jack sat down opposite me and ordered a green tea for himself. As it arrived at our table, his eyes had flickered over my face and widened.

"Yes," he said. "I can see. About the *not-okay* thing."

"I'll be fine. Did you get a chance to call your friends?"

He lifted his cup, his mouth hidden by the rim and the steam. "When you're ready, Max."

"I'm ready now."

Jack's expression had said that personally, he didn't think I could be any further away from *ready*, but he'd kindly refrained from saying it. And he'd driven me straight to the local police station. Thank God again, he also waited until I was done, sitting quietly in an outside office on an uncomfortable plastic chair. And when he thought they'd had enough of me and he knew they weren't going to lock me up, he walked straight to the desk to sign up as my guarantor and took me home.

I had no regrets about the whole thing, you know.

Just a huge fucking pain in my chest where I used to have something that pumped blood around my body.

I TOLD the police lots of things, of course. I gave them details about Baz—as much as I'd known when we were both in London—and a

witness statement about the attack on Stewart. I could see the
policeman making notes to call a counterpart in London, trying to
hide his enthusiasm at receiving a decent lead on a cold case. I also
gave them information about Peck's drugs business and the various
rackets he'd been running around the London club, including attacks
on his couriers like Baz and me, and a few other gruesome rumors I'd
heard on the street. I didn't hold back confirming Alvaro Medina's
involvement in it all, although that was received with more grim
determination than delight. It wouldn't be an easy thing, taking on a
prominent businessman. But I had no doubt they would. In fact, as I
was escorted out, I saw extra activity in the office and a detective
requesting a search warrant over the phone.

They were reasonably decent to me, though they didn't
appreciate the fact I'd kept this information to myself for so many
months. I had to tell them I'd worked for Peck—there's no other way
I could have known enough about the deals otherwise—but they
listened to me when I explained I'd been clean for months and I'd
been trying to get out of the whole business even before Stewart was
killed.

They asked if I thought I was in any personal danger from
informing on the organization. I thought about it for a moment,
wondering why it didn't seem as big a deal now, not like the fear I'd
felt when I left Stewart's body on the pavement or even when Peck
had cornered me in the backyard at Compulsion. *No*, I said. I'd be
fine. I didn't elucidate on that.

They explained they'd have to charge me for the courier
business—for dealing by association. I could go home for the time
being under Jack's supervision, but they'd press the case. They
offered me legal representation, though it wasn't as if I could deny it
was true. But a woman came to talk to me, explaining there were
mitigating factors. She talked about a noncustodial sentence and
probation and counseling. I wasn't thinking very clearly at the end of
my interview, but she spoke briefly to Jack on my behalf and passed
me a few contact numbers. And rather surprisingly, I said I'd follow
them up. Talking to someone else about it all seemed suddenly like a
very good idea.

I didn't tell anyone anything about the previous night at Seve's flat or the work I believed he was doing to cover that up. I wouldn't forget it, but I found I could reconcile filing that away in Seve's world—at least if it kept him safe.

I just wasn't sure if I'd ever know one way or another.

THEY found Baz's body a couple of days later. Jack's friend in the police generously kept us posted as much as he could. The body was rolled in a plastic tarpaulin from a nearby building site and wedged down between two rubbish bins behind a local takeaway restaurant. There was no evidence of where he might have actually died. Rats and foxes rifled around all the bins and there'd been rain during those nights, making forensic investigation that much more difficult—to say nothing of the rumpus over Health and Safety issues for the unlucky restaurant. However, there was still enough left to give DNA samples, and the last I heard, Baz was being matched to two other knife attacks around Soho and several robberies in Brighton. And they were still checking. Baz didn't have any money on him, but there were some stolen credit cards in his pocket, a few items of jewelry, and a red cigarette lighter with an Arsenal crest. I knew this because the police had phoned me directly just to check if I knew any of the names on the cards or owners of the jewelry. I didn't, but I could identify the lighter as Stewart's. There were plenty of those souvenir lighters in circulation, of course, but one of the London kids had scraped their initials on Stewart's at one time. I was able to describe it very clearly, as it was the one I'd borrowed from him—the one that had been in my pocket for so many months. Along with my witness statement, it was vital physical evidence tying Baz to the murder.

That evidence had been a shock to me. I realized Seve must have taken the lighter from me in the flat, picking it out of the stuff I'd left overnight on his living room table. I'd been too disturbed the next morning to check whether I had everything when I left. I was bloody glad it had helped to pin Stewart's murder on Baz, and I was impressed with Seve too. That must have taken some quick-thinking "arrangement."

Jack's contact told us that the Drugs Squad piled into the Medina business empire like it was a day out at the beach—full of enthusiasm and long days involving packed lunches. We got all the news secondhand, but that was okay by me. Despite what I'd said to the police, I *was* worried about repercussions, although it seemed there were no links to Brighton except the fact that Medina had recently opened another club here. Maybe Uncle Alvaro had planned to expand on the south coast but hadn't found the opportunity to start yet. Or maybe there was a reason he'd stepped carefully, unsure of his nephew's appetite for that kind of trade. Whatever, I didn't really relax until they'd found Peck.

They ran him to ground back in London. He must have fled back there as soon as he heard the police were back on the trail. He must have wondered what had happened to Baz—what had gone wrong with his plan to shut us up. I'm sure he thought it was a strategic retreat to lie low for a while. But other people must have heard he was vulnerable and on the run.

By the time the cops came to call at his seedy flat in Hackney, he was no longer available to help with their inquiries. He'd succumbed to an unfortunate accident and was found dead in his bed, apparently a victim of accidental overdose with his own drugs. There were plenty of other supplies and evidence in his place to incriminate him and the London club in the local Soho drug trade.

A quiet word later from Jack's contact told us that the police thought Peck had been into a sadomasochistic lifestyle, because they'd found the marks of ropes and wires on his body. A search of his flat had found a weird selection of sex toys and provocative publications, as they called them. I knew Peck had never been interested in anything like that, but a few of the street kids I'd known would have had no trouble trussing him up, especially if there was a group of them involved. After all, they'd have needed to keep him still while they pumped the drugs into him and scattered damning evidence around the flat.

I had no proof anything like that had happened at all. I just hoped it had. Revenge would have been sweet.

The Medina business empire seemed to fold into itself with little fuss except for a brief shock/horror period in the financial press. I admit I went looking at the library again just to see what was reported. There were no high-profile arrests—presumably the lawyers were good enough to protect the Medina family from that for a while, at least—but it took its toll on the business. The stock price plummeted, several subsidiaries that had been under suspicion were quickly closed down, and the announcement went out that the whole chain of leisure clubs would be divested to new owners. Mr. Alvaro Medina resigned from the board "for personal reasons," which probably included finding the time to fight various fraud and criminal charges—as alleged.

There were a few quotes in the papers from Mrs. Maria Nuñez, Alvaro's sister, currently residing in Spain. She had been cleared of any involvement and had contributed many incriminating documents from her brother's business to the police investigation. She was considering taking control of the board to see what could be recovered from the scandal.

There were no quotes from her son, no mention of him at all. A few gossip columns mourned the fact he'd not been heard of recently. Someone even interviewed the boy band, but whatever little they might have had to say, I didn't bother reading it.

Otherwise, no news at all.

I WAS put on probation in the end. A great relief for us all. It seemed my help in wrapping up the drugs business in London and Baz's nightmare reign had outweighed my criminal time in Peck's employment. Louis did some more blubbing when Jack confessed he'd put in a good word for me. Must have taken a few thousand words, but I was truly grateful. And even more humbling, I found out my boss at the site had spoken on my behalf too. My job was still open, I had my freedom apart from a weekly check-in with my probation officer, and the door was closing on my old, bad past.

Socially speaking, I made a big effort to come out of my shell. I made sure no one saw me moping about too often. I went clubbing regularly with Jack and Louis, joined Harry and the Vs at the cabaret bars several times, and I sat bravely through many more soap opera TV nights with Louis and the gang. His TV character had really taken off with the public. The producers were talking about a romantic storyline with one of the main male stars. It'd be a pleasant change if he didn't play either a token gay man or a tragic loser to be killed off—and I knew Louis was working slyly on making sure that didn't happen. He deserved the success.

And the TV work was a good thing, because his dancing career had stalled for a while. Compulsion had been closed by the police because of the investigation, and it hadn't reopened yet. A couple of other entertainment groups were interested in taking it over—including that well-known club owner with the too-long blond hair and too-orange tan—but with both the Drugs Squad and the Fraud Squad on the case, the Group's assets weren't being allowed on the market any time soon. I didn't miss the club except in unwelcome, very late-night dreams. And its closure was an unexpected help to me. It meant I could relax into being Mr. Honest Citizen in every last sense.

I smartened myself up in other ways too. I started following current affairs programs rather than just watching old films. I did a few DIY jobs around the flat and learned to cook a couple of dishes more than my previous repertoire of grilled hamburger and grilled hamburger with onions. I was even able to entertain the others sometimes. Jack ate anything I put in front of him with quiet approval, though Louis snickered about it the first time I tried, so I had to whap him with the saucepan. Then he threw a fork, and Jack's plate got knocked onto the floor, and everything deteriorated into laughing and yelling and—eventually—home delivery pizza for us all. But I didn't mind, and Louis didn't snicker the next time.

I was happy still working at the site. My boss had been really supportive, and it was familiar enough for me to slot back in while I was sorting out all the rest of my life. But one Saturday I left the flat early and went to a further education workshop on retraining as a youth counselor. I had a reasonable portfolio of exams from the time before I dropped out of Uni, and it looked like I had a chance of getting into a new course. And the idea of helping young people find their way through the shit and struggle that was out there was really appealing.

I went out too, with Will from the library. Well... *he* dated *me*, really. He made a point of coming to say hello whenever I went around there, and in the end I agreed to meet him after work for a drink. It seemed ungracious not to, and he was good company. Plus it felt right to have friends outside of our small group and to do more of the normal things friends did. Watch the football on TV, see a film, browse the record shops on a Saturday afternoon. Will was amusing, not too intense, and good-looking too, with gray eyes and a broad smile. Louis said he was really keen on me, he could tell. Louis had a lust light bleeping in his head at all times. It seemed to work better than any military radar, in my experience. And from the way Will laughed at my jokes—yeah, even some of the lame ones—and touched me whenever he could, I knew he wanted to go further. We were both consenting adults, obviously, so why not?

I admit that I was turned on enough to give him encouragement. My body had been crying out for attention other than my own handshake. I'd left a lot of things behind when I walked out of Sussex Square that day, but unfortunately my desires hadn't moved on as successfully. Sometimes I thought it was difficult to remember being intimate with anyone. But that wasn't true, of course. I could remember very, *very* well—but I didn't dare let that memory in. It led to long, stiflingly hot wet dreams... and anguish.

But when Will kissed me, it was all wrong, you know? He was enthusiastic and he tasted great, but our tongues licking at each other seemed more of a shock than a thrill. He was pleasantly muscled, but when I put my arms around him, his limbs always seemed to be in the wrong place. He was the wrong shape, the wrong feel. Sexy in his own way, but not pressing the right buttons for me. Where I expected the scrape of evening stubble, my lips brushed against a clean-shaven chin. Where I expected taut dusky skin, there was tender pale flesh. I stretched out my hands to his shoulders and found he was much narrower than I thought. When his hands came up under my shirt to run over my chest, his fingers were tentative and his palms weren't damp with that sweat that comes from desperation and pure animal *need.*

It was totally my fault. I should have known it all along. Things weren't going anywhere, and I didn't like to mislead Will. I just wasn't ready for anything more serious, not yet. *If ever.* I hoped we could just stay friends. He was fine about it—well, he smiled and said he understood. Though I didn't see him in town for a while, and to be honest, I thought he might have been avoiding me.

SO THINGS were back on an even keel. I was comfortable with Jack and Louis. I'd offloaded the guilty secrets. I was going to become a Normal Citizen again, and my life was back in my hands. I had a steady, straightforward, and legal job. I was possibly going back to college. Yeah, I was living up to my promise to Stewart at last. I was happy.

Sort of.

I reckoned my head was the straightest it'd ever been. And yet, emotionally, I felt the *worst* I'd ever been. I struggled with moods of depression and often had to be bullied to go out, even if it was in Louis's very charming way and I enjoyed myself when I got there. When Will and I had been going out, I preferred quiet, discreet places. Occasionally the words or gestures of an anonymous person in the street would strike a familiar chord and pure feeling would just swamp me. Sudden exhilarating excitement—then cruel memory—and then just pure *misery.*

The guys tried to help like the good friends they were.

"You need distraction," Louis said. "You still have Will's number?" He wasn't unkind, just pragmatic and always enthusiastic about the next opportunity life had to offer.

"Give yourself time," Jack said. "You did the right thing, and everything's coming together for you, isn't it? Just leave the dating thing alone for a while."

I shrugged, not meeting his eyes. He knew how I felt. I'd have gone mad before now if I hadn't known there was at least *one* person in the world who did.

"Max?"

I shrugged weary shoulders.

"I know you're lonely. I know how that is. But it'll come, I'm sure, one day."

What will? I thought bitterly, though the bitterness wasn't directed at Jack. What *will come? Resignation? Amnesia? Comfortable celibacy?* Jack surely didn't mean *true love.* Only guys like Jack and Louis found that. I was glad I'd never faced more serious criminal charges, that Stewart's murderer had been found, that the bad days with Peck and Baz had been laid to rest. But I still felt punished—and that it had been disproportionately harsh.

I'd been the man who was avoiding anything controversial in his life. And then proceeded to fuck it all up because of one handsome man's nod to me over a drink at Compulsion. All I had left of that were painfully erotic dreams, a fading scar on my left cheek, and the soft touch of a cashmere sweater that I shamefully kept under my pillow most nights. Perhaps this was what a broken heart was like. Bloody well felt like it. Underlying every step forward, every success, every pleasure in life I had, there was a small, still, persistent ache inside.

And never any news from Seve. Even though that was what I'd demanded, wasn't it? Time alone to sort out my life. Time for us both to put things straight. I suppose I thought he'd ignore me like he often had in the past. If this was growing up, I reckoned it was overrated.

But… didn't I say that some things *did* change?

THE call came on an early Saturday evening, on—surprisingly—Jack's mobile. He and Louis were experimenting with new pasta sauces in the kitchen. There was a hell of a lot of laughter and the occasional clatter of a dropped spoon, and I suspected that there was going to be nothing edible out of there for a while. I knew Louis was cooking in nothing but an apron and a pair of cutoffs that were the living embodiment of "shorts." I also knew Jack was too easily distracted when it came to his boyfriend. But they were happy enough, and it left me free to brood while pretending to fix the scratchy reception on the TV in the living room.

I heard the trill of Jack's phone in the background. The theme from *CSI*—it always made me smile. Then I heard the sound of his feet coming up the corridor. The door swung open and he stood there, staring at me. The look on his face was both tentative and excited. I also couldn't miss the smear of tomato sauce on his cheek and the single string of spaghetti on his sleeve. His shirt was half-unbuttoned, and he looked almost guiltily flushed.

"It's for you, Max."

He handed the phone to me, then left the room, closing the door quietly behind him. I was confused. There were people who rang me nowadays. For work, for the occasional night out. But no one rang me this late. And not on *Jack's* phone. I put it to my ear.

"Max?"

The voice was as deep as always, that depth that curled my toes and spoke to the heart of my need. But it was quiet now. Maybe a little nervous.

"Seve? *Shit.* Where are you?"

"I don't... let's not say at the moment."

"You're okay?"

"I'm fine."

There were some muffled noises in the background, but they gave me no clues. What else could I say? I sank down onto the couch again because my legs were suddenly weak. Nerve endings that had been cauterized for months sprang back to life. My gut churned, and not from hunger. "How are... how's your mother? Are you still keeping a low profile?" There'd been a time at the start, when I first went to the police, that I thought they might be bugging my phone in case Seve contacted me. You know, him being a Medina and possibly tainted by association, to say nothing of secretly disposing of a dead body from his own kitchen. Jack had rather drily told me I was being paranoid, and when I saw how much was going on, I realized it was arrogant of me to think anyone was interested in my love life that way. And Seve never contacted me, anyway.

Of course.

So I pretended I'd stopped waiting for it.

"Mama is fine. We're both okay. She's going to do some work for the family business from... Spain." Had he been about to say *here*? Was he still in Madrid with her?

There were a few moments of silence while I wondered what mobile rate Jack was on and if it was going to cost him a fortune if I just kept this line open for the rest of my life, listening to Seve breathing.

"I wanted to call you before, Max, but I wasn't sure."

I marveled that there was a time I'd never have heard those words from Seve Nuñez.

"I didn't want to add to.... Did they give you a hard time?" His voice sounded halting, as if he'd been trying to train himself to be conversational. Trying to phrase words that would be appropriate. It hurt a little to hear Seve like that. I wondered what he'd been through since he left.

"Nah." I smiled, though of course he couldn't see me. "I mean, they charged me, but I haven't had to go to jail. I'm seeing a probation officer each week and keeping on the straight and narrow. I'm Mr. Honest Citizen now."

"You always were," came the murmur.

"Look, Seve. About your uncle—the business... I'm sorry—"

"No, don't be." His voice was sharp. "Mama was angry and distressed, but she understands now that my uncle was wrong. It could not go on that way. Once she realized what was happening, she made sure my uncle was removed from the board. And she passed over the evidence they needed to pursue a case against him."

"I know. I heard." How much had Seve lost? Money, belongings, status? I had no idea how much was wrapped up in the business and how much might have been private. There was silence again, and I threw words into the gap like pebbles into a crevasse. "They found Peck, you know. He was—"

"Don't tell me any more," Seve interrupted. "Don't waste our time on a shit like him."

His vehemence startled me. "So what are you doing nowadays?" I asked. God, it sounded like a something-for-the-weekend chat at the barber's.

Seve gave a low laugh. "I lost my job at Compulsion, obviously. Mama has managed to retain control of a few of the businesses, but only a small number of them were viable. One is in pharmaceuticals, a remarkably resilient industry, and I'm helping to run that now. It's a very small concern, and I am involved at a relatively low management level so far, but it is… surprisingly satisfying." He cleared his throat. "It deals in medical pharmaceuticals, not recreational, before you ask."

I opened my mouth to protest, and shut it again. It was just such a joy to hear his voice, even distorted slightly as it was over the line. "So you're doing well?" I wished he'd say my name again. It sounded so good in his steaming-hot-chocolate tone.

"*Max.*" He sighed. "It's a slow path. Trying to get businesses going again—legitimate ones. I'm… well, I am using another name for the time being. A different history, let's say."

"Wise move. I expect your social security number's flagged at every celebrity magazine. As soon as it appears, they'll be on the quest for a story. Probably bring the boy band with them."

"I expect so." Another small laugh. "Your humor…."

"What about it?"

"Nothing. Just… I miss it."

The brief silence this time was quite companionable. Then I got scared he'd ring off and I started gabbling again. "Are you seeing anyone, then?" How *crass*, I groaned to myself. How moronic, how pathetically clinging—

"No, I'm not." There was a pause. His tone had sounded strangely flat.

"Seve? Are you still there?" *No, please,* please *don't go....*

"Yes, I'm here. What about you, Max?"

"Who, me? Seeing anyone?"

"Yes." The tone was dry now. "Is there a better choice on the honest side of the street?"

"Maybe!" I snapped. The arrogant smartarse—

"Don't!" The phone vibrated against my ear with the exclamation. "I didn't mean...." Another sigh, more like a groan. "I'm still not very good at saying the right thing, Max."

"Yeah," I said. "Perhaps that's what I miss from *you*, Seve." More silence, while I forgave him everything but couldn't tell him. My fingers were numb from gripping the phone so tight. "Seve?"

"What is it?"

"I'm thinking of retraining for the future. Youth counseling."

Pause. "That's good."

I was rambling on. "If it works out for me, I'll go looking for a permanent job somewhere as soon as my probation finishes."

"You might move away from Brighton?" What did that sharpness in his voice mean?

I took a deep breath. My chest felt constricted. Ideas were springing to mind whether I wanted them to or not—whether I thought any of them were good or not. "I don't know. It depends where the jobs are and what I want to do with my life in the longer term. I mean, I like it here, and the guys are still okay with me at their flat. And it's not worth moving lock, stock, and barrel until I know where to go... even what country," I added rashly. "But I wouldn't rule it out." This was the first time we'd talked at length about the mundane things of life—about work, money, somewhere to live. This was weird. "Seve?"

"Yes?"

"What's the job situation like in Spain?" My heart was hammering so hard I couldn't hear my words clearly.

"It's… it's not good." Maybe he heard disappointment in my silence. "But that's the same everywhere. You could find something, I'm sure."

"I could learn the language. It has a lovely sound. Of course, at the moment I only know *two beers, please*, and that's because Pedro in the site office taught me for a laugh—" Fuck. *Talk some more crap, why don't you*. My hand was shaking around the phone.

Seve's voice broke in. "Don't move without telling me."

"I'm on probation, Seve. I can't go anywhere without letting everyone and their dog know." I sounded just a little too sharp. "Why, are you thinking of calling again?"

There was a hissed breath on the other end of the phone. "If that's a brush-off, I know I—"

"No!" I yelped. "*Call me*, Seve. I mean it!" *God*, did I mean it. *God*, was I scared of fucking things up!

More silence. I was terrified I'd lost the connection. But it seemed that neither of us was putting the phone down just yet.

"Max…."

"Yeah?"

"It's no good. This is not working for me."

"Sorry? What isn't?"

"Everything. I miss you."

"Seve." I didn't know what to say.

"I understood that you wanted to be alone—that you had things to do. That… maybe it had come to an end for us. That it was just…."

"Just what?" *A casual fuck*, like I'd once said?

He didn't rise to my bait. "I have tried to move on. I have tried to keep away."

"Seve...."

"It's no good. Like I said," he continued doggedly, "I don't want any other."

And look at me, I thought. I dragged my way through the days like I really was in jail. I did my work and I paid my dues, and I ached throughout it all. I brooded, I obsessed on the pain inside me, and I wallowed in the loss of one of the few things I ever truly wanted. Some days I never contributed more to a conversation than a couple of sentences. I reckoned I was a better wooden spoon than I was a friend to Jack and Louis.

I wanted to say it all aloud, but my throat felt dammed. I couldn't date anyone else—I couldn't forget Seve's skin, fragrant with its unique musky smell; his soft dark hair; his lips tangling with mine. His delight in touching me, in running hands through my hair, his strong fingers gripping my arse. I couldn't forget the feel of his strong arms round me—his legs pushing between mine—the incredible, anguished ecstasy of being fucked by him. My nights were a mess of frustrated tears and aching balls. I wanted all those things I told him about—the company, the argument, the teasing, the sharing. And I wanted them with *him*. Yeah... it was pretty obvious I felt the same.

I took a deep breath. "So... how often do the flights go to Spain?"

"What?" He sounded startled.

"I'll come to you as soon as I can. If you still want me."

There was another sharp intake of breath. "Of course I do. But you said you could not travel—"

"Tell me where you are," I said urgently. I was wondering where my toothbrush was and if Jack would lend me the money for the airfare. "Listen to me, okay? I'll find some way to come to Spain. I'll talk to the probation officer, I'll... I don't know, but I'll find a way. And when I get there, I want to see you—no, it's more than that. I want to be with you, whatever. Wherever." I sucked in a last breath before I lost my nerve. "But the thing is, Seve—or whatever your name is now—I don't want to wait for you to call again on the off chance. I want to see you *now*! The only way you'll keep me away is to tell me you don't want the same."

The door to the living room was opening, and I cursed whoever was interrupting me. But it was Jack, holding a travel backpack out to me and pointing to his watch. "Cab arriving in ten," he said in a stage-whisper. "To the station. There's a train every twenty minutes to the airport!" He backed out quickly.

"Jack?" I gaped at his retreating back.

Seve's voice spoke at my ear, laced with tentative amusement. "He told me I could ring you. I called him first—I didn't know what else to do."

"You called Jack?"

"Yes. I remembered his name from when he booked the club. I still had his number. I didn't know how you'd be if I contacted you first, after all this time. I thought you wouldn't want to hear from me, not when I had fucked up so badly. But I thought *he* might know how I'd be received. You said he was a good friend."

Yeah, I thought wildly. The best! "Um... look, I know I said I'd get there somehow, but I can't fly out right now." I was silently screaming, wishing I had some way of transporting my molecules that'd bypass the probation check on Friday.

Seve made a tutting noise. "Of course you can't. And you don't have to. I am in England, at Gatwick Airport. I have just arrived from Spain. I can stay for a week this time, maybe longer after things settle further...."

I was already pulling my jacket off the back of the couch and shrugging into it. "I'm on my way."

"Max, I must tell you, I only have a little money. I'm in a cheap hotel. It's not like the flat."

I smiled to myself. What an arrogant prick he really was. *My* arrogant prick. "You reckon you fucked up badly, right?"

He made a growling sound. "I try to understand you, Max—"

I interrupted quickly. I was sure he'd hear the happiness in my voice. "If I cared about furnishings, Seve, I'd fuck a cushion, okay? I have almost a week until I have to check in again, and I'm owed some holiday at the site. I'll meet you anywhere. Hotel room, airport coffee shop, car, park bench…." *Just meet me*, I prayed. Then—sudden panic. "You want to spend that time with me?"

"Yes," he whispered. "Yes… please."

My heart shrieked its joy. Thank God they never gave a cock a voice. "We'll talk about it then, okay?" My heart was hammering again, but this time it was with excitement. "I said I'll meet you anywhere, Seve, and I meant it. We'll work something out on the logistics."

"Work something out," he echoed. He didn't say the "yes, please" again, but it was there in his tone. That'd do for me.

I could hear the cab beeping its horn outside the house and a squeal of excitement from Louis in the hallway. "Anywhere, you hear me? Just…."

"What?"

"Just make sure it's somewhere out of the rain!"

I flipped the mobile closed even as I heard his low laugh.

I ran for the door.

CLARE LONDON took her penname from the city where she lives, loves, and writes. A lone, brave female in a frenetic, testosterone-fueled family home, she juggles her writing with the weekly wash, waiting for the far distant day when she can afford to give up her day job as an accountant.

She's written in many genres and across many settings, with novels and short stories published both online and in print. She says she likes variety in her writing while friends say she's just fickle, but as long as both theories spawn good fiction, she's happy. Most of her work features male/male romance and drama with a healthy serving of physical passion, as she enjoys both reading and writing about strong, sympathetic, and sexy characters.

Clare currently has several novels sulking at that tricky chapter three stage and plenty of other projects in mind... she just has to find out where she left them in that frenetic, testosterone-fueled family home.

Visit Clare's website at http://www.clarelondon.co.uk and her blog at http://clarelondon.livejournal.com/.

Romance from CLARE LONDON

Also from CLARE LONDON

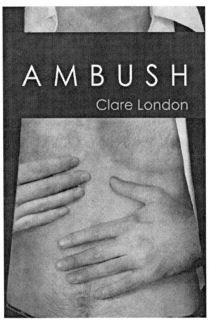

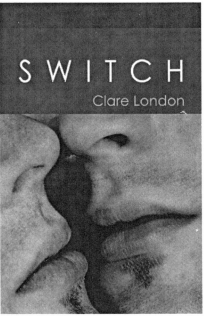

http://www.dreamspinnerpress.com

CPSIA information can be obtained at www.ICGtesting.com
Printed in the USA
LVOW100509241012

303999LV00001B/4/P